Cleave To The Crown – ISBN 978-1-3999-7424-0

Copyright © 2023 Bridget Beauchamp and Arcanum Press Ltd
Published in 2023 by Arcanum Press Ltd.

Cover illustration: © Shutterstock Image 1291628647

This novel is entirely a work of fiction although a great many of the historical details and characters are factual.

Printed and bound in England.

Arcanum Press Ltd. Is registered in England & Wales, company number 10704825. Arcanum Press LLC is a wholly owned subsidiary of Arcanum Press Ltd. and is registered in the State of Kansas, United States of America, entity number 8681348.

Learn more about Arcanum Press at www.arcanum-press.com

CLEAVE
TO THE
CROWN
✝

A sequel to Maid of Middleham

By

Bridget Marguerite Beauchamp

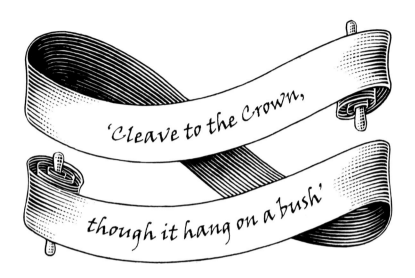

'Cleave to the Crown,
though it hang on a bush'

A Tudor proverb alluding to the legend that
Richard III's crown, having been torn from his
helmet, was found lying in a hawthorn bush
after the battle of Bosworth on 22nd August 1485.
Lord Thomas Stanley took it and placed it upon
Henry Tudor's head.

Bolton Castle, Wensleydale

Nappa Hall, Wensleydale

HOUSE OF YORK (simplified)

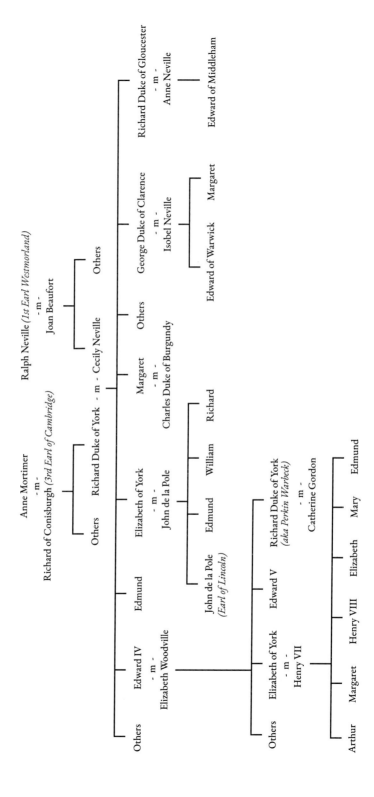

FICTIONAL CHARACTERS

Eleanor Metcalfe *(nee Wildman)* – *widow, former 'Maid of Middleham'*
Elizabeth (Bess) – *Eleanor's daughter by* Richard Duke of Gloucester (Richard III)
Philippa and Isabella – *ladies in waiting at Middleham Castle*
William Metcalfe – *Eleanor's son by* Will Metcalfe *deceased*
Edward and James Wildman – *Eleanor's brothers*
Robert Dinsdale – *Wensley farrier*
Stefan Bauer – *German mercenary captain*
Hugh Broughton – *Cumbrian Marshall at Millom Castle, Eleanor's 3rd husband*
Joseph and Martha - *Minster Lovell servants* ~ Edith – *Cumbrian maid*

MAIN HISTORICAL CHARACTERS

Henry Tudor – *King Henry VII*
Richard III (Duke of Gloucester) – *brother to Edward IV and George, Duke of Clarence*
Anne Beauchamp Countess of Warwick – *mother to* Isobel *and* Anne Neville
Francis Viscount Lovell – *nobleman, Richard's closest friend,*
Anne Viscountess Lovell – *wife of Francis Lovell* ~ Frideswide Lovell – *Francis's sister*
Richard Fitzhugh – *Anne Lovell's brother*
John de la Pole Earl of Lincoln – *nobleman, Richard III's nephew and heir presumptive*
Margaret Duchess of Burgundy – *sister of Edward IV, George Duke of Clarence and Richard III*
Martin Schwartz – *German mercenary commander*
Elizabeth Woodville – *Edward IV's queen*
Elizabeth of York – *Edward IV's daughter, Henry VII's queen*
Edward V – *eldest son of Edward IV* Lambert Simnel – *(John) youth impersonating Edward V*
Richard of York – *son of Edward IV (aka Perkin Warbeck)*
Edward Earl of Warwick – *son of George Duke of Clarence*
Henry Percy Earl of Northumberland - *nobleman*
Lord John Scrope of Bolton – *Yorkshire nobleman, husband of* Elizabeth Scrope
Thomas Metcalfe – *Yorkshire gentry of Nappa Hall, husband of* Elizabeth, *father of* James Metcalfe
Robert Markenfield – *gentry of Markenfield Hall, brother to* Sir Thomas Markenfield
Sir Thomas Broughton – *Cumbrian knight,* Sir Henry Bodrugan – *Cornish knight*
James IV – *King of Scotland*
Jasper Tudor Duke of Bedford – *nobleman, uncle to Henry Tudor*
Baron Thomas Stanley Earl of Derby – *brother of Sir William Stanley*
Lady Margaret Beaufort – *Henry Tudor's mother and wife of Thomas Stanley*

Chapter One

Eleanor had no recollection of those next few days. She felt numb. Her lover was gone. The man she had adored for 16 long years lay dead, slain treacherously and callously on Redemore plain, the crown of England snatched from the thorn bush where it had landed, as blow after blow rained down on the stricken King. This bravest of young men, only 32 years old, consumed by a fearful resolve with no thought for his own safety, had charged his steed into the melee, at the head of his faithful knights. Thrusting and thrashing his way towards the cowardly pretender who had dared to see fit to expunge the last drop of Plantagenet blood from its rightful place on the throne, Richard rode on. Sadly, at the very moment when the king had almost reached his adversary, he was brought down by the sheer weight of numbers. Personal greed and treachery amongst the ranks had facilitated Henry Tudor's usurpation and cost a fearless young man of loyal disdainful courage his life. The date of 22nd August 1485 would live forever in Eleanor's mind as the day her meaningful life ended.

The young maiden, who had aroused the passions of the teenage Richard Duke of Gloucester, had borne his child before he left Middleham Castle at the age of 16. Unaware of Eleanor's predicament, Richard returned with his new wife Anne Neville four years later to claim the Neville patrimony, endowed upon him as 'Lord of the North'. Eleanor continued to raise Richard's child as that of her soldier husband Ralph, who had been killed at the battle of Barnet in 1471. Remaining in service for the Duke and Duchess of Gloucester, Eleanor matured into a desirable woman, while her daughter Elizabeth, blossomed into a fine featured delicately framed teenager, reflecting her father's genes, quiet temperament and serious blue grey eyes, unaware of the secret of her birth. Later, marrying a local huntsman Will Metcalfe, in service with the Scrope's of Bolton castle, Eleanor bore him a son but found herself widowed for a second time, when her husband met his death hunting a wild boar.

Now amidst her grief for her first love, the man she had worshipped for half her short life, Eleanor was consumed by guilt. She had allowed her daughter to grow up without the knowledge her father was a nobleman of the highest standing, brother to a King, then ultimately King of England himself. Vacillating between prudence and panic, she had put it off, the right moment never seeming appropriate but now she felt the burden of regret and self-recrimination, remorse eating away at her conscience as she looked into her daughter's eyes. Too many years had gone by. It was time for Bess to know the truth. 'Elizabeth, sit down, I have something of the utmost importance and secrecy to tell you', Eleanor instructed her daughter, as they prepared for bed in the chamber they shared at Middleham Castle. Bess sat down obediently beside her mother, wondering to herself why King Richard's death ten days ago had affected Eleanor to such an extent. Her mother had been inconsolable, barely eating, lamenting day and night, distracted and distraught to the point where a sleeping draught had been prepared to afford her the blessing of a few hours' oblivion.

Bess herself was sorrowful of course, as was the whole household, numb with shock at King Richard's death and fearful of the new Lancastrian owners who may shortly be arriving. She had admired the late King, who was kind to her and always attentive when he was in residence and had often remarked on his handsome looks. Attracted to those same looks in his illegitimate son John, who had briefly resided at the castle, Bess had harboured innocent fantasies of a romantic liaison with the teenager before he left. Thankfully her flirtation came to nothing, for what she was about to discover would render any such relationship impossible, if not illegal.

'Our king Richard was a brave and courageous man of the utmost integrity, Bess', Eleanor began, grasping her daughter's hand, her eyes red from weeping, her cheeks white, pleading for compassion and understanding, nervously anticipating the inevitable onslaught of her daughter's wrath.

'Aye, I know mama, I loved him too, we all did. It's so sad. He was so brave'.

'I must ask your forgiveness Bess but firstly you must not tell a soul what I am about to reveal to you'.

'Of course, not mother, but why would you need my forgiveness?' Bess frowned, perplexed.

'I know I should have told you this a long time ago but I lacked courage and it was better you remained in ignorance until you were able to understand'. Her mother continued, ignoring the question. Elizabeth was beginning to become irritated at her mother's evasion.

'Understand *what?*' she snapped in exasperation.

'Ralph was not your father, Bess'.

'Oh!' Bess stared, taken aback by the sudden mention of Ralph, the image of a man she had never seen but oft envisaged, resplendent in his soldier's uniform, the Earl of Warwick's emblem emblazoned on his chest, marching off so confidently to fight for king and country, coming to mind. 'Who IS my father then?' she retorted glumly, rather hoping he was not some local peasant farmer of little repute and even less appeal. Her mother took a deep breath and blinked a tear from her eye.

'King Richard was your father' she declared quietly. Bess stared at her nonplussed.

'What?!' she exclaimed aghast, wrenching her hand away in disbelief. 'Is this some sort of jest mother?'

'Nay Bess, t'is no jest, t'is true. We were teenage lovers before Richard left for London to join King Edward in the year '68. I loved him very much and I was so proud you were his daughter'. Bess sat in stunned silence, her mind racing; she thought of the Duke of Gloucester laughing and playing with her, teaching her to ride with his son Edward and how she had oft caught him gazing at her thoughtfully in moments of reflection. Suddenly it all began to fall into place. *Richard Plantagenet was her father!* Somehow, she felt she had always known. There was a bond that she had sensed from an early age but dismissed as childish nonsense, but now her instinct told her that such wishful thinking had been correct.

'So, he knew about me then?' she rejoined, resentment building in her voice at the knowledge neither of her parents had thought to tell her the truth before now.

'Not at first Bess. I kept it a secret. Richard guessed when he returned four years later with Lady Anne as his Duchess, but by that time you had been brought up as Ralph's child. He had no wish to shame me, or you, for that matter, so it was best left unsaid. He made sure we were provided for though'.

'So, no-one else knew then?'

'Just the Countess'.

'The Countess of Warwick knew about me? Bess stared up at her mother perplexed.

'Aye, she arranged for me to wed Ralph, to save my shame'. Bess frowned as immediately another thought struck her. *How many more people knew?*

'What about Lady Anne? She must have known then too?'

'Nay, not for some time Bess but like Richard, she eventually guessed. You have his eyes, his semblance and slender frame, you know'. Bess knew her mother spoke the truth. She had always been slim but with a stalwartness not apparent in her looks and from her classic profile, she was so clearly her father's daughter. Ignoring the reality she had herself already perceived, Bess got up and paced the floor.

'So, you *all* knew!' Feeling naïve and humiliated at being the last to be told this most important truth, Bess struggled to make sense of her circumstance. *King Richard my father? He was here all along! All those times when I longed for a papa to hold me and love me. He was here! The king, my father!* She felt sick, the enormity of the revelation sinking in as her mind raced. *How could they keep this from me?* Her eyes filled with tears of blame and hurt, as she turned to face her mother angrily.

'Why didn't you tell me?!' she raged against her mother. 'All these years, growing up fatherless, thinking papa was a soldier who died in battle, never having seen me! Now you tell me he was right under my nose all that time – a man I looked up to, admired as a nobleman, so far above me in status, to whom I could only curtsey and call 'your Grace?!' *He* was my father???' Her voice swelled with indignation, angry, hurt words spilling from her in an unstoppable torrent. Bess stopped pacing and stared at her mother, fists clenched. 'Do you realise what you've done mother? You've denied me his love! You've denied me his embrace, the chance to call him papa, to kiss his cheek and sit on his knee, to run to him when he came home, to wave to him as he rode off to war! All those years in ignorance, when I so longed to have a father! My God! How could you do that to me?!' She covered her face with her hands, collapsed on the bed and wept.

'Richard would have acknowledged you had I not wed Ralph.' Eleanor answered wretchedly, attempting to ease her daughter's anguish and shoulder the blame herself. She thought of her second husband Will and how he had tried to treat Bess as his own. '...and Will did his best to be a father to you Bess', she added.

'Aye but he wasn't, was he?' came the muffled response from the pillow, before another thought struck the tormented teenager. 'Did *he* know?'

'Aye, I'm sure he guessed, although we never discussed it', her mother admitted, as deep sobs convulsed her daughter. Eleanor wept too, silent tears running down her cheeks. She didn't need reminding, the guilt of hurting her daughter wounding her like a sword through her heart, as if the pain of losing her lover were not enough to bear. After a few moments, Bess raised a tear-streaked face, choking on her words. 'Did papa ...love me? she pleaded, the word 'papa' sounding so incongruous on her tongue when referring to the king of England.

'Aye of course he did, Bess.' Eleanor answered without hesitation, pleased to offer her daughter some solace. 'He loved you, *very* much. He said you were beautiful and he was proud of you.' her words prompting further wails of woe from Bess.

'Oh my God! Prince Edward was my half-brother!' Bess realised propping herself up with a start. 'And John too!!' her cheeks reddened as she thought of the attractive young man she and the other girls had openly flirted with.

'Aye' Eleanor sighed, the relief of having told her daughter the truth, now easing her conscience. *Thank goodness it never came to anything!* Bess breathed silently to herself, although with growing annoyance at her mother for failing to warn her of the blood affinity she shared with John.

'So I'm a bastard too!' she retorted flatly.

'Aye, forgive me Bess, I was young, younger than you are now ...'

Eleanor closed her eyes, brushing away a tear. Bess stared into space, digesting her new status before remembering the king's gift to her.

'The prayer book!' she gasped. '*That's* why he gifted me the prayer book! I wondered why he would single me out for such a favour!' Leaping off the bed, Bess ran to the coffer, taking out the small volume King Richard had given her, the words '*For Elizabeth, may the Lord keep you, loyaulte me lie*' written on the flyleaf in his neat hand. 'Oh papa!' she wailed, sinking to her knees, clutching the cherished volume to her breast, his words now ever more precious and pertinent. She ran her fingers over the ink as if to feel his presence therein. *He gave this to me! He wrote this for me, his daughter! I'm his daughter!* A thrill of excitement ran through her but then almost simultaneously reality dropped like a thunderbolt. He was dead. She would never see him again, never be able to return his love as she should, as she *could* have, had she known.

'Oh mother, why didn't you tell me?' she repeated, anger towards her mother welling up in Bess up once more. 'Now he's DEAD! I will never see him again!' she screamed, as the realisation of what she had missed hit home with crushing finality.

'None of us will Bess. The Lord has seen fit to take him from us and who knows what fate awaits us now'.

'When were you going to tell me?' Bess snapped bitterly.

Eleanor sighed sadly, 'When he had won the battle and England was at peace. I was going to tell you then but God had other plans. Forgive me Bess, I have been too consumed by my own sorrow'. She got up and raised her trembling daughter to her, embracing her tenderly as both women wept for the man they had loved and lost. They stood for a while, tormented by grief, Bess in particular, searching her memory, trying to recall all the precious moments she had spent with Richard, all the while not knowing the truth. The heroic father figure she had dared to dream of was every bit the champion she had imagined, *a Knight of the Realm, nay,… even more than that, a King of England!* She thought about the last time she had seen him at Sheriff Hutton, when she had glimpsed her mother watching Richard at weapons training in the inner bailey. How skilled he was, how confident and strong, willing and ready to lay down his life in defence of his Realm. She realised at that moment how much Eleanor had loved him and her heart softened towards her mother, despite the blame she still laid at her door.

'Were you with him that night at Sheriff Hutton mama? You didn't come back to our chamber did you?' Bess asked, raising her face from her mother's shoulder. her tone more kindly now, recalling how sad and forlorn Richard had appeared that last evening and how her mother had gone to attend to him and not returned until morning.

'Aye, my sweet, I was' Eleanor admitted, swallowing hard as the treasured memory took her back to that blissful night, when Richard had been in her arms again and she could show him how much she desired him. 'He was a broken man, he had lost everyone, his wife, his son, his brothers. He needed comfort. Oh Bess,' she sighed, closing her eyes, 'I loved him… *so* very much', the image of those precious last hours not so long ago, when Richard was hers once more, imprinted so vividly on her memory. How she had kissed away his tears, thrilled to his touch, revelled in his body entwined with hers; her brave knight, the man of her dreams, who had desired her again, not as the naive teenager who had once given herself to him in her innocence but as a woman who could fulfil his needs and assuage his pain.

'I'm glad' Bess admitted, encircling her arms around her mother in a sudden rush of empathy, with hindsight now appreciative of Eleanor's heartache but pleased to know her parents had enjoyed one final night of love together. Despite her outburst, Bess felt for her mother, although it would take time to forgive her. Later as they climbed into bed, Eleanor reminded her daughter of the necessity to keep this new knowledge to herself.

'You must *never* reveal this, Bess. Promise me! It must never come out you have Plantagenet blood in your veins, or it could mean the end for all of us. We are the vanquished and must obey a new ruler. Any of Richard's blood will be sought out and killed. They cannot risk rebellion, though there will be plenty of it fomenting in men's minds. For now, we must stay silent to stay safe Bess. Promise me!' She grasped her daughter's hand in earnest. 'Don't even tell your brother William yet. He's too young to understand and anyway he doesn't need to know his father was not yours.'

'Aye, I promise mama. Let us pray for papa. I want to pray for him'. Bess opened the prayer book and mother and daughter sat together on the bed, reciting the verses they knew, fresh tears coursing down their cheeks as the enormity of their loss registered once more.

Chapter Two

The household at Middleham had erupted into turmoil following the news of the King's death. There remained only a reduced guard, most of the soldiers having left to fight at Bosworth, either having died or escaped and would not be returning, many of those pledging allegiance to the new king, in order to save their lives, or their livelihood. The servants still at the castle were fearful for whom would take up residence and how they would be treated and were planning to leave as soon as possible. The late king's personal staff who had followed him to Nottingham including his Secretary John Kendall, had all perished beside Richard. Francis Lovell, who had not been at the battle, had initially been offered pardon but with no sign of him and no response forthcoming, the Viscount had been attainted and all his property restored to the crown. With Henry Tudor already making his way to Sheriff Hutton to take charge of Edward of Warwick, his sister Margaret and any other Royal children who may still be there, his adherents were expected to progress North without delay. They would be keen to consolidate the Tudor claim and could arrive any day.

Messengers had arrived almost daily with news of the aftermath of the battle. The Countess, concerned for the welfare of her grandchildren at Sheriff Hutton, was shocked at the death of such a number of Richard's most loyal knights and followers.
'So many good men lost', she gasped, the missive quivering in her hand as she read it out to her ladies in waiting. 'The Duke of Norfolk, Sir Robert Brackenbury, Sir Robert Percy, Sir Richard Ratcliffe all died in the battle and William Catesby was executed afterwards!' she read

on. 'Lord Lovell was reported dead but nay, he is apparently missing!' She let the dispatch drop to the table and stared out of the window. 'I'm sure he wasn't at Bosworth!' When we dined with king Richard at Sheriff Hutton, he told us Francis was down at the Southern ports preparing the fleet to await Tudor's landing!', The Countess of Warwick drummed her fingers together, pacing the floor of the Solar agitatedly, as her ladies fussed around her.

'I can't stay here Philippa, I'm going back to Beaulieu', she announced suddenly. 'The Lincolns will see to the children's welfare. Middleham can no longer be my home and as King Richard's mother-in-law, I will be seen as the enemy. I have to seek sanctuary again. There is nowhere else for me. When I am there, I will plead with King Henry to allow some restitution of my property. That's all I can do.' she bemoaned, brushing away a tear with a trembling hand. 'Come, help me make ready.' Looking around at the frightened faces staring back at her, she felt it best to keep them occupied. 'Make haste now', she commanded, the shooing motion she made with her hands prompting the pages to spring into action. 'I must be gone as soon as is possible.'

'What will happen to us my Lady?' Isabella enquired nervously.

'You won't be harmed my dear. You are servants and will be treated accordingly. It's up to you of course if you wish to stay but there may not be wages paid in the interim and you will no doubt be expected to avow your fealty to the new king.' *The new King! Ugh! - Over my dead body* thought Eleanor defiantly, *swear loyalty to the man who killed Richard! Never!* Her lips curled into a sneer of distaste. *How dare he call himself such!* Glancing around at the expressions of disgust on the worried faces, it was clear she was not alone in her sentiment.

'Who will take over the castle my Lady?' Philippa interjected, voicing everyone's fears.

'I hope it won't be the Earl of Northumberland!' Isabella expostulated. 'Objectionable man! He failed to support the king in battle. He's a traitor!'

'Aye, and no doubt will be well rewarded for it!' Philippa scoffed.

'Hush my dears,' the Countess put her finger to her lips, 'Do not voice your opinions so openly. I know not who will take the castle but it will no doubt revert to the Crown, as will all King Richard's possessions. He was defeated in battle, so to the victor the spoils! The new king will decide Middleham's fate'.

As she lay in the darkness of her chamber, Eleanor wept for the reality that had come to pass. All her fears had been realised; the wheel of fortune now firmly set in another's favour. *What did fate have in store for them now?* She gazed into the darkness, her thoughts turbulent and chaotic. *My poor brave Richard, where are you? Why did the good Lord see fit to take you from us? Already the Tudor propaganda machine is spewing out monstrous calumnies, branding you a murdering tyrant, when nothing could be further from the truth!* Eleanor curled herself into a ball and fell asleep embracing the pillow as if it were flesh and blood, *his* flesh and blood, no longer staining the soil of Bosworth field but still living and breathing, even now coursing through her fair daughter's veins.

The Countess left before the week was out, accompanied by Philippa, a small retinue of guards and a priest who would escort her to sanctuary. She stopped initially at Markenfield Hall near Ripon, where she had been welcomed only a few months earlier on her way to Sheriff Hutton. She was treated with respect but Sir Thomas who had survived Bosworth, had subsequently pledged allegiance to the new king and her host Lady Eleanor felt she could not allow her guest to stay more than a couple of nights at the Hall, especially with Tudor's men approaching York.

'We had no choice...' Lady Eleanor offered tearfully, as she embraced Anne Beauchamp '...unless we were to lose everything'.

'Do not fear reproach, my dear. I understand. I would do the same if my lands were still my own', the Countess admitted. 'Thank you for your hospitality and please convey my thanks to Sir Thomas'. The Countess knew that Sir Thomas's brother Robert Markenfield had been sent by Richard III to a remote manor in Devonshire on an important mission, two year's previously and had not returned. The Markenfields, she was sure were staunch Yorkists, albeit covertly and in the event of an uprising, they would be certain to assist the rebels, while maintaining an outward appearance of loyalty to the crown.

That same afternoon in Wensleydale, Eleanor packed up her possessions and together with Elizabeth and 9 year old William made their way back to the Wildman Manor Farm, farther up the valley, where she had grown up in the care of her maiden aunt Mabel. Mabel had died some years ago before Eleanor married Will, the huntsman from Bolton Castle and she was sad her aunt had never got to know her gentle nature-loving husband, who had courted her after Ralph's death. The farm had passed to Eleanor's elder brother Edward Wildman but he, along with their brother James were amongst those who had not yet returned after Bosworth. Their wives and children still resided at the farm, hoping daily for any news of their husbands. The brothers had gone missing years before after they fought for the Earl of Warwick at Barnet in 1471 but had eventually turned up to pledge their allegiance to Richard Duke of Gloucester when he became the new Lord of Middleham. Eleanor prayed they were alive, and on the run once more and not lying amongst the dead on Redemore plain. Her sisters-in-law welcomed her and the children, commiserating with

Eleanor on her previous widowhood and sharing their own concerns, quite unaware their relative's grief for Richard was anything more personal than sadness for the untimely death of a loyal and courageous king.

'I have to find work, now that the Countess has left'. Eleanor told her in laws. 'I will go to the Scrope's at Bolton. Will was employed by them when I met him. He was related to the Metcalfe's of Nappa Hall. They won't turn me away and I am confident they can find positions for me and Bess. Would you favour me with little William's care until he is old enough to join me? I will pay for his keep. I still have money from his father'. Mother and daughter caught each other's eye with a knowing look but to their relief it went unnoticed and with an answer in the affirmative, Eleanor embraced her relatives warmly, grateful for their charity. The fact her money originated from Richard and not Will, need not be acknowledged.

Two days later in a tearful farewell to Will's precious son, Eleanor cupped her child's boyish face tenderly in her hands, kissing his cheek and ruffling his hair affectionately, before watching him run off happily to join his cousins, unaware his mother may not return for quite some time. *So like his father!* she mused wistfully, smiling to herself at William's eagerness to get away from his mother's cosseting. Not only her son but both her children, enduring reminders of the men she had loved and lost.

It was a fine September morning and the colours of Wensleydale, were still predominantly green and lush, not yet tinged with the golden hues of autumn, though the heather blossom on Penhill had begun to fade from purple to brown. The thickets along the bridleways hung heavy with ripened berries, soaking up the last of the summer sun. Swallows and house martins, swooping earthwards, gorged themselves in preparation for their long flight to warmer climes, stocking up on the dwindling insect supplies before gathering on rooftops and castle ramparts, a sure sign winter was on its way.

Riding over to Bolton Castle 7 miles up the Dale. Eleanor wore a plain riding dress given to her by the Countess from her own redundant wardrobe. 'I shall not be needing this where I'm going' her mistress had remarked sadly. She had also given Bess one of Anne's silk dresses, aware that the teenager had lost her blood father and would appreciate the gift. She knew Anne was saddened having never had a daughter to whom to pass on her apparel but with Eleanor being Richard's natural daughter, it seemed appropriate to allow the girl a gift from his family. The rest of Anne's gowns and jewels, the Countess sent to her granddaughter Margaret at Sheriff Hutton.

As Eleanor rode, inhaling gulps of fresh autumn air, she recalled her first months at Middleham Castle and that euphoric evening of teenage passion when she had submitted to Richard and lost her heart to the man of her dreams as they lay together on the hillside. Eleanor still could not quite believe how fate had thrown them together as teenagers, the reserved young nobleman and the shy serving maiden, whose paths were only briefly to cross before being rent apart by class, duty and circumstance. It seemed a lifetime ago, the day she had watched the king's brother ride away, leaving her with child, having to wed a soldier in order to preserve her dignity. *Poor Ralph!* she sighed, remembering her first husband with some gratitude, for despite his indifference to her, he had agreed to wed her and did not deserve to die at Barnet before his adult life had even begun.

Trotting along on the familiar path beside the river Ure, Eleanor recalled her first widowhood and her meeting with Will Metcalfe, the Scrope's quiet huntsman. He had proposed to her by Aysgarth Falls, before their blissful married life together - a few short years of happy contentment until fate intervened when he was cruelly taken from her by one of the wild creatures he so respected. That angry boar which had gouged deep clefts in Will's side, a strange irony and unwitting reminder of Eleanor's one-time lover, Richard Duke of Gloucester, who's emblem was that same proud and protective beast, its bearer destined to be raised to the exalted heights of King of England.

There was something about approaching autumn that Eleanor loved, not only its reminder of the men she had lost but the relief of the freshening breeze as it cooled the cloying air of high summer before turning the sea of uniform greenery into every imaginable hue of yellow, gold, copper and rich brown. The smell of the newly ploughed earth, the roaring torrent as the many falls punctuating the river's course, cascaded over the stepped limestone contours, where in summer there had lingered but a trickle. The mists that clung to the backbone of the Pennines, the early snows that dusted the summits, the dying bracken clogging the hillsides in a mantle of terracotta coloured undergrowth, the kaleidoscope of nature's ever evolving cycle. Every creature hurrying to stock its larder for the coming winter; the promise of a warm fire and hearty broth awaiting riders back from an invigorating gallop; comforting memories of the closing months of the year, now advancing once more.

Baron Scrope, Garter Knight, had been a loyal supporter of king Edward IV, having fought at Towton and Hexham, before serving Richard Duke of Gloucester faithfully as he succeeded to the crown. Eleanor had waited upon the Scropes at Middleham on several occasions and she felt confident the family would secure her employment, if not with them, with one of their many retainers. As they reached higher ground, Bolton Castle hove into view, the oblique rays of the lowering sun sinking in the West, gilding the stone ramparts of the Scropes' family seat, in an aurous light.

Nearing the imposing four walls of this sturdy rectangular fortress standing proudly in its commanding position on the slopes of Wensleydale, its extensive gardens and deer parks, reaching forth across the vale to Penhill, Eleanor was struck by the castle's dominating presence and symmetry. Uprising proudly from its base, perched on ground that fell away steeply to the South, the castle lay sheltered from the North by the bulk of Pickerstone Ridge behind. It felt warm and welcoming, not as large as Middleham Castle but nevertheless conveying an air of grandeur, enhanced and embellished by well-tended South facing gardens, affording a panoramic vista for miles over the far-reaching Dale.

As they approached, the high walls appeared to lean back against the hillside, suspended motionless as if about to fall, giving the illusion of being taller than they actually were. Feeling suddenly giddy as she gazed upwards, Bess was relieved when she could adjust her focus in the shade of the Eastern gatehouse, the only entrance to the castle. Eleanor and her daughter were ushered through the double portcullis into the rectangular internal courtyard, permanently enshrouded in the shadow of the high towers surrounding it, except for a few brief weeks of high summer, when the golden light would warm the cobbles. While their horses were taken into the vaulted stables to await return to Middleham as soon as it could be arranged, the visitors awaited their host in the Great Hall.

'Goodwife Eleanor Metcalfe and her daughter Elizabeth' a page announced, when Baroness Scrope, a middle-aged noblewoman entered shortly afterwards. The two women curtsied politely as Elizabeth Scope held out her hand in greeting.

'Eleanor, my dear, how are you?' she smiled condescendingly, recalling Eleanor from the Duchess of Gloucester's riding party many years ago when their young huntsman first courted the Countess's maid. 'We were so sorry you were widowed. Will was most dear to us and is sadly missed'.

'Thank you, my Lady. This is my daughter Elizabeth my Lady'. Bess stepped forward and bent her knee respectfully.

'Pleased you meet you my dear. You have inherited your mother's looks and will not be short of admirers I'll wager!' Bess blushed and studied the floor.

'Pray be seated' Lady Scrope indicated a low settle by the fireplace for her guests and sat herself down opposite in a high-backed chair. 'The Dowager Countess of Warwick informs me you are seeking employment now that she has left Middleham.'

'Aye my Lady' Eleanor confirmed, relieved to know that the Countess had written to ask the Scrope's to assist her lady in waiting, as she had promised.

'Such an unforeseen turn of events with King Richard gone'. Lady Scrope sighed wearily, pausing awkwardly, as Bess focussed on her hands and Eleanor stared ahead, suppressing the lump in her throat that threatened to undo her carefully staged composure. 'Still, we have a new king now and we must make the best of it,' their hostess continued. 'Thankfully John, Lord Scrope survived the battle and is awaiting release, having pledged his allegiance to the crown, as we will all be obliged to do, if our property is to be spared'. Eleanor couldn't speak and dared not look her daughter's way. She had heard The Countess of Warwick discussing Elizabeth's Scrope's relationship, as half-sister to Margaret Beaufort, the new king's mother. She had questioned the Baroness's adherence to the Yorkist cause, despite the fact Elizabeth had been godmother to Edward of Middleham. 'It has been a great shock to us all but life goes on.' Elizabeth was commenting, her somewhat haughty demeanour beginning to rankle her guests. 'The battle has been won and we will do what we can to carry on as normal'. *How can life ever be normal again?* Eleanor brooded in mute irritation, steeling herself to stay calm and direct the conversation away from the subject of Bosworth and the vision of Richard's last moments that haunted her every waking moment.

'Everyone is leaving Middleham my Lady', she responded. 'With the Countess gone, I have no position. I fall on your benevolence, as does my daughter Elizabeth. We can provide any service, whatever you may require of us my Lady'.

'Thank you my dear. Of course, you are welcome here, although I will have to discuss our needs with my husband when he returns. For now though, you may assist wherever needed and we will find you some accommodation, perhaps with the Metcalfe's. Do you have any means of your own?'

'Aye my Lady, a little from my late husband's will'.

'Good, that will tide you over for the time being'.

'Thank you, my lady, we are indebted to you.'

Lady Scrope stood up, as did the two women. 'Now, off you may go down to the kitchen and get yourself something to eat, you must be in need of refreshment after your ride.' She beckoned to a page who escorted Eleanor and Bess out of the Hall and across the courtyard to the kitchens.

'She seems quite accepting of the situation. I thought the Scrope's were supporters of York'. Bess remarked resentfully to her mother when they were alone.

'Ostensibly aye, Baron John supported Richard most definitely; he fought for him at Bosworth but like many, will have to submit to the new king, or lose his property. However, I know the Countess of Warwick had her doubts about Lady Scrope's affiliation. Hush now though Bess, we must not speak of it. Keep your private thoughts to yourself'.

Two days later, the two women found themselves riding the five and a half miles West towards Nappa Hall, near Askrigg. In the absence of her husband, Lady Scrope had arranged for them to join the Metcalfe's household, where the owners lacked experienced ladies' maids and would welcome the widow of their distant cousin. Their party followed the familiar track beside the Ure, stopping to rest at the clearing beside Aysgarth falls, where Will Metcalfe had asked for Eleanor's hand and she had ridden away pondering upon her answer. A dark cloud obscured the sun and Eleanor shivered, the cold breeze soughing through the trees, its mournful moan prompting past memories and echoing her present anxieties. She stared into the gloomy black depths of the water, reflecting on her life and the men she had loved and lost, the unappealing prospect of years ahead as a widow, away from the grandeur and excitement of Middleham, weighing heavily.

The squires and young huntsman who had accompanied them were amusing themselves, happily engaged in skimming stones across the water, while Bess stood laughing at the youth's competitive taunts as they searched around for the perfectly shaped trajectile. Eleanor smiled, watching her fair daughter proudly, whose solemn blue/grey eyes offered a constant reminder of her noble father, a bittersweet likeness that would forever haunt her mother, yet which she would not wish away – the pain and the pleasure, both a burden and a blessing that she would never willingly lay down.

Resuming their journey Westwards, Nappa Hall, soon hove into view. The fortified manor house, constructed of local stone, had been built by Sir James Metcalfe, who had received it for military service rendered to Richard Le Scrope at Agincourt. Forming part of the Lordship of Middleham, above the River Ure, a 400 acre estate surrounded the Hall, which itself was of modest size. It's single storey central hall abutted by substantial West and East towers, crenelated for defence, was set on a commanding Southerly aspect, on gradually sloping ground, enclosed within a perimeter wall. Across the vale to the South, the distinctive profile of Addlebrough hill protruded into the skyline, while behind the house, the imposing ridge of Nappa Scar uprose steeply to a stepped limestone escarpment, where buzzards wheeled and the shrill trilling of the curlew echoed across the slopes. Eleanor could hardly imagine a more peaceful spot, as she looked about her, the gentle bowl of the dale sweeping away in front of the Hall down to the river Ure and Westwards, the elevated land becoming ever more rugged, with a stark, wild beauty, as it climbed its way towards the boundary of the Westmorland fells.

Proceeding through the arched stable block entrance, Nappa Hall already felt like home to Eleanor, as she recalled Will's fond account of his relative's manor house. The travellers dismounted and were ushered into the great parlour to await Elizabeth Metcalfe, the lady of the house and wife of Thomas Metcalfe. Thomas a loyal Yorkist, was Chancellor of the County Palatine and keeper of the seal, as well as Chancellor of the Duchy of Lancaster and Surveyor of the Bishopric of Durham. He had been a member of the late king's Council, had supported Richard's accession to the throne in 1483 and been rewarded for faithful service in supressing rebellions and insurrections. He had fought for Richard at Bosworth and his brother Miles, an experienced lawyer, Recorder of York, and Edward IV's deputy in the Duchy of Lancaster, had been a trusted member of Richard's Council of the North. Eleanor knew that the Metcalfe's, despite an outward appearance of conformity, were, nevertheless staunchly loyal activists to the Yorkist cause.

Elizabeth Metcalfe, a comely middle-aged woman, well dressed but not opulently, entered the parlour smiling warmly and holding out her arms in greeting. 'Eleanor, welcome my dear! I am pleased to meet my late cousin's widow at last! We were so sorry to lose Will in that tragic misfortune. He was a consummate huntsman and sadly missed at the Hall.'

'Thank you, Madam' Eleanor bobbed a quick curtsey before accepting her host's embrace. 'This is my daughter Elizabeth, Will's step-daughter. Her father was my first husband'. Bess stepped forward to take her host's hand politely, pursing her lips in a look of grudging resignation at her mother, for what she now knew as a falsehood but knowing she had no choice but to continue the charade.

'A lovely girl, my dear! Where is your son?' Mistress Metcalfe enquired, somewhat transparently displaying a preference for a blood relation, over a girl of no connection to her family.

'William resides with my sisters in law, Madam, at Manor Farm. They have offered to care for him until he is of age for employment'.

'Well, we would like to meet him one day and perhaps he can come and join us as an apprentice, so as to follow in his father's profession'.

'I have long harboured such hope Madam, thank you'.

'He is a Metcalfe; he is one of us and will be welcomed as such.' their hostess smiled. 'Now my dear, Jacob here will show you to your accommodation, which we hope will suffice for now. Not as luxurious as that to which you will be accustomed at Middleham but comfortable enough I am sure'. She gestured to the servant who was waiting patiently by the door. 'Make yourselves at home my dears, send for victuals if you wish. Come and see me tomorrow morning and we will discuss your duties and upon my husband's return, we will discuss your wages. Again, it may not match that to which you are accustomed – we are not royalty but we are fair'.

'Thank you, Madam, you have been more than generous and I am indebted to you.'

'Nonsense my dear you are family now and we are obliged to provide for our own.'

As they settled into their modest, low-ceilinged chamber above the stables, Bess couldn't hide her annoyance. 'Clearly, I'm of no interest to Madam Metcalfe!' she snapped indignantly at her mother, as they unpacked their belongings into an empty coffer.

'Hush Bess, enough of such talk,' Eleanor reminded her daughter, 'we are indebted to the Metcalfe's and they were supporters of Richard. Be thankful I married into Will's generous family and have employment! I dread to think where we would have been had I not had such privileged relatives.' She looked across at her daughter's puckered lips. 'Don't start getting ideas above your station Bess! Despite the circumstances of your birth, we are not at liberty to take advantage of it now, unless you wish to endanger us all', she admonished, irritated at the teenager's display of pique. Eleanor was beginning to regret telling her daughter the truth about her royal blood, thus endowing Bess with a sense of entitlement. She had noticed a change in her attitude which was already giving Bess an illusion of superiority over her mother and she realised she would have to impress upon her daughter the magnitude of the secret they held and the danger it posed. Eleanor knew it would be hard for Elizabeth to suppress her natural pride in her father, as she herself had to do, when all she wanted to do was to proclaim her love for Richard from the rooftops. Nevertheless, Eleanor was good at keeping secrets and her daughter would learn to do the same.

She walked over to the open window and stared Eastwards in the direction of Middleham. Rooks were gathering in the nearby trees, their loud gregarious clucking signalling approaching nightfall, while a great flock of starlings wove their shifting clouds of synchronised flight back and forth across a blood-orange sky. Somewhere beyond the wooded horizon, in the old castle, torches would be being lit for the remaining staff, though the candles in the Great Hall would not. No Lord nor Lady now to serve, servants drifting away as supplies diminished, no horses left in the stables, no flag flying aloft, though soon certain to be replaced by the red dragon of Wales or the insignia of some Lancastrian knight.

I'm glad I'm not there, Eleanor mused sadly. She could not bear to see Richard and Anne's possessions purloined by some obsequious Lord, undeserving and uncaring for the lives of those once so happily housed therein. *Although, if Henry Tudor was deposed and a Yorkist king re-instated....!* Eleanor smiled at the treasonable notions bubbling up to the surface of her subconscious, sighing wistfully to herself. *Oh Richard! If only you had lived! Life would be so different now! With the Lancastrian threat gone once more, you could have ruled your people with justice and loyalty and with a new queen, you could have founded a new dynasty of peace and prosperity...and Bess would have known her father!* Eleanor swallowed, her guilt still lying leaden in her gut.

Eleanor thought about Richard's young son Edward, who had died so suddenly, leaving Richard and Anne with no heir. She recalled the monks from nearby Coverham Abbey arriving to lay the child to rest but *where was he now?* A tomb would have been commissioned for the little Prince of Wales but with Richard gone, *who would see it through?* Richard's grand plans for collegiate chantries at both Middleham and Barnard Castle would now never come to fruition, along with proposals for his own final resting place at York Minster. Instead, the late King of England lay trussed up like a convicted felon, cast into an unmarked grave beneath the Franciscan chapel at Leicester, his hands still bound together, no casket to protect his body from the cold, damp, corroding earth - this shameful treatment of an anointed king, a damning reflection of the morality and integrity of his unworthy successor. Eleanor grimaced before turning back to her daughter in whose veins, her father still lived and in whose solemn eyes his soul was now mirrored.

Chapter Three

Autumn progressed its inevitable tempestuous way towards Winter and forward into Spring. Henry Tudor had returned to London and was crowned king Henry VII at the end of October. He had set up his own personal bodyguard, fully aware that his usurpation of the late Plantagenet king's throne, was opposed, if not openly, certainly covertly by many nobles who were loyal to Richard or indeed Edward IV; his only justification for the crown of England, a victory won by perfidy. Astonishingly, Henry had ensured he could punish Richard's supporters freely by dating his reign to the day before the battle of Bosworth, thus enabling him to try them for treason against the new monarch, much to the consternation and dismay of all. *How could it be treason to fight for one's king before he had perished?*

Edward of Warwick, the ten-year-old son of Richard's brother, George Duke of Clarence, had been taken from Sheriff Hutton along with his sister Margaret, to be housed under the watchful eye of the king's mother, Margaret Beaufort. The Earl of Lincoln, John de la Pole, who was Richard III's heir presumptive and had presided over the Council of the North at the castle, had been detained by Henry Tudor but after a short incarceration had been welcomed into Court, where he could be closely watched for any signs of sedition. Henry Percy retained his Northumberland Earldom, freed from a brief imprisonment but also from his rivalry with the late king. Having persuaded the new king of his loyalty he now held sway over the North unopposed.

Henry Tudor then married Elizabeth of York in January 1486 but not before he had destroyed all evidence of his wife's and her siblings' illegitimacy, as stated in *Titulus Regius*, the late king's parliamentary act of 1484, setting out Richard III's right to rule. With Elizabeth of York now being restored to legitimacy, she was free to become Henry's queen, thus uniting York with Lancaster, a justification and validation of Henry's rule, designed to unite the opposing factions that had led to the past 30 years of conflict. In doing so however, should the sons of Edward IV be found to still be alive, Henry would render his own position untenable in the face of two superior claimants to the throne of England. The upshot of this indisputable fact forced Henry therefore, to mount a sustained and prolonged search for proof that neither Plantagenet Prince lived and if they did, to end those lives forthwith.

Henry's invasion of England, bolstered by carefully circulated propaganda that Richard III was a murdering tyrant and had killed his nephews, left Tudor to maintain this falsehood, if he was to remain king and appear as saviour to the oppressed people of England – Tudor's own tenuous claim and double illegitimacy, paling into insignificance beside the solid Yorkist descendancy from the bloodline of Edward III. By comparison, his victory at Bosworth, remained Henry's only vindication but having come about through betrayal and duplicity, was hardly a solid foundation for a new ruler of a divided country. Rebellion was bound to ferment and the troubled monarch knew it, his obsession with stamping out dissent verging upon paranoia.

Along with the anxieties of the upper classes, who had supported the Yorkist cause and now feared for their livelihoods, was added alarm at the news of a deadly sweating sickness that was sweeping the country, which was rumoured to have been brought over from the Continent by Tudor's foreign forces. Eleanor was pleased to be far removed from the towns and cities where unhealthy conditions and close packed living conditions exacerbated the danger.

Meanwhile ostensibly, life in Wensleydale maintained its regular course. Thomas Metcalfe had returned to Nappa Hall but like the majority of landowners, he had initially sought pardon from the new king, in order to secure his family's livelihood and legacy. Now Surveyor of Middleham Castle and Lordship, including all manors in Richmond, Thomas could continue his life at Nappa Hall, as could his eldest son James, who had married Elizabeth Scrope, daughter of the 5th Baron and together with their two daughters and his brothers Ottiwell and Francis and their families, made up the household at Nappa. Thomas's brother Miles died in early in the new year, after a long-term illness, much to his brother's distress as they had been close, leaving the care of his children Richard and Katherine to his brother and widow Matilda.

Welcome news had come to Eleanor that her brothers had returned home from Bosworth, safe and well. Edward and James had been with Northumberland's men waiting on the sidelines on Ambion Hill, when Richard had been brought down. Though relieved they had not had to engage once again in bloody warfare, they were shocked the Earl had failed to deploy them to assist their fallen king, feelings of guilt and shame at not being given the chance to resist the invaders pricking their conscience. It had all happened so quickly that inauspicious day - Richard's valiant charge, as he espied Tudor's standard being borne through the ranks, foot soldiers leaping aside as the king's knights bore down upon them, victory seeming a distinct possibility. All of a sudden, William Stanley's reserves charged down into the melee but to the horror of Richard's waiting troops, not in defence of their king but fighting instead for Tudor. The beleaguered king disappeared underneath a hail of enemy blows from assorted weaponry; his horse having collapsed beneath him and before the Royal army could react, the battle was lost and it was every man for himself.

Standing stationary, surveying the field, Northumberland had surrendered, his soldiers never having raised a weapon, rumours abounding the Earl had cut a deal with Tudor to save his own skin. Watching their king's broken body, slung so shamefully over a horse's back, naked for all to see, his curved spine exposed and accentuated as he lay, the disfigurement now presented as undeniable evidence of wickedness and villainy, Edward and James wept for the young nobleman who had trained with them at Middleham as teenagers. They had been forced to kneel in obeyance as Henry Tudor rode by in triumph, Richard's crown upon his head, a sight so sickening it made them turn away in disgust. They had served the Duke of Gloucester faithfully, facing their first baptism of blood at Barnet and then on Border skirmishes and into Scotland. They learned their skills with him, served him as Duke and later as king and now that loyalty would not so readily be transferred to his murderer and traducer. Returning to live as farmers in their beloved Wensleydale, they steadfastly resolved not to take up arms again unless it was for the Yorkist cause.

Eleanor and her daughter had already proved their usefulness at Nappa Hall by adapting to almost any task allotted to them, be it attending upon Elizabeth Metcalfe, helping in the kitchen, stables, or buttery, no task seeming too lowly or onerous for the diligent pair. With less servants than at Middleham, there was always a multitude of chores waiting to be done and Eleanor and Bess soon learned there was no room for pride or pretension here, just a willingness to pitch in as required. Despite this, Eleanor found she was afforded a certain amount of respect, as a widow of a Metcalfe and experienced a warmth of feeling she had not felt before. She sensed in this easy-going household, relief from the haughtiness oft displayed amongst Middleham's attendants, many of whom would not stoop to take on a duty they considered below their status.

Thomas had been pleased to meet the new additions to his wife's attendants, remarking upon how the view had improved considerably with the appearance of two such fetching females in the household. James had been equally taken by Will Metcalfe's widow, never missing an opportunity to flirt with her when away from the jealous gaze of his wife. He was not an unattractive man but Eleanor was careful not to encourage him, or be seen as a coquette, thereby endangering her position. Eleanor knew James Metcalfe from her years at Middleham, where he had been Richard's faithful retainer in the Border conflicts against the Scots. He was Master Forester and Master of Game in the forest of Wensleydale and keeper of Woodhall Park adjoining Nappa and with James being good friends with Will, they had often come into contact.

Before the winter was out, encouraging news had reached Wensleydale that Francis Viscount Lovell, Richard's closest friend with whom he had shared his wardship at Middleham, had fled from sanctuary in Colchester – the East Anglian town being not far from Gipping Hall, where the sons of Edward IV had been sheltered after Richard's coronation. Francis had vowed to assure the boys' welfare, should Richard perish and with Henry Tudor now king and the boys legitimised, their survival was paramount if a plot to restore the rightful heir was to succeed.

Eleanor was familiar with Francis from her time at Middleham castle, when he and Richard would share knightly training and hunting. He had acknowledged her, although she had never spoken to him directly but she suspected Richard would have confided in him about their union. Her young companion Jane, from the farm, had once been enamoured of Lovell's youthful looks, as were many young serving maids, who watched the Earl's wards from afar. Eleanor knew enough of this most loyal knight, to know he was never going to swear allegiance to the usurper who had killed his dearest friend and benefactor. Unwilling to accept defeat, the Viscount would do his utmost to rally support, albeit still very much under the surface, for the Yorkist cause. Even those who had opposed Richard's reign, would now welcome the return of at least one of Edward IV's sons and if he could stay free from Tudor's clutches, Francis determined he would be the one to facilitate this. He had joined with the Stafford brothers, Humphrey and Thomas of Worcester who had mounted an armed uprising in the West, which had subsequently failed. The unfortunate Stafford's were pursued and forcibly evicted from the abbey in Abingdon after the king procured the Pope's agreement that sanctuary could not be claimed in the case of high treason. Humphrey suffered a traitor's death, while his brother was pardoned but lost his property.

Meanwhile Lovell made his way North, through Ripon and towards Middleham, assisted along the way by those still loyal to the Yorkist cause, albeit covertly. His wife Anne's family, the Fitzhugh's of Ravensworth were being closely watched, though his late father-in-law had been a loyal Lancastrian under Henry V and VI but had rebelled with Warwick in 1470. Anne Lovell's brother Baron Richard Fitzhugh had recently been appointed Constable of Barnard Castle but as cousin of the late king Richard, he supported his sister's errant husband and would not hesitate to shelter him if he returned.

With the news that Lovell had reached Yorkshire and was gathering support against the new king, rumours of an uprising gathered pace and with Lovell reported in the vicinity having amassed a large following, Thomas Metcalfe was among those who joined him.

On his progress North, Henry Tudor had reached York by April of the new year, in time for the first Garter feast of his reign. He was accompanied by the Earl of Northumberland and other previous retainers of the late king, who thought it expedient to curry favour with the new regime, encouraged by promises and pardons. However, John de la Pole, Earl of Lincoln who was with the royal entourage and now back in his home county, was secretly able to make contact with Yorkist sympathisers and those who recognised him as Richard's heir, including his loyal friend Francis Lovell. Francis had been a ward of John's mother Elizabeth, Duchess of Suffolk in the '70's and the young men had formed a close friendship with John being Richard's first cousin and lionising the older Lovell. Now, being part of Henry's retinue, Lincoln was ideally placed to pass on information to the rebels about the Royal itinerary, without yet being under suspicion, a fact Tudor would later discover to his detriment.

By Easter time Eleanor and Bess were shocked to learn that the Scrope's of Bolton and Masham, together with Thomas Metcalfe, Lord Fitzhugh and the recently reinstated Lord Clifford of Skipton, had all participated in the St. George's day feasting at York in the presence of the new king.

'How could they?' Bess had exclaimed to her mother upon hearing the news and for once Eleanor couldn't disagree, though she understood the reasoning behind the nobles' actions. So long as a semblance of loyalty to the new monarch was maintained, what went on behind closed doors could stay hidden and unsuspected. Their disappointment soon turned to delight however, at word from the great Yorkshire city. An attempt had been made on the king's life and although he was only saved at the last minute by the timely intervention of Northumberland, it showed that there was enough support for the rebels to enable an assailant to gain access to Henry without detection. Had the assassination plot been successful, with Tudor dead, Henry Percy knew he would be next in line for Yorkist revenge, thus saving the king, he deemed an act not only expedient but an essential prerequisite to his own survival.

The household at Nappa heard that Thomas had been amongst those arrested in York but after seeking pardon and pledging allegiance, he was released and, on his way home again, much to his family's relief. However, despite outward appearances both the Scrope's, the Metcalfe's and many other Yorkshire families were biding their time and would welcome a Yorkist resurgence, should it prove to be successful. These Northern families would maintain a semblance of obedience to the new king but behind closed doors, old loyalties were still in place and with them an underlying current of defiance was beginning to smoulder, soon to ignite and feed the flames of rebellion and renewed hope.

The Stanleys of Lancashire and the Percy's of Northumberland however, both of whom controlled vast swathes of the North, were happy to support the new Tudor regime and take advantage of the rewards offered for their allegiance. Both Thomas Stanley, his brother William and Henry Percy had all betrayed Richard at Bosworth, engendering resentment and resolve for vengeance in those who silently augured redress. However, the new king's policy of appeasement and gratuities, tempted many a rebel to submit to him and as time went on were less and less inclined to endanger their positions and livelihoods. After all, they could do nothing for Richard now he was dead and to fight an anointed king, no matter how tenuous his dominion, was treason, punishable by a hideous death. Nevertheless, hope still lingered amongst the faithful.

As the weather warmed into May, Eleanor and Bess were woken

in the early hours by the sound of riders clattering on the cobbles below their chamber. It was just after dawn and Bess craned her neck at the narrow casement, to try and make out the figures but they were hooded and spoke in whispers. Upon rising, Eleanor was asked to take some refreshment to a guest occupying one of the small chambers in the East tower but instructed not to enquire the visitor's name. She knocked and entered the room, where she saw a young man in his late 20's seated at a desk writing. He looked weary, his hand resting on his temple, his shoulders hunched, his hose muddied, and his hair unkempt, though his clothes were of fine quality. However, as he looked up and Eleanor could see his face, she caught her breath in a gasp of recognition.

'My Lord!' she bent her knee respectfully. Lord Lovell smiled, put down his quill and ran his fingers through his shoulder length fair hair, although it had darkened from his youth, when Eleanor had last seen him at Middleham. He had several days stubble on his chin and his skin was weathered from exposure but his good looks were still evident, as in the teenage lad the young serving girls at Middleham had desired, as they spied on the young men at arms.

'Eleanor! I am right aren't I?' he questioned, looking her up and down admiringly. 'It's been a long time!'

'Aye my Lord'.

'What are you doing here Eleanor?' Francis asked.

'The Countess of Warwick has gone into sanctuary, my Lord. There's no-one left at Middleham to serve. I am widow to a Metcalfe and they have kindly taken us in'.

'Oh aye, I remember William, a fine huntsman. I am sorry for your loss. You have a daughter do you not?'

'Aye, my Lord, Elizabeth is here with me. I also have a son but he resides with my sisters-in-law.' Eleanor placed the food and ale on the table, filled the mug and set it before him.

'Thank you Eleanor'. Francis smiled warmly.

'It is good to see you my Lord', Eleanor ventured with sincerity. She hoped he wouldn't object to her being so familiar. This young man was now her last link with Richard and she could almost feel her lover's presence in the room, as she sensed the late king's memory forming an invisible connection of affinity between them.

'You also Eleanor'. Francis smiled wanly and put his finger to his lips, though there was no need, Eleanor already knew she must keep the secret of their unexpected guest, as she bent her knee and turned towards the door. As she lifted the latch and glanced back at Richard's friend, his eyes met hers with an unspoken sadness, both cognizant of their shared affection for the man they had loved and served with an almost obsessive loyalty. Closing the door quietly, Eleanor leant against the wall, fighting to contain her emotions, as memories of Francis and Richard in happier times flooded back, reminding her of what they had lost.

Later that day she was summoned back to his chamber. 'Eleanor, I have a favour to ask'. Francis picked up a letter fixed with the Metcalfe's wax seal and handed it to her. 'Would you take this to Viscountess Lovell at Ravensworth? I cannot go there as her family will be watched.'

'Of course, my Lord. I will go at once'.

'Do not mention my name, or why you have come. If you are questioned, tell them you are seeking employment with the Viscountess but hand the letter *only* to her'.

Of course, my Lord'.

'I cannot stop here long but I would like to see her'. His eyes misted over and his hand trembled as he took a draught of ale, as he stared dejectedly into space. Eleanor wished she could have comforted this brave young man, Richard's most loyal companion, with a tender embrace but instead curtsied politely and eagerly hurried off to prepare herself for the journey, happy to be of service to her lover's liegeman. Confiding in Bess that she had an errand to do for their guest, she attempted to hide her eagerness to be trusted with such a mission, knowing her daughter would be curious.

'May I come mama?' Bess asked hoping for the chance to get out of the confines of the Hall.

'Nay, I'm sorry Bess. I have to do this alone, though I will take one of the grooms with me for protection. It should only take me a couple of hours on a good horse and I hope to be back before nightfall. If not, I will stay overnight and come back tomorrow'.

'Where are you going?

'It's best you don't know Bess, that way you will not be complicit'. Bess regarded her mother askance.

'You know him, don't you, mama?' she asked astutely, noticing the renewed sparkle in her mother's eyes and her eagerness to serve the reclusive guest.

'Aye, he was a friend of your father's from Middleham but tell no-one Bess. He is in great danger.'

The ride to Ravensworth was a pleasant one. Everywhere the lush new growth of Spring erupted into bloom and leaf, cascades of white May blossom bursting from the hawthorn trees along the waysides. The groom accompanying Eleanor knew the shortest route to follow, over the moor to Swaledale, through Reeth and by mid-afternoon they had arrived at the 14th century moated Castle, the ancestral seat of the Fitzhugh's, set in extensive walled parkland. Entering across the moat bridge and through the arched gatehouse inside the curtain wall, they dismounted in the wide courtyard, overlooked by 3-storey corner towers and a narrow belfry tower. While the groom waited at the stables, Eleanor was ushered into a large reception Hall and stood waiting for lady Lovell. A lady in waiting offered to take the missive to her mistress but Eleanor held it tightly and insisted on handing it to the Viscountess in person. The woman regarded her disdainfully and left to summon her mistress, who came directly.

A small, slight, petite lady in her twenties, with a somewhat pale but pleasant elfin face entered the hall and hurried over to Eleanor with a look of excited anticipation on her flushed cheeks, her light brown hair neatly braided underneath a short-veiled headdress, a close-fitting lilac gown emphasising her slight figure. She could have passed for a teenager and Eleanor observed a strong family likeness to the deceased Neville sisters, Anne and Isobel, whom she had served at Middleham and whom she knew were Lady Lovell's first cousins.

'I am Viscountess Lovell, you wished to see me?' Anne asked cautiously, as Eleanor curtsied and held out the letter.

'Eleanor Metcalfe, my Lady, from Nappa Hall. I have a letter for you of a most personal and confidential nature'. Anne took the parchment and turned to her lady in waiting who stood behind her, the woman clearly inquisitive as to the nature of the message.

'Thank you, Joan, that will be all. I can see to this'. Lady Lovell commanded curtly, her authoritative tone surprisingly at odds with the timid demeanour Eleanor had assumed. The waiting woman flashed a look of annoyance towards Eleanor, pressing her lips together disdainfully and reluctantly left the chamber, as Anne Lovell sat down on a settle beside the huge unlit fireplace and proceeded to break the seal.

'Oh!', she exclaimed, as she read the contents. 'At last!', her hand shook and she trembled but as she looked up Eleanor saw exhilaration in Anne's wide eyed stare and a tear welling up, threatening to spill over her lashes.

'He is at Nappa Hall?' she whispered to Eleanor, casting a glance at the door through which her maid had gone.

'Aye, my lady but not for long'.

'I must go to him! Does he seem well?'

'Aye my lady, so far as I can tell'.

About an hour later, a small, mounted party left Ravensworth for Wensleydale, the Viscountess ostensibly on an impromptu visit to the Scropes of Bolton, a trip she had done before but which would not be commented upon as unusual. With Eleanor's promise to Anne that Bess would attend to her needs, there was no reason to bring another ladies' maid. The less people that knew about the Lovell's reunion, the better. By the time they reached Nappa Hall, the sun had set and in the dwindling light, torches one by one flickered into life, illuminating the cloaked figures but ensuring the dark shadows prevented identity.

Eleanor showed Lady Lovell up to her husband's chamber, shutting the door quietly behind them, the fleeting image of the couple entwined in a tearful embrace catching Eleanor unawares with a sudden burst of emotion welling up to the surface. She swallowed, the lump in her throat constricting her breathing, forcing an involuntary sob of envy, as she ran back to her chamber and sank down on the bed, tears of longing now flowing unchecked - the sight of two people in love, only serving to underline the emptiness of her own situation, twisting the blade of hurt once more into her heart for the men she could never hold again.

Bess, having waited on the Viscountess for the night, found her mistress kind and considerate, while Anne found the pretty teenager charming and attentive, her honey-coloured hair, and fine features somehow reminding her of someone she had seen but not quite coming to a conclusion, until her husband confirmed her suspicions. Anne had attended Richard's coronation in '83 and the king had visited Ravensworth later when his wife was dying. Anne Lovell's sister-in-law Frideswide who had resided at Ravensworth with the Fitzhugh's since she and her siblings were orphaned, had been attracted to the grieving king and had spent time with him in their home. Now Anne saw those same Plantagenet facial characteristics, those solemn blue/grey eyes and slim frame in the teenager who served her. She had mentioned it to her husband who confirmed her conjectures as they lay together through the night.

'Richard was a dark horse! It seems many a young lady fell for his charms - your sister Frideswide being no exception! 'Anne giggled, to her husband while he sprang to his friend's defence.

'He was not like his brother, Anne. Richard deplored the loose morals at Edward's court but after his wife became ill and there was no hope, he might have strayed and who could blame him? He was barred from her bed and yet still a young man. Frideswide marriage was less than happy and I can quite see how she would have fallen for Richard. As for Eleanor's daughter, she was born long before Richard wed Anne Neville and besides, he was not told. When he returned, he couldn't acknowledge Elizabeth, because Eleanor had married a soldier and had brought the girl up as his'.

'You kept each other's secrets, Francis. I'm glad.' Anne smiled, 'We all need someone we can confide in, someone who will not betray us.' She reached for her husband's arm and pulled him to her. 'I don't mind if you have secrets from me Francis. I know I can't...' she hesitated... 'bear you children but you have my permission to stray if you so wish.

Such is my love for you.'

'Hush, do not speak of it my love, I am content. You will have all my possessions, when I die, if there is anything left, that is! My attainder reverts everything to the Crown of course but when our plan succeeds and Tudor is vanquished, it will be mine once more and you will have it *all* I promise you! There are no issues of my body waiting in the wings to inherit, I assure you!' Francis chuckled, caressing his wife affectionately.

'Oh Francis, I'm so afraid for you!' Anne replied, her voice muffled, as she pressed her head into his chest.

'Be of good cheer my love! I have many options and many loyal friends - Richard's friends - they won't betray me. Support is gathering pace beyond Yorkshire. I will lie low until we can re-group'. He had filled Anne in on the many months since Bosworth, his mission to secure the Princes' safety, tasked to him by Richard should he be killed, his months in sanctuary in Colchester, his escape and progress North with the rebels, the abortive attempt on Tudor's life at York. 'We will not fail again!' he assured his wife.

As he lay in the darkness, Francis prayed he was right, for facing the enormity of the task ahead of him and the horror of the punishment should he lose, was fearsome but a burden he could not relinquish if he was to avenge Richard and return the house of York to its rightful place. Lady Lovell left the next morning after thanking her hosts for their kindness and support for her husband. She thanked Eleanor and Bess, extending an open invitation to visit Ravensworth whenever they were in the vicinity. Before he left, Francis spent some time in private conversation with Thomas Metcalfe who had just returned to Nappa Hall, and Eleanor noticed her employer embrace the young man fondly, despite his purported allegiance to the new regime and his recent incarceration. He had been released after a brief imprisonment and pardoned on his pledge to the new king but behind closed doors Eleanor was relieved to see he had not abandoned his former loyalties.

Eleanor and Bess waited on Francis as he prepared to leave. Bess now recognised Lord Lovell from seeing him with Richard at Middleham when they were preparing for the Scottish campaign in '81, the intervening years evidenced in his matured face. The teenager immediately sensed a bond with her father's champion but was under strict instructions not to show her feelings or give him away to the other servants. Eleanor noticed Francis seemed encouraged and full of renewed resolve, since spending time with his wife. He had written a number of letters, which he stressed to Bess must be delivered urgently, tasking her with ensuring they went to the appropriate messenger. Bess beamed with pride at being asked to assist her father's closest friend and hurried off with a barely disguised air of self-importance for her mission.

'She has her father's eyes and fine features' Francis remarked casually as soon as Bess had left the room. Eleanor looked up with guarded surprise. *He knew?*

'Aye, I knew Eleanor', Francis grinned, affirming her unspoken question. 'Richard told me in confidence. We kept each other's secrets'. He winked, echoing his wife's words as Eleanor blushed and cast her gaze downwards, her cheeks burning.

'I loved him very much my Lord' she offered in explanation, needing Francis to understand Richard meant more to her than just a casual liaison.

'Moi aussi' he replied softly, staring out of the window. After a moment's silence he took a deep breath and slapped the wall with his hand. 'I *will* be avenged, if it is the last thing I do, so help me God!'

he vented, gritting his teeth with forceful resolve. He hung his head in mute prayer, pinching the bridge of his nose and pressing on his eyelids to suppress the tears that were threatening to emerge, before turning to strap on his sword, encased in its jewelled scabbard. He threw on his mantle fastened with a silver brooch, cast with the image of a wild boar. As Eleanor watched him, her eyes strayed to Richard's emblem. Francis saw the direction of her gaze and smiled.

'Loyaulte me lie' he winked, taking her hand and kissing it gently. 'I am indebted to you, fair lady. Keep your daughter safe. God bless you both'.

'My prayers are with you my Lord and I pray you will have success' Eleanor whispered her eyes still fixed on the image. She had her own boar badge, carefully concealed in a casket, the last gift Richard had left for her after their final night of love, the totem forever remaining a symbol of devotion and dedication to her lover's cause.

Francis picked up his saddlebag and hurried down the stairs and out to the stables, where a groom was waiting with the Viscount's horse. Eleanor watched from above as he trotted away through the archway and prayed for this courageous young man, who's loyalty was such that he held the whole nation's future in his hands. 'Fare thee well brave Lord. May God keep you and protect you and may your cause be victorious, for all our sakes!' she murmured, before seeking out her boar badge, kissing it softly, her hands clasped in fervent devotion against her lips, as she recited the rosary prayer.

Chapter Four

After the trouble in York, Henry Tudor based himself at Kenilworth, satisfied for now this latest resistance had been quashed. He now had a son, Arthur, born to his new queen to be, Elizabeth of York in September '86, in whom Henry's hopes for a new dynasty rested. Over winter however, Francis Lovell had disappeared into the wilds of Lancashire and with help from Sir Thomas Broughton of Furness, the Huddllestons of Millom and the Harringtons of Hornby, all staunch Ricardians, the elusive Viscount remained very much a threat and that threat was soon to materialise.

Francis had been visited by Richard Simonds, a priest from Oxford, who was acquainted with Robert Stillington the retired Bishop of Bath and Wells who had exposed Edward IV's bigamy, consequently legalising Richard III's accession to the throne. Oxford was close to Minster Lovell and Magdalen College housed the Lovell family chapel. Not only the Lovells but the De La Pole family were prominent in the area and had not forgotten their Yorkist blood. Simonds was involved in an audacious plan to introduce a boy who could pass for Edward of Warwick, now held prisoner in the Tower, where at some point a switch would be made, releasing the real Warwick and replacing him with the imposter. The identity of a ten-year-old boy of the same height and colouring could easily be mistaken, before the child's features matured into a recognisable and verifiable personality. Once garbed in the same clothes, with the same length of hair, one pre-pubescent boy would appear much like another to those not intimately familiar with him. With the Royal children largely kept out of the public eye, there were few who could swear as to their identities.

As January 1487 arrived, news that Francis had left for Holland came as a relief to those concerned for his safety. He would no doubt proceed straight to Richard's sister Margaret, the dowager Duchess of Burgundy who unfailing support for the Yorkist cause had always been indisputable. Already in Flanders was the young Prince Richard of York who had been residing at Gipping Hall with his brother Edward Prince of Wales when Henry Tudor's army invaded. Sir James Tyrell had been responsible for Prince Richard's safety and in 1484 had been sent over to Flanders by king Richard, 'on great matters concerning our welfare', which could only mean the relocation of one or both of his nephews. Edward meanwhile however, had been separated from his brother and according to local hearsay, quietly conveyed to Portugal by Sir Edward Brampton, the Portuguese Jew who had faithfully served both Edward IV and Richard III. Had Henry known the whereabouts of Edward IV's sons, their fate would have been sealed, for their prior claim to the throne of England and the impotence of his own.

At Court, with much speculation and falsehood concerning the recent discovery of Simonds' plot, both the priest and the retired bishop Robert Stillington were arrested and interrogated. In order to authenticate the young Earl of Warwick currently languishing in the Tower as the real issue of George of Clarence, Henry was forced to have the boy paraded at St. Paul's as proof. However, had Henry known it, an astonishing manoeuvre of subterfuge was about to take place.

After being exhibited, young Warwick was held at Lambeth palace overnight then transferred to the care of the Earl of Lincoln at Sheen Palace, on the River Thames, before being taken back to the Tower. Whilst in the care of his cousin, (an extraordinarily careless oversight by Tudor), Lincoln substituted Warwick for the boy chosen by Simonds to impersonate him, who was domiciled in Lincoln's household. Once returned to the Tower, no-one was keen eyed enough to spot the change and the young 'Prince' was assumed to be safely back under lock and key.

Earl Lincoln, having been summoned to attend the Privy Council meeting at Sheen Palace on 2nd February, appeared for one day, then made his excuses, saying he was going to visit his father's estates in Suffolk, whereupon he immediately set sail for Holland accompanied by no other than the genuine Earl of Warwick, now dressed as a servant. With Henry's net tightening around the conspirators and with the arrest of Bishop Stillington and Simonds, it was time for John de la Pole to assert his true allegiance and join his friend Francis, who was already at his aunt Margaret's Burgundian court.

The approach of winter at Nappa Hall seemed warmer than those Eleanor had endured at Middleham, the manor being comparatively small and compact, the rooms quicker to heat. Farming life had gone on uninterrupted by the change in monarch and supplies were plentiful, farmers not being in a position to pick and choose who bought their produce. One Lord was a good as another to the poorer folk, who notwithstanding their personal allegiance, needed to make a living and as the year turned, the stores at the Hall were well stocked and the household comfortable.

Nothing had been heard from Francis since his flight to Flanders but talk of another uprising continued to ferment and grow. With Elizabeth of York now Henry Tudor's queen, Eleanor marvelled at how quickly fortunes could change. She thought of that vivacious teenager, stripped of legitimacy and title, playing innocently with her young cousin, Edward of Warwick in the gardens at Sheriff Hutton. Now exalted by her mother's ambition, the tables had turned once more, with Elizabeth catapulted towards the throne of England and seen as the lynchpin uniting York and Lancaster. Gossip had filtered through from Court however, that Queen Bess, was simply doing her duty, having submitted meekly to her somewhat unappealing husband. Her previous infatuation with her handsome Uncle Richard, now dashed by his sudden death, had given her no choice but to resign herself to her destiny as unifier of two opposing factions. In her heart however, she remained staunchly Yorkist and would not stand in the way should her brothers return. Under constant scrutiny by her scheming mother-in-law, Margaret Beaufort, however, the young queen wisely kept her feelings to herself.

One of the most surprising pieces of news to come out of London was that Elizabeth Woodville, the queen's mother had suddenly and inexplicably been stripped of her possessions by the king and banished to Bermondsey Abbey, ostensibly for her having made peace with Richard four years before. This somewhat implausible excuse gave rise to whispers that the dowager queen had been found to be in league with Lovell and the rebels in a plan to re-instate one of her sons, or at the very least to ensure their safety. She must have regretted pushing her daughter in the way of Tudor, for Elizabeth of York would lose her crown in favour of her brothers should they re-appear and at the same time lose her husband. Still needs must, the dowager queen reasoned, her daughter would be compensated and either way, at least one of her children would retain the crown of England.

Having struck up a respectful friendship with Lady Lovell, Eleanor hoped she might hear some useful news, so was pleasantly surprised to receive an invitation in late February from Ravensworth, to stand in for Anne's ladies' maid, who was unwell and had been instructed to keep away for fear of contamination. It may not have been the sweating sickness that was rife in the South but it was wise to be precautious. *If the Metcalfe's can spare you, I will send my groom with a horse to collect you on Friday next* the Viscountess wrote. *We will provide your keep and a wage. There is no need to bring anything. We have all you will need here.*

The day Eleanor left for the Fitzhugh's dawned cold and cloudy, the previous night's snowfall already turning to slush, as a pale winter haze broke through the eddying mist. In the courtyard Eleanor donned a heavy mantle and embraced Bess before mounting the saddle of a sleek chestnut mare from the Ravensworth livery. The mare, sporting a white blaze on her nose and three white stockinged feet, had been affectionately named Chausette by Francis's sister Frideswide, Eleanor patted her mount's warm neck and stroked her ears, as the mare snorted and stamped on the hard ground. Bess ran up with an apple for Chausette, watched appreciatively by the Fitzhugh's groom, who was eyeing up the teenager lustfully.

'Perform your duties for Madam Metcalfe well and remember your manners, Bess.' Eleanor instructed her daughter. 'You will take my place while I'm gone, so no more gossiping in corners with the kitchen girls, she glanced at the groom and lowered her voice, '…and keep away from the farm hands and stable lads too! They will be quick to take advantage, given little encouragement!' Eleanor didn't care if the man had heard her, she needed him to know his attentions had been noted. 'Oh mama, 'I'm no longer a child!' Bess rolled her eyes in embarrassment. 'I can handle the boys!' She was excited at the prospect of a few weeks' freedom from her mother's reproachful gaze. She knew very well she was an object of desire for the young men at the manor but none of them appealed since she had caught the eye of the local farrier from

Wensley. Now with Eleanor absent for what could be weeks, Bess was looking forward to continuing her flirtation unobserved.

'Mmm, well, we all *think* we can!' her mother remarked, as much to herself as to her daughter. As Eleanor rode away, she felt somewhat ashamed for her stricture, she had been younger than Bess when she succumbed to temptation with young Richard Duke of Gloucester and Bess was herself an adult now. However, she would not wish on her daughter the shame of an unplanned pregnancy and the need to marry a stranger for appearances sake.

Approaching Ravensworth castle, a lowering cloud base obliterating the surrounding hillsides, the valley appeared featureless and cold. A patchwork of boggy ground had frozen in sheets of grey ice, forming a monochrome backcloth to the stark silhouette of the castle, the bare branched sentinel like trees surrounding it, reaching heavenwards into the mist. Eleanor shivered as they crossed the moat, riding through the arched portcullis entrance and into the courtyard. Returning to a castle once more, she couldn't help but recall the life she had left behind at Middleham and the bittersweet memories of love and loss that haunted her. Shaking off her reminiscences with an involuntary shudder, she followed a page up an external staircase to the first floor in the South East tower, where a small chamber had been set aside for her, along the corridor from Viscountess Lovell's parlour and bedchamber.

Anne Lovell welcomed Eleanor warmly and she was reminded again of the young Neville sisters upon whom she had waited almost twenty years ago, though Lady Lovell was several years her cousins' junior. Chatting amicably about Anne and Isobel and how the Neville girls had both struggled with their health, which ultimately claimed their young lives, the two women soon formed a friendship transcending the class difference between them. Anne enjoyed having a confidant who would not sit in judgement upon her and Eleanor felt privileged to be party to her employer's hopes and fears, heartened by a shared loyalty to those they loved and the secrets they kept.

A few days later Eleanor was introduced to Frideswide, so named after the patron saint of Oxford but oft known to family by her childhood nickname of Frith. She had been married at sixteen, to Edward Norris, the nephew of the Earl of Oxford. Eleanor had seen the twenty-one-year old with her newborn child and 3 older children in the nursery quarters of the castle and was struck by the young woman's beauty. Similar in colouring to her brother, Frideswide's long blonde locks braided prettily at her neck, wide blue eyes and soft features, together with feminine curves, ensured she attracted much attention from men, together with glances of envy from women. Her second youngest child however, stopped Eleanor in her tracks. The child's older siblings had slightly darker colouring but little Anne at nearly 3 years old was the double of Bess at the same age; they could have been sisters! Eleanor had remarked on her observation to Lady Lovell as they sat together the next evening. Anne smiled and lowered her voice.

'I wondered if you would notice' she looked askance at her companion. 'Little Anne is not by the same father. It has caused a rift between Frith and her husband, although they were never close and now they do not speak of it.' Anne leaned closer, staring pointedly at Eleanor. 'I think you might deduce who fathered the child…' Eleanor stopped sewing the headdress she was mending, scanning the Viscountesses' facial expression, a lump already constricting her throat as comprehension registered. She realised Francis must of course have confided in his wife about Bess's parentage. There was only one obvious conclusion.

'Richard!' she managed, swallowing hard, as a stab of jealousy rose in her breast and she felt herself welling up, emotion surging through her, threatening to undermine her self-control. Anne nodded but she could see the revelation touched a nerve in Eleanor.

'Forgive me, Eleanor, mayhap I should not have mentioned it'.

'Nay my Lady, somehow I suspected but I thought not to give it credence.' Eleanor's lip trembled as she put down her sewing and stood up. 'My lady, may I be excused, I'm feeling a little faint. I need to lie down'.

'Of course, Eleanor. I have no need of you tonight. Do please retire to your chamber. I wish you good night'.

'Goodnight my lady'.

As Eleanor hurried away Anne chided herself for her indiscretion. Her companion must still have deep feelings the late king, despite it being at least twenty years since he had impregnated her as a teenager. Anne was not to know of Eleanor's more recent night of passion with the charismatic nobleman, or her enduring obsession with him.

Eleanor lay in the darkness, struggling with her emotions. Fridewide's daughter must have been born in the summer of '84, a whole year before her own last night with Richard. At the time, he would have been in deep grief for his recently departed son and with Anne's failing health had clearly sought comfort with his best friend's beautiful teenage sister. Eleanor could hardly blame him, nor Frideswide for that matter – Richard was in the prime of life and the young mother would have been awed by his attentions, while her somewhat indifferent husband was absent. Richard's reserved demeanour, refinement and noble appeal would be attractive to Frideswide, who herself was unfulfilled, her desire enhanced by her king's obvious need for comfort in his distress. Besides, she would hardly refuse her king!

'*Huh! Unlike myself!*' Eleanor almost laughed out loud, for she was instantly transported back to Middleham when Edward IV had been held by the Earl of Warwick, just after Bess had been born. She had waited on the handsome monarch but had refused his amorous advances, agonising about it afterwards until she observed he was never short of willing courtesans from amongst the castle's ladies. Now, she remonstrated with herself, *after all, I am no different!* as despite refusing king Edward, she had not refused his youngest brother, that blissful evening on the hillside when she surrendered her virtue to Richard. It was only afterwards she found out to whom she had lost her heart.

Staring into the dark, drying her jealous tears, Eleanor censured herself for her feelings. Naturally Richard would have been attracted to many ladies at court and they in turn to him. He already had two illegitimate children from before his marriage and as he matured, a nobleman of his standing and appeal was hardly likely to remain abstinent for long, especially during his wife incapacity. Anne Neville was always so frail and Eleanor knew enough of Richard's character to know he would not think to force himself upon his failing queen, who in any case was no longer able to bear another child. When faced with a youthful beauty who so clearly looked upon him favourably, the temptation of a fleeting tryst would be hard for him or any virile young man to resist.

As Eleanor came to terms with this new revelation, she felt a bond with Frideswide, now that she knew they had both loved Richard and borne him a child. She watched Francis's fair sister as she played with her children, trying hard not to picture her with Richard but failing miserably. She could see Richard pulling Frith to him in a passionate embrace, his lips pressing against hers, his body craving hers until he could hold back no further. She shut her eyes but the image was still there imprinted upon her brain. *What was it that made these sons of York so attractive to women?* Eleanor pondered, a smile playing around her lips - Edward with his stunning good looks and animal magnetism that drew both sexes to him like moths to a flame; tragic volatile George, whose engaging wit and physical appeal had attracted Isobel Neville, the 'Kingmaker's eldest daughter before sickness sent her to an early grave. Lastly, the youngest brother Richard, the quiet, studious, accomplished soldier, who strove to emulate his eldest sibling, quite unaware his family's physical attractiveness ensured he too was an object of suppressed desire by the opposite sex.

Eleanor knew she would have to deal with her jealousy, her only small recompense being that she had shared Richard's bed at least a year later than Frideswide and he had still found her as desirable as at their first liaison – hopefully more so, she smiled at the memory of him caressing her womanly curves and how he had complimented her desirously. She was almost regretful that she had been infertile and unable to conceive since a miscarriage some years before with Will, when she lost a daughter. She would have loved another child to nurture while she was still young enough and especially with Richard. Had he lived, *(if only!)* she knew he would now be betrothed to a foreign princess and their paths would never be likely to cross again. She had come to terms with this fact before Bosworth but since his death the finality of never seeing him again, even from a distance, was a loss she found hard to bear. *For Bess it must be worse!* Eleanor realised, though at least her daughter could picture her father, his smile and his voice imprinted so vividly on her childhood memory.

Eleanor thought about Frideswide's child Anne, who would

never know her father and she wondered if her mother would ever tell her the truth. The girl was largely ignored by her stepfather, whose allegiance to the Lancastrian cause meant he was committed to join Tudor's royal forces should the rebels return. The Fitzhugh household was careful therefore not to openly show support for the Yorkist cause, especially since Richard Fitzhugh had been stripped of his office of Steward, Constable and Master Forester of Barnard Castle for his previous association with the rebels.

While at Ravensworth, news of an astonishing nature emerged, glimmers of new hope and optimism spreading rapidly through the Dales. Francis had sailed to Ireland from Burgundy where he had been sheltered by Margaret, Duchess of Burgundy, who backed his campaign. Accompanied by the Earl of Lincoln and with the support of the Earls of Kildare and Desmond, the rebels had crowned a teenager in Dublin on 24th May, as King Edward V and were sailing to invade England. There was some confusion as to whether the youth was Edward of Warwick or in fact Edward V, who had disappeared with his brother Richard of Shrewsbury, or even a pretender impersonating one of the Princes but for Yorkist sympathisers this was exciting news. Edward V would have been fifteen by now and eligible to be crowned king, whereas Edward of Warwick was still a minor and under his father's attainder, so the assumption was an obvious one.

Lady Lovell eagerly shared with Eleanor what she had heard. It seems that Margaret, the Dowager Duchess of Burgundy, sister to the York brothers Edward, George and Richard, had financed and provided an army of German mercenaries and ships for Lord Lovell and the Earl of Lincoln, which had set out for Ireland. They had with them a young teenager, John from Oxford but later rather oddly known as Lambert Simnel, who had been schooled to impersonate a

Yorkist prince and would be used as a decoy for Prince Edward. The real Edward V, having waited in a safe haven in deepest Devonshire, had been escorted to Dublin by Sir Henry Bodrugan, one of the late king's most trusted adherents.

Lady Lovell told Eleanor that following the death of his only son, Richard had made enquiries into the possibility of Edward V and his brother being re-legitimised, once they were of age. He hoped such an action might unite the country once more and encourage those Yorkists who had defected to the enemy to return. Had Richard not died at Bosworth, those plans might have been put in place when the time was right. Having lost all his immediate family Richard told Francis he had no real wish to continue as king but first he must save England from an unworthy usurper. Sadly, his plan would never be realised, thwarted by the treachery of those who professed loyalty while intending no such favour.

However, Richard being the practical man he was, had also made plans in the event of his death. He knew if he was killed in battle, the victor would assume the crown and his brother's sons would be in great danger, therefore Lovell had to stay alive to facilitate the welfare and eventual return of his nephews. Having already named another nephew John de la Pole, his heir, who would remain in place until Edward's sons were of age, Richard knew his loyal best friend and his sister's son would do their utmost to facilitate his plan. Much as he might wish to support his king, Richard determined Francis must not fight the invaders in battle, he *must* stay alive to save the house of York. He therefore sent the Viscount South to guard the port of Southampton and prepare resistance in case of enemy action.

Eleanor thought of the young knight she had seen riding out from Nappa Hall, the colossal burden of his vow to Richard weighing on his mind, the fate of a whole dynasty resting on his shoulders, the hope and expectation of every loyal Ricardian hanging on his every move. She couldn't help but fear this burden would prove too much for Richard's young advocate and crusader, so committed to his cause and the pledge of loyalty he had made to his beloved benefactor.

Chapter Five

Sir Robert Markenfield, of Markenfield Hall near Ripon, had been assigned stewardship of the manor of Coldridge and its Royal deer park by Richard III following his coronation in 1483. Sir Robert's secret mission, to convey Prince Edward to safety in this rural Devon hamlet, just North of Exeter, until the king had been victorious against the Lancastrian usurper, there to live in anonymity until he was of age to inherit the crown. Sir Henry Bodrugan, had been granted the Lordship of Coldridge in 1474, which after Bosworth, was returned to Thomas Grey. Bodrugan however, had escaped Tudor's clutches, making his way to his West Country estates where he could carry out Richard's orders regarding the care of his nephew. Renowned as a somewhat wary and villainous rogue, Bodrugan could be relied upon to act with courage and resourcefulness but at the same time with unwavering loyalty to the Yorkist cause.

Now from his safe sanctuary at Coldridge, Edward V had been conducted by Sir Henry and his son John Beaumont, to Dublin for coronation, as the true king of England. Here they were to meet with Lovell's army, arriving in Ireland from Burgundy, his invasion force of 2,000 German mercenaries, Swiss trained soldiers, known as landsknechts, notorious for their masterly fighting skills and a certain ruthlessness. They were commanded by Martin Schwartz, a dynamic and fearsome soldier whose reputation for gratuitous violence preceded him. Schwartz's well-disciplined professional army were trained to fight with 18ft long pikes and two-handed zweihänders, six-foot undulate swords with which they would mow down their opponents like scythes through wheat. By contrast, swelling the rebel numbers before they left Ireland, came an assortment of Irish kerns, Gaelic warriors, retainers of Clan chiefs Gerald Fitzgerald and his brother Thomas. Lightly armed and lacking protective clothing but nevertheless filled with enthusiasm and defiance, the kerns' boldness was encouraged by the experienced and well-equipped mercenaries leading them. Also, amongst them, was John, the teenager who was poised to impersonate Edward V in case of capture.

On 24th May 1487 at Christ Church Cathedral in Dublin Edward Plantagenet was crowned king, in a formal ceremony using a crown removed from a wooden church statue of the Virgin Mary. The fifteen-year-old was acclaimed and accepted by the Irish people, not only as claimant to his father Edward IV's throne but as the Grandson of Richard Duke of York, who had been popular as Lord Lieutenant of Ireland in 1449 and had fled back there ten years' later, before being killed at Wakefield in 1460.

There was still some confusion as to the identity of the newly crowned king with many assuming he was the Earl of Warwick, despite the age difference, or even an impostor, the uncertainty, suiting the rebels, who used the misapprehension to their advantage. As it was, Edward V and his impersonator young John were interchangeable, being so alike physically and those not familiar with them would be hard pushed to make a distinction, including Tudor.

The suspicious king, having learned of the goings on in Dublin, sent a Herald to investigate the so called 'pretender' to the throne and expose him as a fraud but to his chagrin, his agent returned with the news that the teenage king appeared genuine, passing the interrogation with flying colours. Henry was perplexed. He was certain he had the Earl of Warwick safely incarcerated in the Tower, so the other alternative was either a new pretender, or more worryingly, the real Edward V.

The next news to reach Kenilworth was that Lord Lovell's invasion force had crossed the Irish Sea and landed at Foulney island harbour on the Furness peninsular of Lancashire on 4th June and was rapidly making its way Eastwards, the numbers of armed men exceeding those who had landed with Henry in 1485. Henry was incandescent. This had alarming parallels with the battle of Bosworth, only now the roles were reversed. Now it was his turn to defend his throne against an invading enemy and *would he suffer the same fate as his predecessor?*

Henry slept fitfully that night, disturbed by visions of king Richard's body, broken, defiled, slung across the back of a horse like a common felon, cast into a hole in the ground with no casket, no ceremony, no honours. He awoke in a sweat, his conscience pricked, visions of the late king's bravery, while he himself cowered in fear behind his French pikemen, etched indelibly on his mind. He had won the crown by the actions of others, not by his own prowess. *Was he about to receive his just deserts for the insults on his predecessor? Who would mourn for Henry Tudor if he perished? His mother of course, Jasper probably, Oxford, maybe, Stanley* nay – all he craved was title and riches, the duplicitous Earl of Derby would pledge loyalty to any flag that paid him well enough. *His queen?* Nay, she was a Yorkist, he could see the hatred in her eyes as she succumbed to her marital obligations; a victim of her mother's ambition and his own, in uniting the red rose with the white. *His son Arthur?* Nay, he would not even remember him.

Henry had no way of knowing how many members of the country's notoriously fickle nobility would support him. *Would the*

Earl of Suffolk come to the aid of his son Lincoln, would those who had lost their lands after Bosworth want revenge? Upon hearing that the capricious Marquess of Dorset was on his way, Henry had him put in the Tower for safekeeping, despite having done no wrong. Those who had turned against Richard so easily, could just as easily turn again and Tudor wasn't taking any chances, especially with Thomas Grey.

Have I done enough? The uneasy monarch agonised. *Will the fickle English Lords stand behind me? I am no soldier, no brave champion, what can I offer them save riches and property?* Then he remembered the crown of England - a sacred state, to which every pious man would pay homage, regardless of the wearer. *I am King! God's anointed!* he smirked with overweening pride, obdurately straightening his back against the bedhead. *If they cannot love me, they will fear me! No man of means wants to commit treason! They dread that grisly death too much.* Immediately he felt better and called for his page to dress him.

Eleanor was back at Nappa Hall by the time local gossip had confirmed the rebel's return. Anne Lovell's lady in waiting had recovered from her illness and Eleanor's services no longer needed at Ravensworth. She had enjoyed the change of scene and especially Lady Lovell's company but she was eager to see her daughter and return to her beloved Wensleydale.

Eleanor noticed a change in Bess upon her return. Her daughter had a sparkle in her eye and a new-found confidence, in part due to her elevated position as Elizabeth Metcalfe's maid but Eleanor guessed there was another reason – Bess was in love. During her mother's absence, Bess had used every opportunity to meet with Robert

Dinsdale, the blacksmith's son from Wensley, who was smitten by the fetching teenager from Middleham, with her amber-coloured locks and mesmeric grey-blue eyes. Bess had a certain poise and presence, lacking in the uncultured village girls who competed for his attention and Robert was encouraged to find this engaging maiden clearly found him attractive in return.

Eleanor had met Robert when he came to shoe the Metcalfe's horses. He had learned his blacksmithing skills from his father at the village forge but preferred to keep his focus on equine care, rather than the explore the full range of metal working techniques in demand at the smithy. Eleanor could see why her daughter was attracted to Robert. A fine-looking lad, well built, muscular, tanned, with hazel eyes and shoulder length brown hair, Rob's natural affinity with horses demonstrated a kindness and sensitivity often lacking in working men. *She could do worse*, she thought to herself and if Bess were to settle down as this young man's wife, her daughter would live in reasonable comfort, her husband's skills being in constant demand. She also felt Richard would approve. With his natural daughter safely under the radar of the warring nobility, Eleanor felt sure he would be content to know Bess was out of harm's way amongst the good honest folk of the working classes.

Chapter Six

With Lovell's invasion army landing in Furness, an area that remained a hotbed of hostility to the new Tudor regime, the country was on high alert. There was much excitement and speculation that a repeat of Bosworth might be on the cards, only this time with renewed hope the Yorkists would be victorious. A campaign of deliberate misinformation was soon being spread by the rebels with news that Henry Tudor had fled or died, which had the desired effect of making it harder for the king to summon support and subsequently delaying his departure Northwards.

Edward V, newly crowned in Ireland and awaiting his destiny, was taken from their landing point at Furness harbour to nearby Gleaston Castle by Sir Henry Bodrugan, who was charged with his safety. Gleaston, originally built by the Harringtons, was now owned by the Marquis of Dorset, Thomas Grey, Edward's half-brother, through his marriage to Cecily Bonville. Here, they were to await the rebels' much anticipated victory, which would allow Edward to once again, take his place on the throne of England. He could not be allowed to fight for fear of capture or death but even as an observer he was too prized to accompany the rebels. They had his proxy John for that; Edward's youthful illegitimate half-brother, poised to impersonate him. Instead, he would wait for news from this remote Furness peninsular. However, should their cause be lost, Edward could quickly make his escape to the West Country unobserved.

The mood was one of optimism and fervour as the rebel army camped at Swarthmoor near Ulverston and after only four days of marching, the force entered Wenselydale, having progressed through the Lune valley, stopping at Hornby Castle, where the Harringtons added reinforcements and thence Eastwards into the Dales.

Morale was high with the tantalising prospect of victory, though some landowners were still reluctant to commit openly against the king, the punishment for treason weighing heavily. Sir William Parr of Kendal, Francis's brother-in-law, having married Anne Lovell's sister Elizabeth, had died in 1483, so his household was unable to provide support as the army passed through the town and though Francis was disappointed, he was undeterred. His troops were buoyant and had every hope of success with the formidable presence of Schwartz and his seasoned fighters at their head, as they marched on through Sedbergh.

The household at Nappa soon heard the rebel army was approaching from the West, having encamped near Hawes the previous night. Francis had meanwhile sent word to Ravensworth of his army's progress in the hope of meeting with his wife along the way.

'Mama, come quick! They're here!' Bess called from the stairwell leading to the roof over Nappa Hall's East tower, just as the sun came up on 8th June. Eleanor hurried up the steps after her daughter, accompanied by several other servants. They peered out across the dale to where a column of dust rose from a procession of mounted cavalry, foot soldiers and heavy-laden carts, marching and trundling its way along the valley floor. The column of riders and men appeared to stretch Westwards for miles, following the course of the river and Eleanor could see the banners held aloft at the front of the cavalcade as the sounds reverberated across the vale; the clatter of many hoof beats, the chink of harness, the rhythmic thud of striding men, their pace almost a jog, the creak of cartwheels and gun carriages, rising towards them like the sound of an approaching storm.

'Where are they going?' Bess asked, leaning her arm on the parapet.

'I should imagine they are making for York', Eleanor replied absentmindedly, shading her eyes from the sun, trying to make out the figures on horseback at the front of the retinue. She was looking for Francis and also for the Earl of Lincoln whom she had last seen entertaining Richard at his Sheriff Hutton castle but the figures were too far distant to identify any individual. The surrounding trees masked much of the view and the distinctive banners they held aloft hung limp in the still morning air, where fingers of mist clung to the course of the river.

'There's so many of them!' her daughter stared in wonderment, never having seen such a large body of men in one place. 'Are they going to fight the king?' she looked up at her mother, wide-eyed, revealing a little too much eagerness in her voice.

'Hush Bess' Eleanor glanced around at the other servants but to her relief they were chatting amongst themselves pointing and gesticulating animatedly. 'Aye, that's why they're here', she answered her daughter with a sense of foreboding. At Bess's age she would have found such a spectacle as thrilling as her daughter but instead she thought of the young men and what they would soon have to face, recalling her brothers' words after they escaped from Barnet; the carnage and horror of hand to hand fighting, the blood and butchery, which neither victor nor vanquished could avoid. Every battle a fight to the death, or if not immediate, resulting in a slow and painful decline from some hideous injury. Though she fully supported their cause, these men were opposing an anointed king and no matter how undeserving of that exalted estate he might be, if they lost they would face execution, or worse, suffer a traitor's death. Eleanor quickly blocked the image forming in her mind and as if on cue to distract her fears, a small party of riders clattered into the courtyard below, one of them Eleanor recognised as Viscountess Lovell. Jolted into action, she grabbed her daughter's arm. 'Come Bess, we'll be needed…and tie your hair back before you present yourself', she added, drawing her daughter's waist long auburn hair away from her face, Bess not having had time to dress herself properly, so eager was she to see the army march past.

After greeting the Metcalfes, Anne Lovell, summoned Eleanor to a small parlour, adjacent to the main reception hall where her brother Richard Fitzhugh, was in animated conversation with Thomas Metcalfe. Anne clasped Eleanor's hands warmly, her eyes sparkling, her face flushed with elation.

'Eleanor! He's back! Francis is here, I must see him! Would you accompany me to Masham tonight? He has sent word to me that they will pitch camp there by sundown'.

'Of course, my lady, I would be happy to'. Eleanor was almost as ebullient as the Viscountess.

'Richard my brother is joining him, along with Thomas and James Metcalfe and the Scropes, we can go with them and then return here together tomorrow. Francis is going to face the king Eleanor! He is going to restore the house of York!' Anne clasped her hands gleefully, like a child who had been promised a coveted gift.

'I pray he succeeds my Lady – we are all behind him'.

'Aye, he has amassed a sizeable army and Lord Lincoln is with him'. Anne exclaimed eagerly, hurrying to the window, as the seemingly unending columns of men marched, jogged and rode by, the sun glinting off polished sallets in the early morning haze. 'I must go to him tonight Eleanor! …If the worst should happen and they fail, I may not see him again!' she swallowed, suddenly serious as her eyes brimmed with tears.

'I pray that won't happen my lady. They have so much support here in the North'.

'Aye, though some are reluctant to oppose the king for fear of losing their property. Huh', she scoffed, 'When Francis is victorious, he will remember those who came to his aid and those who didn't!'. she exclaimed, pursing her lips defiantly, fists clenched, as Eleanor attempted to suppress a smile, at Anne's impromptu display of stubbornness.

Eleanor went to tell her daughter the news of her imminent departure but found Bess prostrate on the bed, sobbing into a handkerchief. 'What on earth is the matter?' her mother asked concerned. 'Why do men always have to fight?' Bess replied tearfully. 'They always go away and leave us to grieve. It's not fair'. Supposing Bess was referring to her father and to Francis, Eleanor thought to instil a sense of pride in her daughter and not to imagine the worst, though she had oft been guilty of that herself.

'It's what men do for us Bess. They have to fight to keep us safe and provide for us. How else are they going to succeed? No use them sitting at home with the womenfolk! We should celebrate their bravery and ask God to give them courage'. Eleanor kissed her daughter's head before selecting a few belongings for her night away.

'I shall be back in a couple of days Bess. Be of good cheer. Things may be about to change for the better! Just think of that! Now, dry your eyes my dear and don't show your feelings to Madam Metcalfe. She will be worried for her husband and won't wish to see your tears'. Bess ignored her mother and continued weeping into the pillow. Eleanor was quite glad she had no husband to wave off to war though part of her was beginning to miss the excitement of male company and that physical union, which made her feel feminine and coveted. She would have been surprised therefore if she had foreseen what would shortly be in store for her.

After some refreshment, Lord Fitzhugh, Anne Lovell, Thomas Metcalfe, Eleanor, and a large contingent of retainers left to rendezvous with Lord John Scrope at Bolton, five miles down the valley and from thence past Middleham and on to Masham, a total of about twenty miles. Eleanor's brothers joined their party, eager for the chance to assist the rebels in opposing the king. They knew Francis Lovell from their time at Middleham, when learning their military skills, under the Earl of Warwick and though the Earl had been defeated, they had returned to serve Richard Duke of Gloucester. This was their opportunity to show their fealty to the Yorkist cabal had not changed. As the host neared Middleham castle, the Lancastrian guards were left with no choice but to flee as the army approached, for to offer resistance would have meant certain death, but to allow them to pass unchallenged would have inferred approbation.

Eleanor felt a lump rise in her throat as she rode by the old fortress – so many memories of past magnificence, the Earl of Warwick's ostentation, the Duke of Gloucester's luxury, the splendour of majesty, the hustle and bustle of this once Northern stronghold now silenced - as impotent as the Tudor flag wrapped limply around its pole. Eleanor looked away, haunted by the ghosts of those with whom she had lived, laughed and cried, the family she had served, the men she had loved; all gone, mostly dead or if not, never to return. This had been her home for sixteen years, the birthplace of her children, a place of safekeeping and sanctuary, now empty and soulless, as cold and unwelcoming as the impregnable stone of its ramparts. Eleanor shivered despite the warm day – *how abruptly the wheel of fortune had turned!*

As the army marched on, they passed the great 12th century Cistercian monastery of Jervaulx Abbey, where the monks came out with flagons of ale for the dust choked troops, the Abbot adding his own armed tenants to their number. The beautiful abbey, a comforting haven of peace and serenity, nestling in extensive parkland, its huge church and extensive monastic buildings gleaming in the sunlight. Jervaulx had prospered under Richard III, providing Middleham castle with battle-trained horses from their renowned equine stud farm. Richard had purchased the more expensive destriers, strong stallions bred for warfare, along with swift-footed coursers, ideally suited for fast-paced hunting. Eleanor recalled the time the Countess of Warwick had ridden over to Jervaulx to purchase a pony for young Prince Edward of Middleham. She had returned in tears when she discovered she had lost her costly devotional locket somewhere along the pathway. Despite a prolonged search the jewel was never found. Now with around 8,000 marching men treading the byways, the golden reliquary would no doubt be lost forever, crushed deeper into the mud with every step.

It was late in the afternoon by the time the riders approached Masham and made for the Fitzhugh's manor of Tanfield castle, where the nobles would spend the night. They had caught up with the tail end of the rebel lines, now slowing pace as they dispersed to set up camp at various points along the river Ure.

Marching at a blistering pace across the country, picking up support along the way, the mood amongst the men was of optimism and resolve, their confidence increasing with every addition to their number. It appeared every pasture, common and riverbank around the market town was taken up by soldiers, tents, horses, carts, guns and weaponry. The German *landsknechts*, distinctive in a colourful assortment of striped and slashed uniforms, busily making camp, unloading wagons, lighting fires, settling down for the night, filling the air with a cacophony of strange voices. As the party from Nappa passed close to the camp, a clamour of raucous whistles and unintelligible remarks emanated from the ranks at the sight of two pretty women riding by, causing Anne to blush and turn her head away embarrassed. 'I hope they weren't being vulgar' she remarked coyly.

'I'll wager they *were*, my Lady!' Eleanor chuckled, staring back defiantly as one of the soldiers grabbed his crotch suggestively and shouted out in an unfamiliar language. She wasn't offended. She knew enough of men at arms going to war, that any excuse for titillation provided a welcome distraction from the coming tableau of butchery they would soon have to face. The man was immediately reprimanded by a captain who turned to see the object of his soldier's profanity and stared fixedly at Eleanor. She meant to look away but she found herself returning his gaze and her heart skipped a beat. He was exceedingly handsome and it was the first time in a long time she felt that frisson of attraction for one of the opposite sex. In fact, not since that last night with Richard had she allowed herself to feel that tremor of womanly desire she had suppressed for so long.

The captain bowed theatrically, grinning admiringly at her and she found herself smiling back, her cheeks colouring with the warm glow of gratification. She'd almost forgotten she was still a young woman in her early thirties and still fair enough to turn heads. After all, had Richard not told her she was even more alluring that last night, than when he had first loved her as a naïve teenager? Their tryst at Sheriff Hutton was not even two years ago yet it seemed like an eternity and Eleanor had since dismissed all thoughts of carnal concupiscence from her consciousness and had ceased to think of herself as desirable. Now however, she was reminded that she was not yet done with the thrill of the opposite sex and feelings she had suppressed could easily be regenerated. Thankfully, the Viscountess in looking the other way, had failed to notice Eleanor's preoccupation with the prepossessing soldier.

Approaching their destination, Eleanor was still picturing the charismatic captain as they neared Tanfield castle, a castellated manor house, enclosed within a high perimeter wall on the banks of the Ure. The riders entered via a battlemented gatehouse with chambers over, featuring an attractive oriel window, which appeared to be a recent addition. A large group of soldiers were congregated outside, a line of gun carriages and carts standing in the road, fully laden with a variety of armaments, armour, stacks of 18ft long pikes and *zweihänders*, their blade's curvilinear form designed for causing the maximum amount of damage as they sheared the enemy down. Seeing these fearsome weapons up close, Eleanor cringed at the thought of their use on the battlefield. She had heard they had been used at Bosworth to great effect, protecting a cowering Tudor, while Richard bore down on his enemy in a selfless display of valour and prowess, with no thought for his own safety. She thought of the devastating efficacy of this bristling wall of sharpened spikes against man and horse and was reminded why these men were here. They knew what they were about to face and for many, for no other reason than monetary reward. She had to admire these young soldiers' courage but at the same time recalling her daughter's words, *Why did men have to go to war?*

Dismounting in the central courtyard, the Fitzhugh's ushered their guests into the Great Hall to await Francis and the Earl of Lincoln, who were refreshing themselves in their private chambers. Lord John Scrope greeted Lord Thomas Scrope who had just arrived from his castellated manor at Clifton, while Lady Lovell was shown upstairs to be re-united with her husband. Along with them, prudently kept out of sight, was the young man primed to impersonate the Yorkist king.

As Eleanor collected her mistress's belongings, she was surprised to see Robert Dinsdale amongst the retainers gathered in the courtyard. He was examining the hoof of a large grey courser, picking out a stone wedged in the sole. Smiling warmly in greeting she went over to him. 'Are you joining the army Robert?' she asked in puzzlement. He flicked the stone away with his hoof pick, placing the animal's leg gently back on the ground and smiled back.

'Well, I'm not sure madam Metcalfe. Lord Scrope has asked for a farrier to accompany them but if I am required to fight, of course I will do so'.

'That's very brave of you Robert. Have you told Bess?'

'Aye madam, we have said our farewells'. Eleanor realised at once the true motivation for Bess's tears.

'Thank you, Robert. You will be much missed but we pray not for long.' She touched his arm gently. 'May God go with you Robert and may you return safe'. She hoped this young man would not have to witness the bloody initiation now facing novice soldiers, yet to experience the reality of close combat.

'Thank you, madam, I fully intend to!' he grinned, handing the horse he was holding over to Lord Scropes' groom, who led it into the stable.

Eleanor went inside and was shown up to a small chamber on the first floor, adjoining a larger one selected for the Viscountess. The single narrow casement faced South, the late sun's rays illuminating the room with a soft warmth. Outside, the flames of a hundred camp fires lit up the fields, where every foot of space was taken up by a prostrate soldier, their energy spent from the march. Eleanor had nothing but admiration for these men who would be on the move again tomorrow and the day after that until they met an opposing force with which they would have to engage in battle. *How do they do it?* she marvelled before falling back on the bed, closing her eyes against the shaft of sinking sunlight streaming through the casement, her body weary from her ride, though her mind remained too active for slumber.

She thought about Anne Lovell reunited with her husband once more, envying the couple's closeness, recalling her own marriage to Will and she wondered if she would ever have that again. Her thoughts strayed to the handsome captain in the field and the shiver of excitement she had felt. She smiled at the idea of intimacy with a man she would most likely never see again. Part of her thought *Why not?* while the God-fearing part of her recoiled at the notion of behaving like a harlot. A while later, interrupting her reverie, Anne Lovell entered the room. Eleanor could see she'd been crying.

'What ails you my Lady?' she asked gently, though it wasn't hard to guess.

'I fear for my husband Eleanor. I'm beginning to wish he'd taken the king's pardon after all. We'd be living happy at Minster Lovell by now.' She clicked her tongue. 'Tch, no, I don't mean that really! I support him, of course I do! Francis is so brave and loyal to Richard's memory and the vows he made to him before Bosworth. Seeking pardon from Richard's vanquisher, would be a betrayal worse than death. He would rather die than renege on his promise to his dearest friend. Now he's marching against the king and we all know how that could end!'

'How does he seem my lady?'

'Oh he's brimming with confidence!' Anne declared somewhat grudgingly, blowing into her handkerchief. 'He has over 8,000 men with him and some of the best fighters in Europe, as well as the Earl of Kildare's men. They're not so well equipped as the German mercenaries but they're spoiling for a fight and full of Irish pride.' She stopped speaking and drew a shuddering breath. Eleanor attempted to dismiss the vision of bloody battle that was unwittingly coming to mind and distract Anne's attention from the coming conflict.

'May I get you some refreshment my lady, or are you eating in the Hall?'

'Thank you, Eleanor, I'm not very hungry, my stomach's in knots. Perhaps a little wine and some fruit in my chamber. Francis is at his ablutions now but he will dine with the Lords in the Hall. They have tactics to discuss. I have no wish to join them and anyway they won't expect women there. My husband will share my chamber tonight though Eleanor, so I won't need you, later'.

'Very good my lady'. Eleanor knew the Viscountess intimated that the couple should not be disturbed and as well as the bonus of an evening to herself, she was pleased it would allow them a last night of wedded bliss before the army departed. She wished Anne would eat a little more, her slight frame akin to that of her Neville cousins but Eleanor understood only too well how anguish and concern for the coming conflict could dampen any appetite.

Making her way down to the kitchen, she found it full of soldiers, chattering loudly in a guttural language she didn't understand, their voices alien and intimidating, each man eagerly devouring the cold meats, cheeses and vegetable broth on offer. They were well accoutred in colourful and flamboyant clothing and Eleanor figured they were men of rank, having been given access to the castle kitchens, while the infantry had to make use of their field rations and what they could glean from villagers and farms. As she selected victuals for the Viscountess and for herself, she was uncomfortably aware all eyes were upon her and from the chuckles and guffaws, she knew the men were making lewd comments, though thankfully the unfamiliar tongue spared her blushes. As she passed back through the doorway with her hands full, she was forced to avoid two soldiers engrossed in conversation.

'Excuse me sirs' she said politely, waiting to be allowed past. The soldier with his back to her turned his head, his face lighting up with a smile of recognition.

'Guten abend Fräulein' he turned and bowed grinning. It was the handsome captain Eleanor had seen in the field. Eleanor's cheeks coloured and she smiled shyly. She felt like a teenager again as his penetrating blue eyes bored into her with a look of unabashed desire. She felt a sudden thrill of sexual magnetism between them, as senses suppressed for so long burst into life. Weather-beaten and swarthy, he was mature and muscular, a jagged scar branding his temple and cheek but which did nothing to detract from his masculine appeal, indeed embodying the ideal conception of a battle-scarred hero, only adding to his allure. The man he had been talking to smirked and made what appeared to be a salacious remark, which the captain ignored, instead responding with a vulgar hand gesture, prompting mirth from his colleagues. Eleanor could only guess what had been said, her cheeks aflame, as the soldier turned back to her and held out his hand.

'Please, … he said with a thick accent, taking the heavy jug of ale from her, kissing her hand before she could withdraw it.

'Stefan' he bowed, regarding her questioningly, awaiting her response.

'Eleanor sir', she wondered if he could speak enough English to converse with her, or if they would have to resort to signs and gestures.

'Ah, Eleanooore' he repeated as if savouring each syllable. 'Du bist wonderschon Eleanooore'. Eleanor regarded him blankly. She hoped it was a compliment and without responding proceeded to walk on down the corridor, only too pleased to be distancing herself from the soldiers, their laughter echoing in her ears.

'So, Eleanoore, what are you doing here?' Stefan asked walking beside her.

'You *do* speak English!' Eleanor looked up surprised, ignoring his question but somewhat relieved.

'Ja! Enough to be understood, Eleanoore. I have to take orders from whoever pays me. I know French and Spanish too. ...Now, its your turn to answer my question!'.

'I'm waiting on Lady Lovell sir',

'Stefan please, ... ah, you serve my lord commander's wife?'

'Aye sir... er Stefan'. she corrected herself absently, gazing at the soldier's handsome features, wondering how he had acquired that scar, noting a day's growth of stubble on his chin, watching his lips as he talked, aware of his virile presence and the sensual stimulation it now gave her.

'Do you have a husband Eleanoore?' the German suddenly asked as they proceeded down the passageway. Eleanor stopped walking and raised her eyebrows quizzically. *You don't waste any time do you?* she thought, slightly taken aback by his forthrightness. *How very direct!* she chuckled inwardly, a frisson of anticipation arousing her senses. Another time she might have found such directness unsettling but now she felt stimulated by it, knowing it would give him the perfect excuse to proposition her but somehow, she cared not.

'I am a widow' Eleanor told him. She could have lied and told him she was married but she wanted to continue the flirtation. She had been chaste for too long. She knew she was already on the slippery slope of capitulation and the thrill it gave her could not be denied, as she felt a flutter of excitement at the erotic charge of animal attraction between them.

Stefan grinned and stopped walking, placing the jug on the stone floor at the foot of the stairs. He took the platter Eleanor held in her other hand and put it with the jug, then taking her hand he led her outside into the courtyard. It was nearly dark but the torches had been lit, their flickering glow casting intense shadows into hidden corners. Stefan pulled her into the shade, casting a glance around to see if anyone had noticed but there was no-one about, apart from a couple of young boys, sweeping up horse manure into a pile. The boys were too busy discussing weaponry and the merits of pike formations, to take notice of a soldier and a ladies' maid whispering in a dark alcove. The sound of laughter and clattering of dishes emanated from the Great Hall and Eleanor could hear Lord Scrope's voice commanding his guest's attention. She would not be missed for a while. She allowed the captain to take her hand and sit her down on a stone bench against the wall.

'Have a drink with me Eleanoore', he offered.

'Thank you, Stefan but I mustn't be away too long. Lady Lovell is expecting me'.

A soldier approached making for the kitchen and saluted to Stefan, who clicked his fingers and spoke to the man in German. A few moments later the man returned with two tumblers of ale and handed them to the captain. Stefan offered one to Eleanor, who thanked him and feeling the need to initiate a conversation, asked politely where he had come from. The European town of Mechelen he mentioned meant little to her and as he seemed disinclined to expand on it, she began to tell him about her life at Middleham Castle. He listened intently, surveying her face and figure all the while and although he made the right responses, she knew he was expecting more than just polite discourse but instead of feeling offended by it, as she might have been in the past, this time she felt aroused by it. As he drained his tankard, he shifted himself closer to her, taking her hand in his and kissing her fingers desirously, watching for a reaction. Encouraged by the absence of a rebuff, Stefan pulled Eleanor to her feet and leant his arm on the castle wall entrapping her against a buttress. She knew what was coming next.

'Eleanoore, may I kiss you?' Trembling, as he tentatively put an arm around her waist, Eleanor had already vowed she must either accept Stefan's kiss and the expectation it held or refuse him at the start. It was an easy choice. She recalled the time when she had allowed herself to be kissed by Philippe at Middleham but had then run off in shame, leaving the hot-blooded bowman angry and frustrated. This time she knew she wasn't going to decline this tantalising man's request, a man who may indeed soon lose his life on the battlefield. He was fighting for the restoration of the Yorkist crown and for Francis, which meant for Richard too. She almost felt she owed him his moment of pleasure; there would be little of that where he was going. This was no time for false modesty, especially when, in all likelihood, they only had this one night together.

'You may, Stefan', she smiled invitingly, her mind made up, as he lifted her chin, his mouth immediately and urgently enveloping hers with the vigorous passion of one starved of female company for quite some time. She allowed herself to relax into his embrace, returning his kiss with equal fervour as her own long-suppressed desire overtook her senses, thrilling to the feel of his body thrust against hers and his evident arousal.

'Well my English rose,' he ventured, as they paused for breath, 'I am only here for one night and it would be a shame to waste it with a troupe of foul smelling soldiers,' he chuckled, 'especially …as I might die tomorrow!' He watched her expression from under his lashes before studying her with a measured gaze, which she returned, surprising herself at her composure.

'Aye it would!' she laughed, knowing only too well what he was going to ask. He drew her closer towards him, his arm encircling her waist tightly.

'I want you Eleanoore! Lie with me tonight', he whispered in her ear. Eleanor smiled, at the request she fully expected and the decision she had hitherto made. He stood back, raising his eyebrows expectantly. Eleanor nodded; she certainly wasn't going to refuse this man now. She was enjoying this too much and she wanted him, as much as he wanted her. *After all, who would know?* Their paths were unlikely to cross again. Allowing him to kiss her once more, she then eased herself away from the wall and out of his embrace, suddenly aware of the time that had passed.

'Follow me to my chamber Stefan and wait for me there. I must take Lady Lovell her supper first'. Eleanor almost surprised herself with her composure and boldness at having just agreed to submit to a stranger at such short notice.

'Danke meine liebe'. he grinned, kissing her hand as she pulled away. Stefan followed Eleanor upstairs to her chamber and waited inside while she attended Anne. Francis was dining with his commanders and would join his wife later, the Viscountess advised her. When Eleanor returned to her room, Stefan was sitting on the bed, having removed his outer clothing, weapons and belt, his shirt falling open to the waist. She could see his skin was tanned and his muscles toned and firm from the exertions of his profession and she realised she desired him as much as he did her. He patted the bed cover and Eleanor sat down beside him removing her headdress, her long auburn locks cascading around her shoulders. She knew her hair was one of her best features, hoping Stefan would think the same. She wasn't disappointed. He stared at her in wonderment and put out his hand to stroke the silken tresses, running his fingers gently through the undulant strands.

'Mein Gott, your hair Eleanoore! It's like burnished copper!' he grasped a lock and held it against his face, brushing it with his lips, then pulled her to him in another burst of passion, before eagerly unlacing her dress.

'I hope you don't think I make a habit of doing this?' Eleanor glanced at him shyly, under her lashes, suddenly abashed at what they were about to do. Without answering Stefan put his finger to her lips to curtail any further declarations and gently brushed his mouth to her lips, chin and neck down to her cleavage as her gown fell away.

Eleanor revelled in the exuberance of his touch. She felt feminine and desirable again, proud of her womanhood, savouring the pleasure it clearly gave this alluring man. She sat back, watching him from the bed as he discarded his shirt and hose, marvelling at this archetype of male perfection. She ached for him as she had done before for Richard but this time it was pure lust and longing for masculine company. She hadn't had time to fall in love with this man but given time it would not be hard. For now though, he was a stranger and he needed her and for once she felt she could indulge herself without censure.

Allowing the sheet to fall away from her body as he approached the bed, blushing at the sight of his male nakedness and the rush of yearning that surged through her every nerve ending, she fell back against the pillow as he hungrily pressed himself against her, Eleanor felt her reserve melt away, as his hands reverently worshipped every contour of her body. There was something undeniably erotic about a man of gladiatorial strength and latent power, who could bestow tenderness and passion to a trembling butterfly he could crush at will if he so desired. Eleanor almost cared not if he crushed her, she almost wanted to be his victim, the boundary between pain and pleasure blurring the senses in the rapture of total submission.

He loved her more than once that night, their hot impassioned union at first urgent and intense, both starved of that physical contact with the opposite sex they had missed. As they caressed and entwined their limbs, rejoicing in each other's flesh, their juxtaposition arousing senses long dormant, they savoured each contact, each blissful sensation stirred by fingertip and mouth, ardent, lustful, erotic, neither one constricted by familiarity – two strangers filling a need, no guilt, no shame, no apologies. Eleanor felt liberated and unrepentant, revelling in the physical sensation of erotic love, unrestrained by formality or cordiality. She would most likely never see this man hereafter but she could leave him a memory to warm him before he fought his last battle and gave up his life in service for others to whom he had no particular loyalty. She wondered what motivated this professional soldier and whether he squared his conscience with himself or with God. In one of their satiated moments, before they slept, Eleanor voiced her thoughts. 'How do you do it? Time after time, going into battle?' she marvelled. 'You get used to it.' he replied indifferently. 'One battle is much like another. We have a job to do and we do it. We get well paid for our efforts'.

'Are you not troubled by killing another man?' Eleanor had often wished to ask a soldier this question, especially if they were pious and God-fearing, as after all, killing was a sin wasn't it?'.

'Huh! There's no time to dwell on it! It's our profession! T'is not a joust Eleanoore! *Every* man is out to kill you - stop to think about it and you're dead, although not many of our opponents can't match us for skill, they're mostly amateurs or farmers with pitchforks!', he scoffed dismissively. The long summer nights had not yet reached their equinox and the light from the casement lit up Stefan's face just enough to bathe their bodies in a flattering luminescence. Eleanor turned to face him, her finger tracing the scar line on his face.

'How did you get this?' she queried tentatively, somewhat unsure she wanted to hear the answer.

'Just a little disagreement with a German at Neuss' he chuckled. 'He tried to slice my head off but I declined the offer!' he jested flippantly.

'Declined?' Eleanor raised her eyebrows, amused at his levity.

'Ja, I skewered him like a hog on a spit'. Eleanor wrinkled her nose in disgust, the unwelcome image crystallising, as she sank back on the pillow, marvelling at the nonchalance of this trained slayer of men.

'People say your commander is the Devil! Is he really that bad?' she enquired.

'It depends who's side you're on! I would not like to oppose him!' he chuckled. 'Nein, Schwartz is a hard task master but it pays off. He treats us well but he takes no prisoners and suffers no fools. That way he gets respect.' Eleanor thought to ask another question but from Stefan's rhythmic breathing she saw he had fallen asleep.

Eleanor lay awake, her head on his chest feeling it rise and fall with every breath, marvelling at his courage and wishing they had more time together. In a few hours he would be gone, on his way to yet another brutal confrontation and she would be alone again with just the memory of this night to look back on – a night not unlike her last night with Richard. A shudder convulsed her as she fought to erase the memory of that night and the semblance of similitude now nagging at her thoughts, as the dread of the morrow this man would face, lay like a lead weight in the pit of her stomach.

She awoke with a start in the pre-dawn twilight, as the dawn chorus filled the air with a crescendo of sound. Stefan was already dressed and strapping on his scabbard and dagger sheath. She could hear sounds of movement outside as the army broke camp and prepared for another day's march and she knew the Viscountess would be awake and steeling herself to bid farewell to her husband. Eleanor reached for her underdress and pulled it over her head and as she did so, Stefan came up behind her and gently pulled her hair through the neckline, spreading it over her shoulders before kissing her neck tenderly.

'Thank you Stefan'.

'I thank *you* mein leibling' he replied, twisting her round and kissing her slowly, as if savouring a last taste of sweet wine.

'I won't forget you, Stefan.' Eleanor looked into his eyes as they parted and found herself speaking with an unexpected sincerity. 'I hope you will remember me sometimes?' she asked optimistically.

'I will *never* forget you my lovely English rose but just to make sure...' he grinned and with a quick flick of his dagger deftly cut off a lock of Eleanor's hair, much to her surprise and was about to put it in his pocket. She laughed and took it from him.

'Here,' she offered, 'let me tie it together otherwise it will be lost'. She picked up her ribbon from the chest by the bed and wound it tightly around the lock of hair, tying it together and knotting it neatly at one end.

'Thank you Eleanoore, now you will always be with me to bring me good fortune!' he kissed the lock, tucked it into his doublet, holding her in a firm embrace before turning to go. As he reached the door, he hesitated. 'Eleanoore, ...forgive me if I took advantage. A man going into battle has no time for social niceties'. He felt ungracious and ill-mannered, walking out on a beautiful woman who had given herself to him freely, leaving her with nothing but a memory in return.

'There is nothing to forgive Stefan. I could have refused you, had I so wished'. Eleanor smiled but her eyes were full of tears. 'I will pray for you Stefan. May God be with you'. She hated partings, most especially before a battle, when the odds were stacked so heavily against survival. 'He had better be, or there'll be some explaining to do on the day of judgement!' Stefan quipped, relieved at her response, winking affectionately at Eleanor before hurrying through the door and out of her life.

Chapter Seven

Lady Lovell called on Eleanor to help her dress. The Viscountess would say her final farewell to Francis after he had breakfasted with his commanders. Anne noticed Eleanor had braided her hair in a looser, more flattering way under her headwear, her face appearing flushed and animated. It crossed her mind her pretty maid servant may have found company for the night.

'Did you sleep well Eleanor?' she asked pointedly, watching for a reaction.

'Aye, my lady, thank you'. Eleanor looked away, attempting to appear casual, busying herself packing Anne's belongings into a coffer but the Viscountess had noted the evasion in her voice. *Hmmm…* she thought to herself. *I wonder?*

Eleanor retraced her steps to the kitchen where the staff were busy preparing bread and cold meat dishes for the commanders in the Hall. She took a platter through to the diners and placed it on the long trestle table set up for the guests, bending her knee politely as Francis looked up and gave her a friendly wink. Beside him sat a fine-looking young man, expensively dressed, whose chiselled looks echoed his Plantagenet roots and whom Eleanor recognised as John de la Pole, the Earl of Lincoln, Richard's nephew, whom she had served at his home at Sheriff Hutton. He acknowledged her with a smile and she dropped a respectful curtsey, struck by his clear resemblance to the house of York.

Opposite them two Irish noblemen were conversing in soft lilting language Eleanor had not heard before and on Francis's other side, sat Lord John Scrope of Bolton scrutinising a map, beside him a heavily built swarthy looking man. Certainly, a foreigner, with a well weathered, angular face and jet-black hair, dressed in colourful, ostentatious clothing, gesticulating and talking in a loud voice, his broad throaty accent similar to Stefan's. He could only be Martin Schwartz, Eleanor reasoned and had to admit the man sent a shiver of dread through her, his dark soulless eyes boring into her with the arrogant coldness of one without empathy. He made a casual remark in German aside to a man seated on his right, who sniggered lecherously, running his tongue over his lips and raising his tankard towards Eleanor in a somewhat libidinous salute. Lord Lincoln flashed a look of contempt at the Burgundian Commander, who returned his gaze with a sneer of arrogant defiance. Clearly, Eleanor judged, there was no love lost between those two.

Averting her gaze from the foreigners' unwanted attention, her eyes rested upon a teenager sitting quietly next to the Earl of Lincoln, with a man of the cloth seated to his left. The lad was fair and quite slim and had something about him that reminded her of the late king Edward, though not as handsome. Eleanor wondered who he was and what he was doing at this gathering of nobility and militia, evidently not a servant, judging by his courtly dress but seeming somewhat out of place and surely too young to fight? She made a mental note to ask Lady Lovell about him later.

Dawn was breaking and the army was on the move. The lords had finished eating and were dispersing. After a quick bite to eat in the kitchen, Eleanor hurried upstairs to collect her mistress's few belongings but upon entering Lady Lovell's chamber, she found the couple embracing. Anne was weeping on her husband's shoulder but Francis looked up and beckoned Eleanor to enter, seeing her hesitate and start to close the door. Francis seemed confident and buoyant, assured and well rested, cheered by the support he had gathered and the approaching culmination to his ambition of revenge, no longer the sad fugitive who had left Nappa the year before.

'Pray come in Eleanor, I was just about to leave.' he smiled.

'My Lord,' Eleanor bent her knee and waited by the door. Francis whispered into his wife's ear and she nodded, releasing her hold on him and went to stand by the window, turning away so as not to reveal her torment. Her husband's face was full of confidence and intention, as he clasped on his cloak and scabbard and at a loud knock, he marched purposefully to the door. Baron Richard Fitzhugh came in and had hardly uttered the words 'Come brother, its time', before Anne ran to embrace her sibling tearfully.

'God be with you both' she cried, as Richard returned her embrace, then nodded to Francis, who picked up his cap from the table.

'The young man is ready to assume his role and awaits us downstairs' he spoke quietly to the Viscount.

'Good' Francis murmured, then adjusting his hat with a confident flourish, bowed and grinned.

'Farewell ladies! We go to restore the house of York!' he declared exuberantly, then lowering his tone he touched Eleanor's arm. 'Look after Lady Lovell for me, Eleanor' he enjoined gently, 'she worries about me so', then he was gone.

'Aye my Lord, of course' Eleanor replied but he was already disappearing down the stairwell behind his brother-in-law. Eleanor busied herself with packing her mistress's belongings, while Anne sat on the bed sniffing into her handkerchief but neither spoke, both consumed by their own fears and forebodings.

On the ride home, Lady Lovell's party passed by the fields

and verges now empty of militia; flattened grasses, smouldering fires and discarded casks, the only trace left of the colourful army, now marching its way South towards its inevitable rendezvous with destiny. Eleanor thought about Stefan and a warm thrill went through her, their night of passion still so vivid in her mind. She turned her head away in case Anne could see her lips curving into a smile, thankful her thoughts were her own.

Whispering a quick prayer for her brothers, she tried not to think about what they might have to face, recalling the scene of carnage they had described to her after Barnet. Jogging through this pastoral idyll on this sunny morning, fields of ripening wheat swaying gently in the breeze, swathes of multi-coloured wildflowers crowding the banks, it seemed somehow against all laws of nature that mankind should resort to killing each other for no purpose other than to rule and predominate over their own kind. *Surely, we should all live in peace and harmony for the common weal? Wild creatures are not consumed by covetousness, are they?* Eleanor debated with herself, *so why is man so envious and malcontent?* Dismissing her philosophical musings, for which there seemed no answer, Eleanor observed Anne was unusually quiet and she was not sure whether to leave her to grieve or try to lighten the mood. She decided to ask about the young man she had seen at breakfast dining with the nobles.

'Oh that's young John' Anne answered, glad of the diversion from dwelling on her husband. 'He's taking the place of Edward V until the king can be safely returned to London in Tudor's place. Should anything go wrong, we can't risk him being taken by Tudor, so we are using a decoy to confuse the matter'.

'What will happen to him?' Eleanor asked, picturing the reticent teenager, who seemed so incongruous.

'Nothing. He's just a puppet and will be dispensed with once he's served his purpose. He will be well recompensed, do not concern yourself Eleanor'.

'Did you not tell me he was an illegitimate son by king Edward's mistress Jane Shore?

'Aye, could you see the likeness? You met his father didn't you?'

'Aye, I did and yes I could', Eleanor admitted. 'King Edward was the handsomest man I had ever seen!'.

'Aye and didn't he know it!' quipped Lady Lovell chuckling, 'That is, until he let himself go with too much indulgence!' Eleanor laughed in accord but she was already wondering about the king's son.

'Where's the *real* Edward V then? The boy who was crowned in Ireland?'

''Hush Eleanor' Anne lowered her voice to a whisper. 'He's safe, Sir Henry Bodrugan is keeping him out of harm's way. We don't need to know where. He will be sent for when its time'. Trotting her horse along the byway, her mind still dwelling on last night's encounter, Eleanor recalled the mercenary commander she had seen at breakfast. 'Was there some animosity between Lord Lincoln and commander Schwartz, my Lady? They seemed to dislike one another!'

'Aye, Francis told me they had a heated argument when Martin Schwartz accused John of deceiving him about the numbers of Englishmen who would come to join their cause. The German was shocked at the low turnout of those rallying support and said he wouldn't have brought his men all this way had he known. However, he said was a man of his word, having given Duchess Margaret of Burgundy his pledge, so he would see it through.'

'That's very admirable of him'.

'Aye but John felt belittled by him and humiliated, especially when he couldn't deny Schwartz spoke the truth. Francis wasn't keen on the man either but experienced troops are hard to come by and the commander's reputation for excellence precedes him'.

'For sure, you *would* want a man like that on your side', Eleanor mused, echoing Stefan's words.

'Aye, no place for good manners on a battlefield. The days of chivalry are long gone'. Anne sighed ruefully, concerns for her husband playing on her mind. Eleanor thought about Stefan's words and then about Richard and how he had tried to live by the code of chivalry but had been brought down by its very antithesis. She prayed Francis would not suffer the same fate.

'They seem to have a good number of men', Eleanor tried to sound positive.

'The king will have more I fear'. Anne replied dispiritedly. She would not be cheered and with visions of Bosworth playing on both their minds, Eleanor thought it best not to continue the conversation. It seemed no matter how many men you had, or which side you were on, there would always be those considering betrayal or defection and even mercenaries could be persuaded to change sides for the most lucrative recompense.

Arriving back at Nappa Hall, Eleanor showed Lady Lovell to her chamber. She was to stay for a few nights with the Metcalfe's in the hope of hearing good news from Francis. Ravensworth being near Richmond castle, was now Tudor's and Anne worried she might be detained there as a deterrent against supporting her husband, or perhaps interrogated as to his intentions. Besides, Frideswide's husband Edward Norris was fighting in Tudor's army, no doubt instructed to listen out for any news about his elusive brother in law and to report back on Anne's movements.

Bess was eager to hear all her mother's news, especially concerning Robert Dinsdale. She was fearful he might have to fight but Eleanor reassured her that there were plenty of trained soldiers for that and as a farrier, Robert was more useful to the cavalry for his equine skills, than risking certain death at the front line. Heartened, Bess felt comforted by her mother's words, although Eleanor was unsure of her conviction. She knew from what she had heard that the numbers coming to fight for Lovell and Lincoln were less than expected, not that many did not support their cause but those having accepted Tudor's pardon after Bosworth, were reluctant to endanger their future prospects yet again by further treasonous action. Many would sit on the fence until they could be assured of a positive outcome and then opt for the victor. *Surely it can't happen again?* Eleanor agonised uneasily, thoughts of treachery on Bosworth field still haunting her. She had heard the rumours that some men had conspired to desert Richard even before the battle, contemptible acts of betrayal she hoped would not resurface for Francis.

While the occupants of Nappa Hall waited anxiously for word, Lovell's army reached Bramham Moor where Lord Clifford of Skipton's army was encamped outside Tadcaster. The rebels mounted a surprise attack, scattering Clifford's men and seizing supplies and equipment. Buoyed up by this success, the two Lord Scropes took a small force into York but were repulsed at Bootham Bar, although opportunely this tactic had the added advantage of delaying the Earl of Northumberland's troops from joining Tudor. Richard Fitzhugh was with them but not having had time to gather retainers for further battle, returned to Masham, not only that, he was feeling unwell and not in a physical state to fight. The Earl of Lincoln then attacked the cavalry of Lord Scales in several successful skirmishes through Sherwood

Forest before making their way to the River Trent, manoeuvres which unfortunately allowed time for Tudor's forces to progress. Here the rebels forded the shallows at Fiskerton, positioning themselves on the high ground of Burnham Furlong, to await the Royal army now fast approaching from the South.

The Earl of Oxford's vanguard was the first on the scene and in the morning of the 16th June, Lovell, Lincoln and the Irish Lords made the decision to attack before the bulk of the king's army arrived. However, having little or no battle experience between them, having to abandon their advantage of high ground prematurely left them vulnerable. As they charged down into Oxford's men, hoping to break the royal line, they were unaware at this stage, their lack of cavalry and longbowmen was to prove a decisive factor in the eventual outcome.

The English longbow, with its quick draw and superior fire power, soon made itself felt against the slower European crossbow and unreliable hand-guns. It wasn't long before the swathes of lightly clad Irish kerns fell under a hail of arrows before they even reached the enemy. The mercenaries nevertheless initially stood fast, Schwartz keeping his pikemen in close formation, holding their ground in the fierce fighting, with heavy casualties on both sides until the arrival of Henry's fresh troops, when eventually the enemy's superior numbers turned the battle into a rout. The rebel lines broke seeing the Irish fall in such numbers, the remainder fleeing into a ravine only to be slaughtered in their thousands, hemmed in by the terrain in what came to be known afterwards as 'Red Gully'.

Despite putting up fierce resistance Martin Schwartz, finally overwhelmed was slain in the bloodbath. With their commanders gone, the foreign mercenaries surrendered and were allowed to go free, albeit without pay, though many English and Irish soldiers were hanged for their resistance to the king. As battle subsided, the Earl of Lincoln was found leaning against a tree, gasping for breath, his bloodied hands gripping an ugly stomach wound, before one of Tudor's soldiers finished him off with a willow stake through the chest. Had the soldier been identified, he would have faced severe reprimand from the king, who needed the Earl taken alive to determine the extent of rebel support. Thomas Fitzgerald was killed but his brother Gerald survived, to be later pardoned. Young John having been discovered unharmed at the rear of the field in the care of the priest Simonds, was taken to Tudor. Francis Lovell, however, made his escape across the river, as did Sir Thomas Broughton, discarding their armour as they fled.

Chapter Eight

Lovell's horse stumbled into the shallow water, blood pouring from a deep gash in its flank, his rider slumped over the stallion's neck, himself bleeding from a slash to the back of his knee and a puncture wound from a halberd spike deep in his torso. Mid-stream the animal faltered and fell, its energy spent, the cool depths of the river a welcome relief to the exhausted warhorse, now emitting its last failing breath as its lungs filled with blood and its head slipped under the water. Francis slid off its back and stood waist deep, hurriedly discarding as much of his armour as he could, so as not to be dragged under, before limping to the far shore. Despite the warm June day, the river was ice cold and Francis gasped involuntarily as the freezing water reached his thighs and then penetrated his side wound, the knight bellowing in pain until mercifully his flesh numbed. He wiped his eyes with a bloodied hand but the tears kept coming, his laboured breathing emitting deep heart-rending sobs, not just for his pain, or the death of his faithful equine friend but at the horror of his first taste of brutal battle, the carnage, the terror, the exhaustion and the shock of his army's defeat.

How could this happen? How could all this be for nothing? All those months of planning, amassing his army, young Edward's coronation, that punishing march at breakneck speed, the skirmish at Tadcaster filling his men with false confidence; the prospect of one last battle before he would fulfil his vow to Richard, victory so tantalisingly close, yet for the weight of enemy numbers and those devastating bowmen. *Oh Richard, I have failed you my friend and you too John! Forgive me!* Francis dragged his wounded leg onto the far bank as more soldiers ran for their lives, the sounds of battle and the cries of the dying still reverberating behind him. Thirsting for a drink, he cupped his hands into the river but the water was undrinkable, having been stirred into a bloody soup by the corpses of man and beast. Cursing angrily, he wiped away his tears and looked about him. He must get away fast before Tudor's riders caught up with him and carted him away to face the inevitable traitor's death that now awaited him.

In a fog of mental confusion, a conflation of terror and adrenaline cut through the pain of his wounds, propelling him blindly forward as he hobbled on. With the cries of the dying pursued by a vengeful enemy, resounding in his ears, his heartbeat throbbed in his brain, the tumult now diminishing with each breath, as he put distance between himself and that scene of horror. A few hundred yards further on beside the river bank, a destrier stallion stood calmy nibbling some lush grasses, its Lancastrian rider slumped over its back, a heavy metal tipped cross bow shaft piercing the man's chest. Francis reached up and with a groan of agony hauled the body down. 'Thank you, Martin' he breathed as he stuck his boot in the stirrup and heaved himself into the saddle cursing in a spasm of pain as he did so, a wave of nausea causing his head to spin. He retched as bile rose in his throat but to vomit would be unbearable, the contraction enough to finish him off. He managed to fight the impulse but was aware he needed to rest and slake his thirst before deciding his next move. For now his most urgent need was to get away from the battle site before Tudor's army hunted down fleeing Yorkists to face certain death. Digging his heels into the horse's flanks he encouraged it into a trot, each stride forcing an agonised groan as he gritted his teeth against every jarring jolt.

Following the river South for several miles in the direction of Nottingham, recalling childhood days in his maternal grandmother's castle at Stoke Bardolf, Francis realised the old, moated manor was within easy reach and would in all probability afford him a safe place to spend the night. Forcing himself to stay alert and not succumb to the exhaustion that was overwhelming him, he made his way forward. He could feel the life blood draining from every vein and he knew if he lost consciousness now, he would fall to the ground and be found by Tudor's men to face execution, if he were not dead already.

As he rode, every step sending a searing paroxysm through his side, he felt a hopeless sadness, a devastating despair, overwhelm him. Disheartened and heart broken, sickened by the recent scenes of battle he had witnessed and the realisation of his failure, he felt wretched. Not only from his wounds but depressed and weary of the burden he had carried for so many months, his avowed revenge on the cowardly usurper who sat like a cockroach on the throne of England, now thwarted and with it his failure to avenge his friend.

Francis wept uncontrollably, tears of shame, hurt, regret, anger, hopelessness and pain, tears for his dead friends, tears for his sweet wife, whom he may never see again, tears for England. The campaign begun so optimistically, had failed. It was all down to him. He had sent John de la Pole to his death amongst so many loyal Ricardians who had perished with the utmost courage and faith in their leaders. They had paid the ultimate price for their loyalty. He had let them all down and most of all himself. It would have been better had he died on the battlefield, a hero, fighting manfully to the end like Richard but instead he was fleeing like quarry from the hunt, pursued until he could run no more, anguished, wounded, not only in body but in spirit, guilt-ridden and ashamed.

Just as he was on the point of losing consciousness, the familiar outline of the manor rose up before him. Filling his lungs with a deep gulp of air, he blinked his eyes into focus, guiding his horse through the arched entrance and crossing to the stable block, where he dragged himself from the saddle with the help of a young stable hand. A kindly housekeeper ushered him into the kitchen, judging it best not to advertise his presence to the household with the king's army so close by. She could see from his bloodied tunic, glimpses of the Lovell blue and the boar insignia of the late king Richard, that he was a rebel but she failed to recognise the boy she once knew, who had become a man, Francis deciding there was little point in enlightening her. The less she knew the better when the king's men came calling, as inevitably they would, once word of his flight was broadcast, it being likely somebody would have spotted him fording the river. The woman washed and bound his wounds as best she could, while he ate and drank his fill before passing out on a bale of hay in a small storeroom beside the stables.

He came to in the early hours, awakened by the searing pain of his injuries but something else had disturbed him – the sound of riders clattering into the yard and voices commanding a search of the manor. There was no time to think, he had to get away now. Thankfully the kitchen staff were remonstrating with the soldiers, delaying the inevitable search. Francis grabbed the remains of the meal that had been put out for him and made his way round to the stall where he had left his destrier. A groom helped him saddle the horse and mount, wishing him well on his way but just as he passed an empty stall a familiar voice whispered from the shadows.

'My Lord Francis!' Francis twisted his torso round with an agonised groan, his hand on his dagger in readiness for a fight, or for death, which now struck him as a welcome relief.

'Thomas!' he rasped. 'Thank God! I thought you were dead!'

'I thought you were too, my Lord'. Thomas grinned with relief.

'Quickly Thomas! Saddle a horse and catch up with me. I'm heading South. Hurry!' Francis pressed a gold coin into the hands of the groom, who refused it saying, 'Nay sir, take the horse. The soldiers will take them anyway'.

Five hours before, Sir Thomas Broughton had slept as soon as he lay down on the coarse straw. He was utterly spent. Three hours of relentless fighting and then running for his life, he had abandoned his armour crawling through Red Gully, concealing himself under a dead soldier as the Lancastrians charged down the ravine to finish off the fleeing Yorkists. He held his breath until they were gone, before crawling under a bush and down the shallow slope into the cool waters of the Trent. His own stalwart warhorse had died under a hail of arrows, the animal's head shielding him from the lethal trajectiles.

Thomas was a strong swimmer, having spent his youth swimming in the cold Lakes and tarns of Westmorland and was quickly across to the far bank. He was mostly unscathed, apart from a few cuts to his wrist and a slash to his neck where a blade had lifted his helmet in an assailant's attempt to cut the strap but now the cold water eased the sting as the blood congealed. Sickened and dismayed at the rebels' defeat, he put as much distance as possible between himself and that scene of carnage, tears falling freely for his brother John, whom he had seen perish with manful courage, his older sibling's advancing years no match for younger men. Following the course of the river in the same direction Francis Lovell had taken, West towards Nottingham, Thomas intended to lose himself amongst the crowded streets and lie low before returning North. Assuming Lovell had met his death along with his other commanders and their cause was now lost, he knew there would be no coming back from this. All he could do now would be to make his way back to his beloved fells and live out his life amongst family and friends.

He urgently needed rest however and as he neared the manor house, resolved to try and find a safe place to catch a few hours' sleep. Scaling a low perimeter wall he found the stable block, slaked his thirst at a water trough by the door, caring not the cool liquid was insect infested, then sank down in the corner of a stall. Awoken in the early hours by voices and the creak of leather harness as a horse in the adjoining stall was saddled, Thomas was immediately on the alert. He listened intently, determining whether to make a run for it or stay hidden but something about that voice made him stop. It took him a few seconds to register but there was no doubting it was unmistakeably Lord Lovell.

Thomas soon caught up with Francis as he rode South and West. They shared their accounts of the battle and the men who had fallen, before Francis told him of his plan. If he could get to Oxford, he could find sanctuary at Abingdon Abbey where he could recover from his wounds, though this time his whereabouts must be kept secret. He hadn't forgotten the Staffords who had helped him escape from Colchester but who had been taken out of sanctuary at Abingdon by Tudor to face execution for treason. *More deaths on my conscience* thought Francis gloomily as he rode, though now considerably heartened by the company of his friend and collaborator.

Though both battle-weary men emerged into daybreak blood smeared and mud spattered, Thomas was shocked at his friend's appearance. Francis was clearly in great pain, the colour drained from his cheeks, thickening blood oozing down his torso and leg but not only that, the Northern knight could see the spirit and resolve had gone out of this most steadfast and courageous nobleman. This once intrepid leader and most loyal champion of the late king, was quite clearly a broken man, crushed, tormented, consumed by regret and remorse for the men he had sent to their deaths and the cause he felt he had disgraced. For a long time neither man spoke, each wrestling with images of carnage etched in their memory, words of consolation inadequate to describe the sickening despair and utter hopelessness of defeat.

Chapter Nine

Word of the debacle at Stoke field reached Wensleydale a few days later. The people's worst fears had been realised. Battle had been ferocious, the rebel army had been routed, Lord Lincoln slain, the German mercenary commander had gone down fighting, the Irish Lords killed. Lord Lovell had disappeared, last seen amongst those fleeing for their lives over the River Trent.

'Nay, nay! Please God, let this not be true!', Anne Lovell wailed, collapsing in dismay as word came in, her initial denial becoming disbelief, then despair as reality hit home. The army, so confidently promising liberation from Tudor rule had failed, now they were all traitors. The Viscountess paced the floor of Nappa's Great Hall agitatedly as report after report arrived with no word of her husband, except that he had disappeared leaving her with some small hope, for if he had not been reported amongst the dead, he might still be alive. 'He was last seen crossing the river! He must have got away!' she looked up pleadingly at Elizabeth Metcalfe, hoping for reassurance but her host was pre-occupied with the news of her own husband and the possible punishment that may ensue. *Where would Francis have gone? On the run with a price on his head and a traitor's death if he is captured!* Anne shuddered at the thought. 'They'll be watching us all now in case he comes here.' she continued.

'He will know that, Lady Lovell. He won't wish to endanger you or us. He may go abroad and lie low until this is all over'.

'It will *never* be over, Elizabeth', Anne answered with a finality that could not be gainsaid. 'Once a traitor, always a traitor! He led an army against the king, they will *never* pardon him now!' Elizabeth Metcalfe could not deny it, instead she tried to soften the impact of the undeniable with a positive.

'Sir Thomas Broughton escaped too. Perhaps they are together? Sir Thomas sheltered him at Witherslack the last time, I believe'.

'Oh aye, of course!' Anne's face brightened a little. 'I hope so! I hate to think of Francis all alone. What if he is sorely injured?' she exclaimed as a fresh concern struck her.

'He can't be too bad if he was able to cross the river! Be of good cheer my dear. All we can do is wait for word'.

The Scropes had been summoned to Windsor to answer for their actions, Thomas Metcalfe taken to the Tower and the Harringtons of Hornby attainted. Many English soldiers who had survived had been hanged, along with their Irish counterparts, though Thomas Broughton and Sir Richard Harleston had so far evaded capture. Wensleydale and indeed the whole of Yorkshire reeled in shock. The colourful army that had marched down the vale ten days ago was no more, any surviving mercenaries having been sent home without pay. Eleanor was relieved to hear her brothers had been with the Scropes in York and therefore avoided the battle but her fears for the rest of the men were by no means allayed.

In Eleanor's chamber, Bess lay on the bed distraught, convinced Robert Dinsdale must be dead, having had no news of him, either amongst the fallen, or captured. Eleanor tried to comfort her daughter but was herself dealing with her own forebodings of what might have befallen both Lovell and Stefan, though she would not admit to her night of passion with the charismatic foreigner. Although Bess might understand Eleanor's feelings towards a lover, she may not accept the fact her mother had allowed herself to be intimate with a stranger, at such little notice. Besides Eleanor would not wish her daughter to follow her mother's example, at least until she was able to understand men a little better.

Suppressing her fears about Stefan, recalling his commander Martin Schwartz and the other nobles she had seen dining at Masham, Eleanor remembered the youth John – *what had happened to him?* Later, preparing the Viscountess for bed and commiserating with her on her husband's plight, Eleanor enquired after the young teenager.

'What happened to the boy John, my Lady? Do you know?'

'Oh aye, they found him with his priest and took him to the king'.

'Oh dear. I hope King Henry won't maltreat him'.

'Huh! Tudor won't harm him, Eleanor'. Anne sneered contemptuously. 'T'is more than his reputation's worth! He can't be seen to kill a bastard child, when he is accusing King Richard of the very same!'

'Poor Richard! All those malicious untruths flying around about him and he's not here to defend himself!' Eleanor reflected sadly.

'Aye, if Tudor really believed all his own propaganda, he wouldn't be so desperately trying to find the sons of Edward IV'.

'What would happen if he did find them?'

'I imagine he'd lock them up for a very long time, or perhaps find an excuse to execute them when they come of age'.

'But they're his wife's brothers!' Eleanor exclaimed, horrified at the thought.

'Aye, that's his dilemma! When he re-legitimised his wife, he re-legitimised her brothers too! Now they have a more superior claim to the throne of England than he does! He needs them dead if he's going to hold onto his crown and if he can brand them imposters his wife need never know they lived!'

The Viscountess rode over to Bolton the next day to offer her condolences to Lady Scrope on her husband's detention and to see if she had any further news of Francis. She was surprised to find Elizabeth Scrope optimistic and not at all dismayed at her husband's arrest.

'I will put in a good word for my husband with Lady Margaret Beaufort'. Lady Scrope announced proudly, boasting she had the ear of the king's mother. 'She will ensure John is pardoned I'm sure of it. The king is always open to his mother's requests. After all, it was through her persistence he got where he is.' Anne didn't answer, allowing Elizabeth to prattle on, as if trying to convince herself of her husband's innocence and distance the family from any wrongdoing. 'John didn't actually fight the Royal army at Stoke,' Lady Scrope continued, somewhat tactlessly, 'he tried to enter York with Thomas Scrope but they were repulsed and retired home to Clifton, following the arrival of the Earl of Northumberland. So, he can truthfully say he never actually raised arms against the king!'. She almost sounded triumphant in her conclusion and settled back in her chair satisfied the Scrope's future was already assured.

Anne Lovell opened her mouth to speak but decided against it, not trusting herself to be polite. She was furious with Elizabeth Scrope. *How dare the woman gloat at her husband's ability to wriggle out of a treason charge, when all those loyal men are dead and Francis a fugitive!? After all Francis has done to restore the rightful king to the throne of England and all Elizabeth Scrope cares about is her property and her husband's reputation!*

'Now my dear, you must try not to worry. If your husband gives himself up and asks for pardon I'm sure the king will be lenient'.' Elizabeth continued, attempting to console her guest in a show of magnaminity. 'Francis will die before he does that!' Anne leapt to his defence and before Lady Scrope could reply, got up to excuse herself, unable to bear any more of her host's self-satisfied remarks.

'You must forgive me Lady Scrope, I have other calls to make', she lied but it was the only way to leave without being rude, much as she longed to be.

'Of course, my dear. I will pray for Lord Lovell' Lady Scrope offered disingenuously.

'Hmm, I'll wager you won't! Anne found herself retorting silently to herself, as she was shown out. She got the impression Elizabeth Scrope was ashamed of her husband's support for the Yorkist cause and would do her best to make amends with the Lancastrian king.

For the rest of the summer life at Nappa Hall carried as normal on without Thomas Metcalfe, however by the end of harvest, he arrived home, having paid a fine and made promise of good behaviour. The family were pleased to see him and hear of his ordeal and of the battle. He told them that Lord John and Thomas Scrope had also been heavily fined and released but had been bound over to reside South of the River Trent and not to travel home. Anne couldn't help feeling smug at the thought of Lady Scrope's failure to restore her husband to his ancestral home. Apparently, John Scrope had attempted to blame his tenants for forcing him to support Lovell and Lincoln. Anne couldn't help but compare these self-serving Lords to her own most faithful and trustworthy husband, one who's steadfast loyalty could not be doubted. *Better to die for one's cause than to live in shame of selling out one's friends!* she concluded, her pride for Francis only tempered by her fears for his safety.

Thomas had news of Robert Dinsdale too. The young farrier had been with John and the priest, waiting in the rebel camp for the expected victory but after it became clear they had lost and were preparing to flee the field, they were apprehended by Oxford's men.

With John, now dubbed Lambert Simnel, safely under the watchful eye of the king's household, the farrier had been set to attending to John de Vere's cavalry and it was unlikely he would be allowed to go home any time soon, if at all.

There was still no word of Francis, apart from the fact he was thought to be at large, which remained some consolation for Anne Lovell. She returned to Ravensworth to care for her brother, who was ill and had not been well enough to fight in the battle. Richard Fitzhugh was not amongst those attainted, having already been stripped of his offices the previous year. Anne's brother-in-law Edward Norris having been knighted by the king for his part in the battle, only served to increase the strain on family relations, with the Fitzhugh's having supported the rebels and the Norris's on the opposing side. Frideswide was in the difficult position of having to show support for her husband, who had received an injury to his shoulder when, in reality, backing her brother.

Chapter Ten

Having reached Abingdon Abbey after several wearisome days on the road, Francis and Thomas were grateful for the care and relative comfort on offer at the monastery. Sleeping in barns and stables on the way down to Oxfordshire, Thomas had procured food and drink where possible, from shop keepers who had no interest in a battle-weary stranger, so long as he could pay for his purchases, the knight having removed from his clothing any identifying insignia that would mark him out as a rebel, or man of rank. With a price on his head there was no point in enticing poor folk into temptation.

Arriving at the Abbey, Abbott John Sante, who had provided sanctuary for the Stafford brothers and financial aid for the Lambert Simnel deception, immediately recognised Francis, now the Viscount was back in home territory. He had seen Francis with Richard on the late king's progress to Oxford in 1483, having known the Lovell family well but fortunately his association with the rebels had so far been overlooked. As a staunch Ricardian, Sante did not hesitate to offer assistance to his friends who had risked everything to restore the house of York to its rightful place. The Abbey could provide sparse but comfortable single celled accommodation, basic medical care and ample food and drink.

Whilst having had his wounds dressed and cleaned, Francis needed to think. Each morning it had taken him a moment to focus, sometimes in graphic dreams imagining that the battle had been won and Edward V restored to the throne, only to realise with a crushing despair upon waking, that all his efforts had failed and the Lancastrian usurper was still firmly in place. He almost dreaded waking, when reality brought his defeat slamming into sharp focus once more. The worst had happened. If he was captured his fate would be more ghastly than a quick beheading. This was no mere dream, this was a living nightmare. In moments of self-pity he remonstrated with himself. *Why didn't I take Tudor's pardon when it was offered? I would be back at Minster Lovell with Anne, living a comfortable life!* Then he would hear the voice of his lifelong friend and he knew he must keep his promise to Richard, if he were to save his soul from the guilt of betrayal, *Loyaulte me lie*, Richard's motto, resounding over and over in his head. *As if I needed reminding!* Francis reflected gloomily, fingering the silver boar badge he now carried in his pocket.

Francis knew he needed to get away from England and with help from Thomas, he may be able to get to Ireland or Flanders, if need be, taking the young king Edward with him. Upon receiving word of the rout at Stoke, he knew Sir Henry Bodrugan, waiting at Gleeston Castle, with the Yorkist monarch, would then convey Edward back to his estate in Devon, where he would live incognito until he could be reinstated, leaving the imposter to carry on the charade. Francis knew Lambert Simnel would not be harmed by Tudor, it was more than the king's reputation was worth and he would be happy simply to expose the lad as a pretender and not worthy of further concern. To bolster his case, the king had ordered the Irish parliament to destroy all records, on pain of treason, so no proof of the identity of the Dublin king could be found to use against him.

Feeling unable to return to his home territory without assuring Francis's welfare, Thomas was agreeable to his friend's plan to make for Devon, though he was concerned the Viscount's injuries may hinder their progress. If necessary they would split up and Thomas would go on ahead to ensure Edward V's safety. If John had been seized by Tudor, at least the paranoid monarch was bound to assume this was the lad who had been crowned in Dublin and feel no cause to look further. For now, the deception had worked, which would give them time to re-group, Francis consoled himself.

Francis and Thomas left the abbey a week later, despite advice to the contrary from the Abbot. The Viscount's condition had not improved and he remained feverish and in great pain. The physician had tried poultices and honey but the wounds were still putrefying, however Francis was adamant. He insisted he was well enough to travel and his lesions would heal before too long. Against his host's advice however, he had decided to make the short trek North westwards to his manor at Minster Lovell, before turning South, despite the fact it was now in enemy hands. Abbot Sante had told him the new occupant Jasper Tudor, now the Duke of Bedford, had not yet returned to Oxfordshire since the battle and was currently enjoying the king's grateful hospitality at Kenilworth. The chances are the manor would be unoccupied, apart from essential staff, of whom many would be Lovell acolytes. Being so close, Francis could not let the opportunity of seeing Minster Lovell once more, pass him by, having had a sudden premonition he may never see his beloved home again.

'Do you think it wise my Lord?' Thomas cautioned. 'Surely that's the first place the king's spies will look?'

'I disagree Thomas. That's *exactly* why it would be safe to go there. They will judge it too obvious and therefore unlikely. They will dismiss it. Besides... There's something there which I must collect.' Thomas sighed with fatalistic compliance; clearly Francis had made his mind up and would not be swayed, though Thomas suspected the Viscount's wounds contributed in no small way to irrational thought and flawed decision making.

Setting out from the Abbey Francis felt comforted riding through the familiar byways of his home turf and wracked with homesickness, he was resolved to make the detour, despite his companion's misgivings. As they approached the manor house, so picturesquely situated on the banks of the River Windrush, Francis felt the lump in his throat threaten to break into a sob as his lip trembled and he fought away tears. His beautiful home, so full of promise and potential, memories of laughter and sunshine streaming in through the tall windows, a place of peace and plenty, luxury and comfort, a haven of safety and security as the family home of Richard's Lord Chamberlain, now snatched from him, thrust into the hands of another. It felt like a rape, his home, violated, unloved, uncared for, used, usurped. He wanted to weep as he had wept after the battle but with Thomas beside him it felt unbecoming and sentimental to show such emotion for a dwelling place.

He took a measured breath, composing himself, as they dismounted and knocked on the door of the elegant manor house. It was unusually quiet, no sounds of occupation coming from the courtyard, no guards in evidence or faces at windows. After a few moments the door hinge creaked open as a man servant peered through the gap. Francis pulled a neckerchief over his mouth and nose, while Thomas stepped forward. Francis felt sickened that he was here begging at the door of his former home, no longer its master but instead a common fugitive.

'My Lord's not in residence' the man grumbled with a lilting Welsh accent. 'What do you want? The man could see the pair were well dressed and their mounts well accoutred, though the taller man appeared to be in pain, leaning his arm on his companion's shoulder. Thomas requested shelter for the night for two weary strangers, holding out a silver coin.

'You had better come in then', the servant agreed unenthusiastically, taking the coin and beckoning to a stable boy to attend the horses. The man ushered the visitors into the parlour and bade them sit by the open fireplace, then disappeared into the kitchen, advising an old servant he had callers, before repairing to his quarters with the coin safely hidden inside his tunic. A short time later an elderly man with a pronounced stoop, long grey hair and kindly brown eyes entered the parlour with a jug of ale and two tankards, which he placed on the table by the window.

'Some refreshment gentlemen. May I enquire your business here?' All at once Francis stood up steadying himself again on Thomas's shoulder but now beaming with recognition at his old retainer.

'Joseph!' he exclaimed. 'It's me, Francis!' he grinned, revealing his face. Joseph hurried towards his former master, clasping the young nobleman's hands together and bowing his head.

'My Lord!' he uttered as the words caught in his throat and his lower lip trembled. 'We thought you were dead! The old man's eyes watered as he took in Francis's sickly pallor and unkempt appearance. The handsome young man who had gone off so confidently on his king's mission before the invasion, two long years ago, appeared noticeably aged, subdued, devoid of that spark of bravado and optimism, so defining in young men before the horrors of war had had time to break their spirit. Yet that was what he could plainly see - this man was broken, defeated. He bade Francis sit and poured him a drink, his hands shaking, dismayed by the change in his employer, his gaze settling on the bloodstained cloths binding the Viscount's torso and leg.

'You are wounded my Lord! I will get help'. Francis put his hand on Joseph's arm.

'Nay Joseph, thank you but its too risky. I'm on the run with a price on my head. I can't chance it. No-one must know. I'm even putting you in danger coming here. Pray allow us a bed for the night and we'll be gone tomorrow'.

'Very well my Lord, you can be assured of our silence' he leaned forward and lowered his voice to a whisper. 'You may bed down in the under croft, even the new master is as yet unaware of its existence but we keep it ready for just this type of eventuality.' He winked at Francis, 'You remember it my Lord?' Francis smiled.

'I most certainly do! In fact that's why I came, to retrieve something I left there before Bosworth. When are you expecting the owner back Joseph?'

'Any day, my Lord. Pembroke's been at Kenilworth celebrating his victory with the king.' The old man looked abashed as he spoke of the battle that had vanquished his former master.

'No doubt being showered with more Yorkist possessions!' Francis quipped bitterly, as Joseph went to check there were no other servants about. He returned and beckoned to Francis, who got up with a grimace and hobbled uncomfortably to the kitchen. Thomas drained his tankard thirstily and followed his companion, rather wishing they had not made this detour to the manor house, with Tudor's uncle Jasper poised to return at any moment. He didn't trust the man who had admitted them either and hoped Francis's pain had not impaired his judgement, for discovery and capture would mean certain death for them both and probably Joseph as well, for aiding and abetting the leader of the rebellion.

Entering the large kitchen with its expansive hearth, an old spaniel lying on a blanket, awoke from its torpor and began wagging his tail enthusiastically at the approach of a familiar figure. 'Hector is that you old fella?' Francis knelt down gingerly, holding his wounded side and fondling the old dog's grey muzzle gently. 'Hector my old faithful! Good to see you again!' The dog nudged his master and whimpered softly pressing his nose against Francis's face, licking him affectionately.

'He's old now my Lord, not long for this world I reckon,' Joseph commented sadly. 'Aye, I can see that. I know how he feels!'. Francis observed, gently kissing the top of the animal's head, as the servant checked once more they were alone, nodding affirmatively. He hurried to steady Francis who got up with a groan and limped over to the fireplace, whereupon reaching out to the wood panelling by the side of the inglenook, he stuck his dagger into the join where a panel abutted its frame. Sliding it back to reveal a cavity in the brick where an iron bar protruded from behind the adjoining panel, Joseph pulled the bar across and pushed the adjacent panel inwards, at which point the whole section of panelling became a doorway, the hinges disguised by a strip of ornamental beading. The portal opened onto a set of narrow stone steps leading downwards into a black void. The old man handed Francis a candle and they climbed down into a large, enclosed cellar with a low barrel-vaulted roof, a table with a long bench and two beds against the wall. It smelled airless, damp and cold and Joseph lit the fire and the hanging tapers on the wall and went back up to get some food and blankets.

Thomas whistled softly and looked about him in surprise that such a large room could be so well hidden. 'It won't do you any good to stay down *here* too long my Lord', the knight observed, concerned for his friend's condition in this dank atmosphere and not relishing the thought of a night in this gloomy space that felt like a crypt.

'I don't intend to Thomas but you will thank me when you see what I've come for!' Francis walked over to the fireplace and reached up under the mantelpiece. He felt along a hidden shelf inside the recess until his fingers found a metal box. He pulled it out and prized the lid open with his dagger blade. Thomas gazed wide eyed at the contents – a bag full of gold and silver coinage, enough to set a man up for life, a handful of pearls and a garnet cabochon. Thomas let out a vulgar expletive and Francis laughed.

'Aye! Now you see why I came back?' he put his arm around his companion and sat down heavily, as if all his energies had been saved up for this one salvage.

'I was intending to retrieve it after Bosworth had we won the day!' he sighed with resignation. Dividing the coins into two piles, he placed half in a pouch with the garnet and half back in the box before returning it to its hiding place and tucking the pouch into his clothing, wincing from the pain in his side, as Joseph was heard on the steps. Having filled their stomachs and bid goodnight to the servant, the two noblemen lay in the dwindling firelight discussing what to do next. The short journey had exhausted Francis and he knew he had already exerted himself too much, however a plan had been forming in his mind and he needed his friend to carry it out.

'Thomas, you have been a stalwart friend and I cannot express my gratitude enough, but I need you to do this one more thing for me. You must go to Devon alone. I cannot accompany you, I am spent. I need you to call on Henry Bodrugan at Coldridge Manor. He will have heard the battle is lost and will have left Gleaston with Edward. They should be back in Devon by now. If Bodrugan is not there, Robert Markenfield will help you. He lives close by. Tell Bodrugan what has happened and ask him to ensure Edward's safety, if necessary, convey the lad to Burgundy or Portugal. He should be safe under his assumed name but we need to keep him out of harm's way should Tudor's spies get wind of his whereabouts. If Bodrugan is attainted, which he is sure to be, he will lose Coldridge. It's my guess the manor will be returned to Thomas Grey but I can't be sure he is not being watched, so we need to protect Edward. Take the money and use it well, my friend. Give the garnet to Edward, it was Richard's, so it should be returned to his nephew. Take what you need, set yourself up somewhere in the South until you are able to return North. Do this last thing for me Tom'. Francis collapsed back against the pillow, breathing heavily with the exertion, spitting blood and groaning as a coughing fit consumed him. Thomas got up to hold a drink against his friend's lip and was about to speak but Francis gripped his arm. 'I need you to carry on for me my friend'. he rasped. 'I may have lost this battle but I intend to continue the fight, so help me God. Once I am healed, I will go to Burgundy. Duchess Margaret will help us and with any luck we will try again.' Thomas blew out his cheeks and shook his head.

'You're a brave man Francis!' He wanted to tell his friend that he had done enough and to relinquish his cause but he couldn't deny Francis this vestige of hope, which may be the one thing keeping him from utter despair. 'Very well, I will go to Coldridge but I can't promise anything after that. I need to get in touch with my family and secure their livelihoods. I will ensure Edward's safety but I can't get involved in another military campaign, much as I would wish to. I have already lost my brother. There are plenty of younger men who can carry on the fight. Forgive me my friend.' Thomas felt bad in the face of his companion's determination but he could already see Francis was beyond recovery and their only sensible option was to give up and accept defeat. Francis laid his hand on Thomas's shoulder.

'Aye of course, Thomas. Nay, forgive *me*, I should not have presumed. I am sorry about John. You have already done more than enough and

I know how much you miss your home amongst the lakes and fells - which you will have no doubt lost because of me. Keep yourself safe that's all I ask'.

They slept soundly in that dark space, the only radiance emitting from the fireplace, where a glimmer of light from the adjoining kitchen chimney above and the embers in the grate lifted the undercroft out of total darkness. Thomas woke first, at the sound of the bolt being slid back from the top of the stairs and Joseph appearing with some welcome victuals. Hector followed the old servant, lolloping slowly down the steps and over to his master. Thomas shook Francis awake, whom he had heard call out in the night in a fit of delirium, or a bad dream, Thomas was unsure which. He felt his friend's forehead. It felt warm and clammy. *Not a good sign* he reflected, as Francis opened his eyes and cried out in pain as he tried to sit up, collapsing back on the bed in agony.

'You *must* go my Lord! Go back to the Abbey,' Joseph advised, his voice conveying a new urgency. 'Pembroke has sent word to the household he is on his way again today and we must prepare - he will be here by tomorrow.'

'I cannot!' Francis breathed heavily, easing himself upright one more. 'I've got no strength left. I will lay low here until the coast is clear again. You must lock me in here Joseph and let me know when Jasper Tudor leaves again, as he is bound to do. He will want to get back to his Welsh estates and inspect all the other properties he is sure to have bestowed upon him by his grateful nephew! Besides, he knows he's not popular here in Oxfordshire!'

'Aye, my Lord. If that is your wish, I will ensure your sanctuary, though I deem it unwise. I will send Martha to tend to your wounds, she will not betray you my Lord'.

'Ah Martha! Your good lady wife and my faithful housekeeper! How is she Joseph?'

'She is well my Lord, thank you'.

Francis smiled, 'Good, I'm glad to hear it.' He turned his attention to the dog who put his paw on the bed and nuzzled his nose towards his master. 'I'm sorry my Lord, he's been scratching at the panelling'. Joseph apologised. 'I had to let him come down for fear he gives you away.' Francis smiled and fondled Hector's ears.

'Nay problem, Joseph. You can keep me company Hector!', he addressed the dog before turning back to his servant. 'Joseph, would you be so good as to fetch me some writing materials. I need to notify my wife'.

'Very well my Lord', Joseph agreed moving towards the stairs, while Francis raised himself slowly off the bed, leaning heavily on the table for support, feeling inside his doublet for the coin pouch and handing it to Thomas. 'Now go! Hurry Thomas, be on your way, as we discussed and God speed my friend'. Thomas nodded his consent, blinking away the moisture blurring his vision.

'Thank you, Francis. God be with you also'. He put his arm around his friend in a gentle embrace, careful not to cause any further discomfort, clasping Francis's hand firmly before girding on his sword and mantle and following the servant up the stairs and out to the stable where his horse had been saddled.

'Look after him Joseph, I fear he may not come through this', Thomas whispered with glum certitude as he mounted.

'Aye sir, I will. Fare thee well sir', Joseph nodded, both men acutely aware, in the look that passed between them, of the inevitability of the Viscount's decline, no further words being necessary to convey their dread of the certain outcome.

Chapter Eleven

A rriving at Minster Lovell from Kenilworth, Jasper Tudor, Earl of Pembroke and newly entitled Duke of Bedford, ordered a thorough search of the manor. He had planned to search the house anyway upon his return and having received a tip-off from the servant who had admitted two strangers a few days before, he had to make sure. Joseph had assured the Duke the visitors had left and that they were simply travellers seeking shelter but Jasper's suspicions were roused. Every chamber, alcove, roof space and outbuilding was searched but to no avail. All the staff were interrogated but none admitted seeing Lovell or his companion and irritated, the Duke eventually left for Wales, leaving a troop of soldiers to guard the manor should Lovell return. He would have enjoyed apprehending the elusive Viscount and presenting his prize to the king in triumph. With Lincoln dead, Lovell would have been Tudor's trump card and indicator, as to the remaining Yorkist threat. Meanwhile, unbeknown to those carrying on their daily tasks in the manor, below them a young man sat alone, incarcerated in that dark cellar, with just his regrets, his pain and his faithful dog to occupy him.

Francis was tired, his head swam, he wanted to vomit. The pain in his side from his now putrid wound was overwhelming, the sepsis spreading through his flesh at will. He couldn't move his leg where the poison had festered. He wanted to lie down but the effort and pain of hauling himself over to the bed was too much to entertain. His hand shook, he could feel his lifeblood seeping away. He knew he was dying and he welcomed it. *What was the point of living?* He had failed, the burden of guilt too much to bear, death would be the relief and solace he now longed for.

Martha had dressed his wounds as best she could, provided him with ink, a quill and parchment, together with a book of hours and a bible, which she thought may give him some comfort and left him alone. Hector had curled up at his feet, unwilling to be taken back upstairs and Joseph had deemed it better to leave the dog in the cellar where he could not alert the household to his master's presence.

It was not long before Francis heard the sounds of the returning possessor of his property. He could hear the commotion upstairs and knew they must be searching for him. It was unlikely that he and Thomas had remained unseen when they approached the manor and somebody had indeed spotted them, no doubt encouraged by the rewards on offer for information. He could hardly blame them. With the country in turmoil and livings jeopardised, people were too terrified to be seen in opposition to the king.

After what seemed like an eternity however, the banging of doors and scraping of furniture overhead stopped and silence once more fell upon the manor. Francis couldn't remember when he had last eaten or how long he had been alone, it may have been hours, it may have been days. Time meant nothing in this dark space where there was no difference between night and day. He knew he may not stay conscious for much longer. His old dog had lain still for hours, his breaths shallow, showing little interest in the scraps Joseph had left, though occasionally slaking his thirst in the water bowl and relieving himself on a pile of straw in the corner of the under croft.

Francis knew there was not much time left to him now, he must write to Anne while he could still think. He knew she would be worrying but once he could get this message to her, he was satisfied she would come for him. Old Joe would be back soon with fresh food and drink, then he would rest. '*Oh blessed rest. I must sleep,… no I must write*'. He jerked his head up. '*Stay awake Francis! How should I start? Perhaps…My dearest beloved Anne, Forgive me, I have failed you…*' He lifted the pen to write, his eyes swam, he could not focus, his head slumped on his chest, he could feel himself fading, his eyelids closing, '*I must sleep! I will write tomorrow,*' he decided, relief flowing through him as another tide of nausea threatened to engulf him. The candle flickered as the wick burned close to the pool of wax it had made. He felt the darkness envelop him as he lapsed into unconsciousness. Gradually his breathing slowed before a long shuddering breath soughed from his lungs and stopped, then there was no more pain. His muscles relaxed and the quill dropped from his hand.

All at once, he found himself looking down from the ceiling. In the wavering pool of radiance below him, he saw a man sitting slumped over a desk, a blank piece of parchment in front of him, save for an ink blot staining the page where the quill had fallen and at his feet an old dog sleeping motionless. A candle flame beside the man flickered and died, plunging the windowless void into a pitch-black abyss but no, *what was that?* a tunnel of bright light coming towards him, so bright he couldn't see what was at the end. He found himself moving through the tunnel and out into the all-enveloping brilliance. Suddenly he was filled with the most wonderful euphoria, there was no pain, no sadness, no guilt, no physical sensation at all, just overwhelming bliss. Everything was white, shimmering figures suffused with light, were holding out their hands in greeting. A man approaching him spoke. 'Francis, at last!'. His face was radiant, he seemed familiar. *Was that Richard?* and behind him, stood John. Richard held out his hand.

'Your Grace!'. Francis bowed his head, fell on his knees and was gently lifted to his feet as if weightless.

'There's no need for that, we are all equals here. Come,' Richard smiled, 'we've been waiting for you'.

Once Bedford had left, Joseph and Martha waited for nightfall to check on their guest. It had been 48 hours since they had been able to take him any food or drink, the staff having been closely guarded while the search was carried out and by now they knew Francis must be holding on by a thread. As soon as they entered the under croft, they could tell something was not right. The void was in complete darkness and mingled with the fusty atmosphere of the dank cellar, was the smell of decay and death. Joseph held his candle aloft, walked over to the figure slumped over the table and felt his master's hand. He recoiled with a sharp intake of breath. The body was stone cold and probably had been so for some time. Martha, standing by the foot of the stairs covered her nose.

'Is he dead?'

'Aye for certain'. Joseph crossed himself as did Martha.

'What do we do?' she asked her husband, turning her head away from the eerie sight of the corpse still seated as if it were simply dozing momentarily.

'What *can* we do? We can't get him out of here without being seen and will be marked as traitors for assisting him'. Joseph sighed and shook his head. 'Poor man! We can't help him now. He's in God's hands. Come Martha'.

'Are you just going to leave him? And what about the dog?'.

'I don't see we have any other choice, Martha. I'll check on the dog when I can but I can't risk him coming out now. He's not far behind my

Lord anyway'. Joseph pushed his wife up the stairs, slid the bolt back into its housing and closed the panel. At least the Viscount was home, he comforted himself, the secret cellar serving as a perfect mausoleum for his master, until in the unlikely event of a Yorkist restoration, Francis Lovell could be buried with honour in a tomb befitting this most valiant and true knight. One thing was sure, the old servant vowed, he would take the secret of the Viscount's final resting place to the grave if need be. No Tudor king would be able to rest easy in the certain knowledge of his enemy's demise.

Chapter Twelve

In Wensleydale Autumn was well under way. The lush greens of summer, now suffusing to gold, orange and terracotta, as blankets of fading heather and bracken clothing the uplands glowed a rich umber in the oblique rays of the retreating sun. In the woods bright saffron leaves of birch and aspen, blazed out from an artists' palette of colour, occasionally punctuated by the deep green of a solitary sombre yew, a rusty oak or the purple magnificence of a copper beech. Beneath the canopy deep drifts of fallen leaves carpeted the woodland floor, where bursting chestnuts and plump acorns lay in abundant profusion amongst a miscellany of omnifarious fungi – nature's rich bounty, ensuring deer, swine, small mammals and birds would survive the coming winter.

News came from Ravensworth that Anne's brother Richard Fitzhugh had finally succumbed to his long-term illness, leaving his wife Elizabeth with her infant son George to succeed him as Baron. Frideswide's husband Edward Norris had also died from the injury received at Stoke. There was still no word from Francis and as the winter set in, hope began to fade for his wellbeing. Attainders had been levied on many of the Northern noblemen who had fought for the Yorkists, including those who were missing, like Thomas Broughton, to ensure their families paid the price for their complicity in opposing the king.

Another loyal friend and supporter of Francis Lovell, Edward Franke, who had been at one time Sheriff of Oxfordshire under Richard III and had joined the rebels and consequently spent time in the Tower, had recently been released. He travelled North to Ravensworth where Anne and her mother Lady Alice Fitzhugh felt encouraged enough by his loyalty to engage his services in searching for Francis. The two women had written copious letters to loyal Yorkists who may have even the slightest clue as to Francis's whereabouts, at the same time spreading misinformation via Anne's maternal aunt, the Countess of Oxford. The more conflicting reports and rumours, the better to confound the enemy. However, Franke's enquiries came to nothing.

With the whole country on alert for news of the fugitive traitor, it was a testament to the Viscount's popularity that no-one gave away any information and even Anne's mother Alice showed she favoured her son-in-law's safety, over the temptation to betray him to her sister. With every day that had passed, however, with no word from her husband, Anne was becoming increasingly distraught and anxious. *Surely if Francis were alive, he would get word to her?* Though with both friend and foe searching for him and a hefty reward offered for his capture, who could be trusted with a letter?

For Eleanor and Bess there was nothing for it but to immerse themselves in their duties at Nappa Hall as usual but with no report of Robert, Bess remained downcast and sullen, debating with her mother at every opportunity as to what her suitor might be doing amongst the Earl of Oxford's retainers. *Would he return to her, or should she abandon all hope of his return and set her sights on another prospective marriage partner?*

'Oh mama, what do I do? I love Robert but I'm not going to wait around for him until I'm an old maid!' she told her mother in a fit of pique, 'but if I do wed someone else, supposing Robert comes back?' she argued with herself, as much as Eleanor.

'There's no rush Bess. Wait a year or two before making your choice. If you've heard nothing by then, I think you could safely assume he won't return'. Eleanor advised her daughter.

'A *year* or two?!' Bess exclaimed in horror, the prospect of her precious youth wasting away for what seemed like forever to one so young, while Robert was presumably getting on with his life elsewhere, was not an option she wished to entertain.

Lying in bed at night alone with her thoughts, Eleanor could not help but picture Stefan. She had prayed fervently the German mercenary was still alive and if so, perhaps back in his home country with the rest of the hired men at arms who had been allowed to go. She couldn't stop herself wondering about the women he would be bedding and if he would still think of her with affection. She smiled as she remembered the lock of hair he had reaped from her so brazenly and hoped he still cherished the memory of their night of abandon together. Part of her also hoped he would not think badly of her for yielding so willingly to him and to assume she was a woman of loose morals. She had never behaved like that before and did not intend to do so again but *would he know that?* Turning it over and over in her mind, she argued with her sense of morality. If her erstwhile lover were dead it hardly mattered, she had given pleasure to one who was soon to lose his life but *if he lived?...What would he think of her?*

The winter months dragged on, the snow lying in deep drifts on the Pennines, naked trees etched in ebony outline against the bright snow, where huddled in the deep blue shadows cast by drystone walls, full fleeced sheep gathered for warmth against the biting East wind. When the sun shone the beauty of the vale in winter never failed to delight Eleanor as she went about her errands. Excited children piling snow into shapes, pelting each other with compressed balls, squealing and laughing with delight, sledging down inclines, or sliding around on frozen ponds of flood water lying in the fields. Eleanor loved the stark beauty of leafless trees, each one unique, etched in linear form against a white canvas, brighter than any man-made parchment or sun dried linen. Every colour appearing to leap out; a flash of orange as a lone fox raced across a snow-covered field, the wonder of a winter sunset painting the hills in delicate pink, or a frozen waterfall suspended in its descent like the tail of a white charger. Sometimes the rain-sodden clouds would be as dark as lead, the snow blanketed hills appearing even brighter as a shaft of sunlight cast an arc of colour onto the gloom, a fleeting spectrum of hope heralding the returning sun.

Despite no news of Francis, it was widely believed he must still be alive. With no word to the contrary and no body having been found, it was left to people's imaginations and theories to determine his fate. He soon became an almost legendary figure, many convinced this brave young fugitive was simply biding his time before returning to restore the House of York, not the least of which was his wife and even Henry Tudor couldn't bring himself to dismiss him completely. The king cursed at the demise of the duplicitous Earl of Lincoln whom he had brought to Court but who had ultimately betrayed his trust. If John de la Pole had lived, Tudor may have learned the extent of the danger facing him but instead he could only surmise and speculate, relying on a network of spies to alert him.

Sir Richard Harleston had escaped to Burgundy and filled the Duchess in on the events of the battle they had lost. Margaret of York, shocked and saddened by the death of her nephew Lincoln, was convinced Francis was in sanctuary somewhere and would need a safe haven to which to return. She wrote to James IV of Scotland requesting he offer his support to Francis Lovell, Thomas Broughton, and others should they appear North of the border. The whereabouts of Edward V was also unknown. The last the Yorkists had heard was that he was being taken South by Henry Bodrugan and possibly conveyed to the Channel Islands or even Portugal, one rumour suggesting the lad had been sent to Guines but with no positive sighting, he remained an enigma.

Sir Henry, who having left his charge in safe hands at Coldridge, retreated to his manor at Bodrugan Park in Cornwall. Henry Tudor had him attainted and sent Sir Richard Edgecombe to seek him out. Edgecombe was only too pleased to be tasked with apprehending his former enemy, who had hounded him from his Cornish estates, after the Buckingham rebellion in '83. Back then Edgecombe had had a narrow escape, shrewdly casting his hat into the river, whereby his pursuers assumed him drowned. He fled to join Tudor in Brittany but now with the return of a Lancastrian monarchy, at last the boot was on the other foot and he could take his revenge on the agent of his exile.

As the king's men approached his manor, however, Bodrugan slipped out of a rear doorway and ran to the cliff edge at Turbot Point. He had instructed his servant to arrange for a boat to pick him up offshore and upon reaching the grassy headland, flung himself into the sea. Miraculously surviving, he was picked up, escaping to Ireland where he remained in exile. The cliff top thereafter, renowned as 'Bodrugan's leap', the knight going down in history as a charismatic and courageous adventurer. Of Edward V however, there was no further sighting, he had simply disappeared and most who had supported him, supposed he had died at Stoke, despite the continuing propaganda alleging his uncle Richard had murdered him and his brother back in '83.

As Spring arrived and marched on into another summer, Anne Lovell began to lose hope of ever seeing her husband again, despite the thorough search she and her mother had engaged in for the past year. They had written letters to as many people as they could think of who might have word, or who could search on their behalf but not one yielded any information. By June the Scottish king, only too happy to unsettle the English usurper, issued his letter of safe conduct for the rebels, fully expecting one or all of them to take advantage of it but they never did. Francis had vanished and Thomas Broughton likewise.

Eleanor and Bess, with more time on their hands than they had enjoyed at Middleham, would oft on Sundays after chapel, ride out along the bridleways towards Nappa Scar, the limestone cliffs rising nearly 1500 feet to the rear of the Hall. The tops of these flat-topped escarpments lay littered with boulders left by retreating glaciers, stacked at random, many large blocks resting precariously on a much smaller base, yet undisturbed for millions of years. Picking their way along the tracks under Carperby Moor, surveying the wide expanse of Wensleydale laid out before them, mother and daughter stopped to take in the familiar landmarks, they called home. The flat-topped prominence of Addlebrough to the South, the shining jewel of Semerwater, just visible from the heights, Penhill to the East, the wide green expanse of Wensleydale forest carpeting the valley and to the West, the distant Cumberland hills diminishing into a cerulean haze.

Eleanor loved this tranquil dale, her home, her refuge, the kaleidoscope of colour through the seasons, the familiar byways and vistas, places held dear by the men she had loved. She pictured Richard in his youth, riding eagerly through the woods and up on the moorland heights, bathing in the Rivers Ure and Cover with his friends, carefree and careless before the burden of duty curtailed his passion and mellowed his fervour. She could still hear Will calling to his hawk as she returned, Maia clutching a small mammal or game bird in her vice like talons; Eleanor would recall her husband describing the creatures and plants in the forest and how nature looked after its own. It was hard to think these vital young men would never return but at the same time Eleanor felt they were always with her, somehow indivisible from the land that nurtured them, their voices echoed in the sough of a summer breeze, the moan of a winter gale through bare branches, or the gurgle of the gushing falls as their ice cold waters tumbled down limestone terraces in effervescent abandon.

As often as she could Eleanor made her way back to Aunt Mabel's farm, where her son, William, now a gangly twelve-year-old was preparing to join Henry Scrope's pages at Bolton Castle. He would soon be allowed to join the family's hunting party, whose numbers had been depleted by the recent battle at Stoke, many of the local men having not returned, including Lord John Scrope who had been forbidden to return to Wensleydale. Eleanor's brothers Edward and James, however had arrived home safely and now ran their farm together. They had joined the Scropes' in the failed attack on York but afterwards had been sent home, thus avoiding the battle, for which Eleanor was thankful. After conversing with them, she hugged her son and bade him mind his manners, work diligently, paying special attention to the skills his father had possessed, so as to follow in his footsteps and honour his memory.

'Of course, mama. I want to be as good as papa, mayhap even better!' William grinned enthusiastically, as they walked down to the paddock where several horses were grazing. 'Look mama, let me show you how I can ride bareback!' He grabbed a bridle hanging on the gate, ran over to a small fell pony, slipped the harness over her head and sprang up onto her back, trotting around the field, gripping the animal's flank with his thighs and holding onto her mane for balance.

'Well done, William! I can see you've been practising but don't try that yet with Lord Scrope's horses, they will be powerful and not so easy to control'. *He grows more like his father every day*, Eleanor mused proudly watching Will's son confidently manipulating his pony. Soon he would eschew the nurturing of womenfolk and would learn to become a man in his own right, no longer a child, nor her charge to parent; a boy growing up in men's company, learning the ways of men.

At the end of the summer, the blacksmith Walter Dinsdale called at Nappa Hall to ask if there was any way his son Robert could be contacted. The old man was becoming increasingly frail and was finding his Wensley smithy too much for him, despite having taken on a young apprentice. He had always planned to retire and leave his only son in charge but with Robert now retained by John de Vere he needed to request his release. Being unable to write himself, Walter called on the Metcalfe's in the hope they could persuade the Earl of Oxford to return his son to Yorkshire. Thomas Metcalfe suggested such a request would be better coming from Alice Lovell, Oxford's sister-in-law and a letter was soon on its way to Ravensworth to that effect.

As another winter set in, Eleanor was sad to hear from Thomas Metcalfe that the new king had imprisoned Richard's illegitimate son John, to head off any attempts to use him as a figurehead for insurrection. It appeared no-one who had any connection to the late king, could be shielded from Tudor's paranoia. There was some good news for Eleanor and Bess however, that upon the Fitzhugh's request, Robert Dinsdale was being allowed to return home, providing he pledge his allegiance to serve the king when required and not take part in any future rebellion.

Bess was ecstatic at the thought of her one-time suitor returning and by the next Springtime had accepted Robert's proposal of marriage.

He had ridden up to the Hall during Easter week, Bess running to his arms in delight. Robert had matured and bulked out his physique, looking sun-bronzed and healthy and Eleanor was glad to see he still held Bess in great affection and wished to wed her. Clearly his time with Oxford's men had not diminished his ardour and in fact had added martial skills to his accomplishments. His captain had been reluctant to let him go but relented, with his farrier's promise to fight for the king if he was called upon to do so, in return for his freedom.

The couple tied the knot in Wensley church and settled down to life in the blacksmith's cottage, leaving Eleanor on her own at Nappa Hall, thankful her daughter was safely wed to an honest and diligent young man with a thriving business. She felt sure Richard would have approved but with Elizabeth being one of the least entitled of his natural children, she was free to live her life in secure anonymity. Eleanor knew Bess was safest as a farrier's wife in rural Yorkshire, despite her son-in-law's allegiance to the new monarch, though she felt it wise to remind her daughter of the need to keep the truth of her paternity secret, even from her new husband.

Bess longed to wear the fine silk dress the Countess had given to her from Anne Neville's wardrobe but which Eleanor reminded her was not appropriate attire for a farrier's wife and questions would be asked. On the eve of her wedding however, Eleanor allowed Bess to try on the gown and imagine how she may have looked, as a nobleman's daughter and as Bess stared at her image in the looking glass, her eyes filled with tears.

'Oh mama! I wish father was here to see me!' Eleanor nodded, herself unable to speak, as mother and daughter embraced, the presence of both Anne and Richard somehow palpable in the silken folds of the sensuous garment, its faint perfume transporting both women back to the magnificence of Middleham castle's royal chambers and the man now lost to them forever. Gazing at her beautiful daughter, whose looks and bearing would not be out of place in the Great Hall, Eleanor imaged her dancing with her father, as he had done with his young Neville cousins, all those years ago. *If only...* she fantasised sadly. Bess resigned herself to keeping her secret locked away and on the threshold of her new life as a wife, vowed to find happiness and fulfilment with the man she had chosen, content in a loving partnership – the advantage of being a commoner, her mother had reminded her - not obligated, as a noblewoman, to wed for rank or privilege.

Robert like many others of his class, was content to submit to whoever held the highest office in the land, so long as his livelihood remained secure. However, hidden from sight, there still simmered in the depths of men's consciousness, a deep loyalty to the late king, waiting to come to the surface should a new Yorkist challenger appear. The shadow of the white rose would linger in the background for many years to come, as occasionally repressed loyalty and rage held in check for so long, would come to the boil, when pockets of civil unrest found an excuse for violence.

At the end of 1489, as part of a protest against taxes in Yorkshire, a report arrived from Thirsk, announcing the death of the Earl of Northumberland. Henry Percy had been dragged from his horse and killed by an angry mob, some of whom had used this opportunity to show their displeasure for the Earl's failure to support Richard III at Bosworth. As his king fell, hopelessly outnumbered before being hacked to death in the mud of Redemore plain, the self-seeking Earl had stood by impassively, holding his troops on the sidelines. Many Yorkshiremen were not sorry to see the back of Percy, who made no secret of his dislike for Richard, whom he saw as infringing on his authority in the North. Eleanor recalled the Earl's sullen demeanour at Sheriff Hutton and couldn't help feeling his death was some sort of divine retribution. Her brothers felt the same, having harboured a deep resentment towards their self-serving commander for his non-participation at Bosworth and his obsequiousness towards Tudor.

At Ravensworth, Anne Lovell despairing of ever seeing or hearing from her husband again, assumed widowhood and took a religious vow. Even if Francis was confirmed to be dead, she had no interest in marrying again and with no children to bring up she had lost her focus in life. Though still residing at Ravensworth, she donned the russet headdress of a vowess, dressed herself in a plain grey gown, took her vow of chastity and indulged in daily prayer and almsgiving.

Now that the head of the Nappa Hall household had returned, Thomas Metcalfe having received a second pardon for his part in the so-called Lambert Simnel uprising, soon proved himself a useful supervisor of the castle and lordships of both Middleham and Richmond with an annuity from the king. Despite this, he had not altogether forgotten his allegiance to the Yorkist cause, which would re-emerge again before long, with the appearance of a second challenger to the throne.

Eleanor's son William, at last a teenager, was happily ensconced at Bolton Castle with the other pages, pursuing his new skills with enthusiasm and Eleanor felt a sense of relief at having brought up her children safely and securely, leaving them in as good hands as possible. Elizabeth Scrope had died and with Lord John Scrope marrying again, their son Henry, who was wed to Elizabeth Percy, daughter of the 3rd Earl of Northumberland, took over the running of the castle.

Chapter Thirteen

James Metcalfe, having ingratiated himself with Henry Tudor, retained his positions and as Master Forester of Wenselydale, was granted the lifetime herbage of Woodhall Park close to Nappa, safe in the knowledge he would eventually inherit all his father's lands. His relationship with his wife Elizabeth was at best cool, though she had borne him a daughter who had died in childhood. James had a reputation for philandering and trying his luck with any attractive woman he encountered, evidence of which Eleanor was well aware from her time at Middleham, though he had never approached her when Will was alive.

Since she had been widowed however and joined the household at Nappa, James would regularly make advances to his former friend's surviving spouse in the hope of reciprocation. Eleanor found him mildly appealing but he was married, a fact of which she was only too well aware when serving his wife. She would tolerate his suggestions and innuendos, laughing them off as flippant jests, never intending for one moment to take him seriously, though rather suspecting he was. He seemed undeterred by the fact she was older than him by about eight years and she felt flattered he still found her desirable enough to proposition.

Riding out one early Spring afternoon with a large party of the Metcalfe family, Eleanor rode Westwards through Askrigg towards Hardraw force. They stopped to gaze at the impressive waterfall, tumbling 100 feet down over its limestone escarpment, where the cliff fell away abruptly under Hardraw Beck. Standing by the edge of the fearful precipice peering down at the tumbling cascade of water as it plummeted in a long slender stream into the rocky pool below, Eleanor eased her mount away in alarm. She had heard about the force from her brothers, who as children had often teased her that they would drop her from the edge if she misbehaved but this was the first time she had seen Hardraw for herself. The height of the scar appeared every bit as frightening as she had imagined and it was only by retreating a good distance from the others, that Eleanor was able to calm her nerves. One false step by her mount on those slippery rocks and both horse and rider would fall to their deaths.

Dismounting further upstream and allowing her horse to drink, she sat on a mossy boulder lost in visions of childhood. She recalled days riding out with her father and brothers, on the rare occasions he was released from his duties in service for Richard Neville, Earl of Warwick, at Middleham castle. She had worshipped her father, who's death at Towton, left his children orphaned, their mother having died eight years previously, giving birth to Eleanor. She missed the only parent she had known and as his one daughter, had enjoyed his protectiveness longer than her brothers. Preoccupied with thoughts of him and with the drumming of the force behind her, she failed to notice a rider's approach until he dismounted and sat down close beside her. 'Impressive, isn't it?' James Metcalfe had announced, making Eleanor start.

'The force? Oh, aye sir, I'm fearful of looking at it', she frowned, shifting uncomfortably at his proximity.

'What else are you fearful of Eleanor?' he grinned, edging closer, grasping her hand and fixing her with a salacious stare.

''Sir?' She stood up, her cheeks colouring, casting around nervously for the rest of the party but they were alone.

'Do you fear *me*, Eleanor?' James stood up in front of her, her hand still held firmly in his, his frame edging too close for comfort, invading her personal space. Eleanor steeled herself to be polite but resolute, not wishing to give him any encouragement.

'Nay sir!' she announced assertively meeting his gaze in defiance.

'Well then Eleanor, you must know how I feel about you!' He pulled her towards him, his face inches from hers. She gasped and tried to extract her hand from his grip.

'Unhand me sir!' He hesitated, then seeing her resolve, let go. She turned away conflicted. He wasn't unattractive and the temptation unsettled Eleanor as she wrestled with her conscience. However, she had made up her mind since her night with Stefan, she would accept nothing less than marriage from another suitor and this man was already espoused. She glanced at him sideways and James sensed her ambivalence.

'Come on Eleanor, how long have we known each other? How long have you been widowed now? It must be 10 years at least. You must hanker for some male company, a handsome woman like you?' he cajoled.

'Sir, I brook no favour from you! You are married and I am your servant.' Eleanor riposted, ignoring the compliment. 'You should not take advantage of me', she frowned, attempting to appeal to his integrity but was unsure what to do. If she rejected him too forcefully, he could dismiss her but if she submitted to him, she would be an adulteress. She thought of his wife, who already regarded her suspiciously, having noted her husband's preoccupation with the auburn-haired beauty who waited upon her. Eleanor was determined not to be seen as a husband stealer, or a woman of easy virtue. She had come across women like that at Middleham who garnered nothing but contempt.

'Should not?' James snapped irritably at the reprimand. 'As your employer Eleanor I could disadvantage you, or make it worth your while?' he inveigled but then immediately regretting the coercion, detracted his rash statement. 'Nay I don't mean that Eleanor. I don't wish to buy your affections, nor should I use my position as leverage. Forgive me'. He moved towards her again, taking her hand and kissing it, before impulsively pulling her towards him, his arm around her waistline.

'Oh Eleanor! I desire you! I want you! You *must* know how much!'

Just then a rider was heard approaching and James abruptly released his hold on her, cursing under his breath and moving away from Eleanor as his groom rode up.

'I was worried sir, I thought you were lost.' The man knew immediately he had interrupted something, noting the abashed look on Eleanor's face and the annoyance on his master's. 'We are heading back now sir'. the groom added, smirking as he turned away, knowing it was common knowledge amongst the servants that James Metcalfe lusted after his wife's waiting woman. He almost wished he had delayed his appearance and caught the couple in *flagrante delicto*, juicy gossip being hot property in the servants' quarters.

Eleanor breathed a sigh of relief at the fortuitous interruption, for with no idea what to say to James in response, she felt trapped and compromised. She untethered her horse, pulling herself up into the saddle, trotting off to join the main party, distracted by James' admissions and pondering her responses. She was aware however, that the groom would likely make more of what he saw than she wished. Having witnessed James's embrace, the man would naturally assume Eleanor's consent. - that's how gossip ignited, being rarely based on truth, embellishments and exaggeration having far more appeal in the telling, than bland fact.

Eleanor kept her distance from James, conscious she was being observed and a subject of discussion amongst the domestics but remained determined to give them no verification for scandal. A few days later, James, in a state of inebriation, returning with his parents, from an evening with the Scrope's, accosted the object of his desires in a dark corridor, pressing her forcefully up against the wall, determinedly crushing her lips with his. Eleanor tried to push him away but he held her fast, the alcohol giving him false courage.

'Nay sir! Release me!' she cried out, catching her breath.

'Come on Eleanor, be my mistress! You know you want to!' he leered, his breath heavy with a bellyful of his hosts' French claret, his eyes unfocused.

'I do not and I never will! Leave me be sir, or I will be forced to expose your impropriety!' Eleanor had no real intention of exposing his infidelity but he was not to know that. He judged she was serious and at the sound of voices from the stairwell, released his grip on her and stalked off muttering as he went, humiliated at her rebuff.

'Jezebel!' he retorted churlishly.

Eleanor ran to her room, shamed by his inference that she had somehow invited James's attentions despite doing nothing to encourage him. She actually liked him, when he was sober but not enough to compromise her integrity as his doxy, which would inevitably end in her dismissal. Besides, with Bess expecting her firstborn, she would shortly be a grandmother and as such be expected to behave with mature propriety. James, suitably abashed by his behaviour, apologised to Eleanor a few days later, though simply for his drunkenness and rudeness, not for desiring her, for which he offered no expression of regret, from then on avoiding her in sullen indifference.

Eleanor's first grandchild, born in early April, was to his parents' delight, a boy, unsurprisingly christened Richard by his doting mother, 'in honour of the late king', Bess told her husband, who took her choice at face value, only too happy to have a son to carry on his name and eventually his business.

Chapter Fourteen

ow on her own again, Eleanor began to think about herself and her situation. Still appearing youthful, though in her late thirties and fortunately retaining her slim figure, she was even now able to turn heads, younger men being no exception. Despite having no strong wish to marry again, she began to yearn for the comfort of a companion, a like-minded person with whom she could share her life. Though she had once contemplated religion, since her night with Stefan, she felt she had more to give as a woman, before the years ravaged her looks and despite the fact she was unable to bear more children, she felt her time as a wife had not yet run its course. Ideally, she would have wed the German captain had he asked her but he was lost to her, either by the sword, or by distance and any fantasies she might harbour for him had to be dismissed. Though not actively seeking a husband, she was not averse to the prospect of a new partner in life. Besides, as someone's wife once more, she would cease to be presumed fair game by libidinous admirers.

Easter came and went, followed by St. George's day when Eleanor would accompany the Metcalfe's to Bolton Castle for the feasting, at the same time, allowing her an opportunity to check on her son's progress with the Scrope's huntsmen. Amongst the guests were members of Cumbrian families, some of whom had been involved with assisting Lovell's rebellion but who now had submitted to the new king, for fear of further reprisals. Eleanor became aware she was being observed with interest by more than one guest and one in particular had caught her eye. A middle-aged gentleman, his hair greying at the temples, a close-cropped beard delineating his jawline, was seated with the Huddlestons of Millom and she noticed him repeatedly glancing in her direction. A distinguished looking man with a sturdy physique, well dressed, he somehow reminded her of her father. As she waited on the Metcalfe's, she found herself smiling back at him and saw him commenting to Elizabeth Metcalfe, clearly about her, as her mistress turned to look in her direction as he spoke. She could see her name formed on their lips, though the words were muffled by the general hubbub of conversation and she wondered what was being said. Later on the ride back to Nappa Hall, Elizabeth slowed her mount and drew alongside Eleanor.

'Eleanor, I must speak to you. You saw the gentleman I was seated next to at the dining table?'.

'Aye madam'. Eleanor guessed what was coming.

'His name is Hugh Broughton, he is Marshall for the Huddlestons' at Millom Castle. He is a widower and would like to make your acquaintance. He has asked to call on us tomorrow before he returns to Millom. Will you receive him?'

'Of course madam, I would be pleased to meet him' Eleanor replied politely, her pulse missing a beat, as she sensed a new avenue in her life opening up, *for what would a widower want from her except marriage?*

'I have apprised him of your circumstances', Elizabeth continued. 'He is well positioned Eleanor and he seems very taken with you', she looked askance at Eleanor, 'I feel he may proposition you Eleanor and I think you should consider it - you could do worse my dear!'. Eleanor couldn't help wondering if word had got round about James's attentions and his mother had decided her waiting woman would be best married off, away from temptation.

'Aye, madam' Eleanor agreed politely. That night she lay awake pondering upon the prospect of a new future, once more as a wife but to a man she did not know. Her head told her it was a sensible option, she would be more than comfortable, her future secure but her heart hesitated. *Do I really want to marry a stranger again?* She recalled her marriage to Ralph, his indifference and infidelity and whether this man would be the same. She thought about the intimacy of the marriage bed and immediately Stefan came to mind. She smiled ruefully, for the charismatic mercenary was bound to be dead by now. This Hugh was not as handsome but pleasant enough and if he were kind to her, she could surely grow to love him? At least living again as a wife, would mean she was no longer alone and would be provided for. It was the age-old question, when presented with a new path in life and Eleanor vacillated, sensibility fighting with emotion. *Should I take it, or wait for something better to come along? Come on Eleanor, you're not getting any younger!* she remonstrated with herself, before resorting to prayer for spiritual guidance and falling asleep, awaking none the wiser in the morning. Having risen and dressed herself with more attention to detail than usual, Eleanor found Hugh and Elizabeth waiting in the great chamber as she entered.

'Hugh Broughton, Eleanor' Elizabeth introduced the visitor as Eleanor extended her hand in greeting.

'Pleased to meet you sir', she smiled, blushing as his eyes met hers with a look of unabashed admiration.

'Nay, Eleanor, the pleasure is all mine', he replied with a distinct Cumbrian accent, kissing her hand politely as she sat down opposite him. Elizabeth got up and excused herself leaving the couple alone. Hugh filled a goblet with wine and handed it to Eleanor, who sipped at it self-consciously while he outlined his life as Marshall at Millom

Castle and why he had come. His wife had died some years ago and his children were all married now, he told her. He wanted a companion in life with whom to spend his remaining years. She watched him as he spoke, taking in his grey-green eyes, craggy physiognomy and rough work-hardened hands. He was well built and stocky, his midriff swelling from an over-indulgence of ale and good food but she could see he must have been good looking in his youth. Reminding herself she was past the age where physical attraction was paramount, she understood that there had to be something more to a mature partnership. She told him about her own life and service at Middleham castle, her two previous marriages, her children and her connection with the Metcalfe family. It seemed they were both lonely people and as he spoke Eleanor relaxed and found herself picturing a future together.

'Well Eleanor, I am sure you have supposed my intentions.' He took a deep breath and stood up offering his hand towards her. She stood up and took his hand tentatively, as he grasped hers tightly, knowing there was no more time for deliberation. Eleanor's mind raced. *Should I accept or refuse him? Do I live out my years alone, or do I take a chance on this stranger to be my companion?* It would be nice to be cared for once more and as the wife of a Marshall, she would garner some respect from employees under her husband's dictate. Whether it was the wine, or maybe just curiosity that prompted her decision, Eleanor found herself taking a plunge into the unknown, besides it was easier to accept this man than suffer the embarrassment of a denial and the displeasure of her mistress. This was it! She must answer him now.

'Would you accept my hand in marriage Eleanor?'

'Aye sir, I accept, thank you sir' she replied, almost without comprehension as to what she had agreed. Before she could draw breath, he had hauled her towards him, his lips planting a firm kiss on hers, his beard brushing her skin softly. She almost wanted to laugh at the ticklish sensation but deemed it impolite given the seriousness of the pledge she had just given.

'Thank you, Eleanor. I am honoured. You won't regret it my dear'. *I hope he's right*, Eleanor thought, realising she had passed the point of no return. Hugh picked up his hat and kissed her hand again. 'I will make arrangements and send for you as soon as possible.' he grinned and strode to the door with a lightness of step that surprised him. He hadn't expected such a positive response and congratulated himself on his good fortune in securing this local beauty.

'Congratulations my dear!' Elizabeth Metcalfe beamed as Eleanor told her the news.

'Have I done the right thing do you think?' Eleanor enquired of her employer, still unable to process to what she had just agreed.

'Of course, my dear! If nothing else, it will be a step up for you. You will be well cared for and want for nothing, I am sure. He seems like a good man and you will be near the sea and the high hills of Cumberland.'

'Aye but I will miss my children and grandchildren'.

'For sure but you are not that far away. You know you are welcome here any time my dear but you should think of yourself now and not hold back because of others. They have their own lives now'. Eleanor knew she was right. It was time to let go and live her own life.

Two months later Eleanor found herself wed to Hugh Broughton and residing in his quarters at Millom Castle, though he also had a cottage on the Broughton Manor estate which had belonged to his cousin Sir Thomas Broughton. Thomas, in his absence, had been attainted for his part in the battle at Stoke and his properties given to Thomas Stanley, Earl of Derby but this cottage had been given to Hugh some years previously. Although there had been no news of Sir Thomas since the battle, he was assumed dead by many but nevertheless, his family still held out hope for his return, confident he was merely in hiding.

Eleanor and Hugh were wed at Holy Trinity church beside the castle and mass was said for them in the Huddleston chapel. Eleanor wore one of the silk gowns she had been given at Middleham and Hugh presented her with a simple gold and ruby wedding ring engraved with their initials entwined on the inner rim. Their wedding night was no more nor less than Eleanor had expected. Hugh was respectful and polite and though she felt no physical desire for him, she gave enough reassurance for him to feel gratified that his wife was willing to indulge in intimacy. Hugh was in awe of his new wife, who at ten years younger than himself was even now an object of desire for younger men, as confirmed by the admiring glances of his soldiers. He marvelled at her cascades of auburn locks falling over her shoulders to her waist, the rich colour not yet dulled by age, her skin still smooth and relatively unlined. Her once svelte frame more voluptuous now, her hips showing the fullness of child-bearing but in contrast with her husband's heavy build, she delighted him with her youthfulness, his love making intense but brief, for which Eleanor was thankful. She tried not to think of Richard, Will or Stefan but often as she lay awake beside her sleeping husband, she would re-live those moments of ecstasy and vigorous abandon, that sensual thrill that once was all pervading but now distinctly lacking. Try as she might, Hugh could not arouse in her those feelings of physical desire she had felt before but she made sure he remained unaware.

Eleanor was not dissatisfied with her new life, however; she was comfortable and had less to do. Hugh had valets, grooms and pages to wait upon him and she had a ladies' maid to assist her if needed, though being accustomed to attending to herself, it felt odd to summon help for something she could quite easily manage unaided. Her maid Edith, a local girl with a broad Cumbrian accent, was happy to serve the Marshall's new wife, especially one so amenable and considerate. Edith enjoyed braiding and arranging Eleanor's hair, marvelling at its rich colour and silky softness.

'Too good to hide under a veil and wimple madam' she would say as she pinned it neatly back.

'Thank you, Edith, I used to hate my hair as a child but I've grown to appreciate it and have been told it's my best feature.' Eleanor smiled to herself picturing Stefan boldly stealing that lock of hair from her and wondering if it had ever been found amongst his belongings, as he must surely be long dead by now.

Eleanor, for her turn, was expected to serve the Huddleston's but was rarely called upon to do so, for they had their own ladies in waiting. As the Marshall's wife and a newcomer to the area, she would however be invited to ride out with them, up to the heights of Black Combe and Whit Fell, or out to the prehistoric stone circle at Swinside. This was her favourite ride. Following the course of Black Beck as it wound upwards to its source in the hills, the riders would veer West as the ground rose up to a grassy plateau, encircled by hills. There set in a perfect circle stood a ring of ancient stones, set upright like dragon's teeth. This enigma from a bygone age, lay mysterious and silent, a place of ritual or reverence, its significance shrouded in the mists of time, if not the frequent cloud that clung to these high places.

The henge fascinated Eleanor. She wondered who had erected these blocks of stone in this remote place and why. On warm days when they stopped for refreshment, or to rest the horses, she would sit with her back against the ancient slabs, gazing across to the hump of Black Combe fell, brooding over the sea. When cloud cast it into shadow, it lived up to its name, a dark mass against the bright water of the estuary behind. Northwards rose the distant Cumbrian hills, the Scafell massive and Coniston Old Man, wild inaccessible peaks, except to those hardy, grey-fleeced sheep, grazing the steep slopes year in year out. These Herdwicks had rounded, more woolly faces and sturdier legs than the Yorkshire Swaledales, coarser fleeces and lambs which were born black, fading to brown and grey with age.

Compared to the gentle moss-covered moors of Wensleydale, the landscape these native sheep roamed was wilder and less trodden, the time-worn tracks they followed, weaving narrow highways through rugged outcrops of rock. Occasionally a lamb would become crag-fast and must be rescued by the farmer, using dogs to guide him across the mountainous terrain. Rising to the skyline, slopes of jagged slate screes and hardened granite shoulders formed an impressive mountain vista, known only to locals but treacherous and forbidding to those unfamiliar with the paths. On a fine day, each successive ridge lay outlined in ever decreasing shades of blue, fading into an azure sky, as Eleanor's eyes adjusted to the distance – the beauty of the scene masking hidden dangers for the unwary.

Eleanor marvelled at her new surroundings so different from Yorkshire. Casting her eyes Southwards towards the Duddon, the estuary sparkled in a silver ribbon, snaking its way through the mudflats and out towards the huge expanse of sea stretching to the horizon, unbroken as far as the eye could see. Arriving in Millom had afforded Eleanor her first glimpse of the open sea and it made her feel vulnerable. Cocooned in the lush inland valleys of her youth, she hadn't had to think about England's boundaries, or the threat that could come by ship from foreign lands. The huge expanse of water in front of her now appeared terrifying – a living breathing entity, always moving, its constant wave action sighing and crashing on the shore, its unfathomable depths oft stirred into mountainous waves by the winds, while man's tiny ships tossed and tumbled helplessly at the mercy of nature's whim. This area of coastline lay exposed and defenceless in the face of nature's raw energy and when the Westerly gales struck Eleanor would hide herself away within the castle walls and not venture out until the storm had blown itself out.

Living with Hugh, Eleanor soon began to realise the folly of rushing into marital union with a stranger. It was not long before she discovered her husband had a temper, especially when he had indulged in too much ale, which was frequently. He would become boorish and rough with her, demanding his conjugal rights and treating her as an outlet for his frustration. He would apologise in the morning when he had sobered up but Eleanor had begun to fear him and sometimes would be left bruised by his energetic advances. He was a big man and her small frame no match for his brute strength, when he forced himself upon her, his beard scouring her skin, leaving it red and sore. He could tell she did not love him and was just meekly accepting of him as her husband and it enraged him, partly because he knew he had a wife who was probably more than he deserved and who would no doubt, have preferred a younger man. She did her best to reassure him but he watched her constantly, noting the admiration of other men for his comely wife, convincing himself without any foundation she was complicit in attracting male attention. Edith would warn her mistress when he returned from a drinking session with the soldiers in his employ. 'The Marshall's in his cups again madam', she would whisper, as Eleanor prepared for the night, readying herself for her husband's drunken demands.

However, when sober, Hugh and Eleanor found they had common ground in a love of the land they inhabited and the fact they were both staunch Yorkists, loathing the new Tudor regime with equal vengeance. Hugh had not fought at Stoke due to sickness but many of his men had joined Lovell's army on their way through Ulverston. Along with the Huddleston's and the Harrington's of Hornby castle, these families held a long-standing grudge against the Stanley's. Thomas Stanley was a powerful Northern magnate holding sway over much of Lancashire and Cheshire. Despite clashing with Richard Duke of Gloucester, who had sided with the Harrington's in 1470, Stanley had been rewarded by Richard when he became king, holding the position of High Constable. Yet despite his advancement, the baron and his brother William, were to betray Richard at Bosworth. Eleanor hated the man whose last minute intervention on that battlefield had cost her beloved king his life. Now Thomas, elevated to the title Earl of Derby by his grateful son-in-law, had been granted the Broughton estate after Thomas Broughton's attainder, much to the resentment and enmity of the family.

Hugh was concerned for his cousin of whom nothing had been heard so far, though Thomas's brother John had been reported killed at Stoke. He was pleasantly surprised therefore, when out of the blue a letter arrived at Broughton Hall addressed to Thomas's wife Margaret. She arrived at Millom Castle one morning, breathless and exhilarated demanding to see Hugh privately on a personal matter. When they were alone she handed Hugh the letter. It was from Sir Thomas. He was alive and still a fugitive, having been holed up in a remote village in Devonshire since fleeing the battle. He wanted to come home but with his property lost to Thomas Stanley, if he suddenly appeared alive and well, he would be imprisoned and in all probability, executed.

Delighted her husband still lived however, Margaret told Hugh she had devised a plan, which she discussed with him and for which she required his help. They would bring Thomas home to Cumbria but conceal him amongst his tenants at Witherslack, where he could live out his remaining years in obscurity, amongst friends. Excited and thrilled that his cousin was alive and determined he should come home, Hugh set to arranging to collect him, eager to be of service to a veteran of the battle at Stoke. He had much regretted not joining the rebel force when Lovell's army had passed by and now welcomed the chance to atone by assisting in his cousin's escape.

A plan of action was decided upon for Hugh to sail with one of the regular merchant ships plying a trade route between Millom and Bristol, carrying iron from Furness and wool from Kendal. At Bristol Hugh would ride the rest of the way to Coldridge where he would meet Thomas and take him back to Millom, disguised as a ship's merchantmen, of whom no questions were likely to be asked.

'I want you to accompany me Eleanor.' Hugh announced to his wife, not purely for her discretion in keeping his Yorkist cousin safe but also to keep an eye on her while he was away, though he would not admit to such a motive. 'With my wife at my side, we will appear less suspect, besides, I don't trust anyone else here,' he told her. There are too many of the king's spies who would betray Thomas for a goodly sum and I won't have that on my conscience.

'Aye sir, if that is your wish', Eleanor complied, though the prospect of a sea voyage filled her with dread.

'Speak to no-one about this Eleanor, not even your maid. You can't be sure, to whom she might divulge our purpose.

'Edith is a Yorkist Hugh, she knows the score.'

'Maybe so, but tittle tattle amongst servants, spreads like a wildfire through bracken. There's no telling who might overhear.' Eleanor couldn't disagree and despite her trepidation, she welcomed a change of scene and her first sea voyage and perhaps with the stimulus of his new mission, Hugh would be less sullen and ill-humoured. When he was sober they got on well and he was proud to show off his pretty wife, boosting his ego with having bagged such a prize. He was staunchly loyal, to the point of obsession, which pleased Eleanor, though she never divulged her intimate connection with the late king of England, a secret she would take with her to the grave.

Hidden deep in her subconscious, however, Richard would still appear in her dreams, reminding her of the love and desire she had felt for him and which nothing could erase. He was her first love, yet he was never hers, save for those brief moments they had shared. She would see his smile, as he glanced at her sideways, his handsome teenage profile softening as he grinned boyishly, his slim fingers caressing her body, belying the strength within. She would find her dream darkening as Richard became ever more burdened with care and loss, his brow knitted with care, his eyes cheerless and distant. Awed by his persona and presence, an innate nobility shared with his exalted family, Eleanor felt privileged to have been his one-time lover, watching him mature and earn respect as Lord of the North, before being thrust into a kingship he had never envisaged. At Sheriff Hutton she had shared his pain, could still feel his tears upon her cheek as he faced his destiny alone, the weight of the nation upon his young shoulders as he held her to him - his heartbeat so strong but so soon to be silenced, his selfless masterful courage eclipsed by the black void of treachery. Eleanor would wake sobbing, his voice, his touch, so tangible one minute so elusory the next. *My poor brave Richard, who should be hailed as the hero who tried to save England from tyranny but instead is tarnished by falsehood and fabrication. Oh Richard, if only you knew the lies that are being told about you!*

Chapter Fifteen

Suppressing her innermost doubts and regrets, Eleanor determined to make the best of her new life of material comfort and ease. After all, she had much to be grateful for and it was not Hugh's fault he could not arouse those feelings of desire Eleanor craved. She was well provided for and only had to ask her husband for something she desired and it would be hers, like the pretty bay palfrey mare he presented her with, after she expressed a wish to go riding on the sands. The huge expanse of Haverigg beach stretched for miles when the tide was out and she would take Pearl, so named for the single white mark on her forehead, for an invigorating gallop along the shore. Here, where the waters of the Duddon estuary spilled out into the Irish sea, the Isle of Man lay clearly visible on the shimmering horizon. Sometimes on a hot day, Eleanor would remove her boots and lead her mare along the water's edge as the tide ebbed and flowed, enjoying the cool mud oozing between her toes, the surf bubbling around her feet. The radiance reflecting off sea and sand was so bright it would make her eyes water and it would take a moment to focus when returning to the dark edifice of Millom castle. The salty air, so palpable on this Western peninsular, was invigorating and refreshing and Eleanor would arrive back flushed and pink cheeked, her boots, along with her horse's flanks, muddied with splashes of sand and sea spume.

Their mission to fetch Sir Thomas soon finalised, the Broughton's spent a night at Furness Abbey, the monks having facilitated their voyage, before boarding a merchant caravel bound for Bristol, carrying a cargo of wool and locally smelted iron from the

Furness Abbey bloomeries. The ship's cabin was cramped and dark and once in open water the craft pitched and rolled nauseatingly, forcing Eleanor to frequent the deck where she felt less bilious. The salty air and constant wind filling the sails, brought a pink flush to her cheeks which soon felt dry in the glare of the sun and she could quite see how the crew had developed their leather-like skin, exposed for long hours on the deck. It took an interminable four days to sail Southwards, hugging the rugged Welsh coast, until at last they entered the wide Severn estuary and secluded reaches of the River Avon, before anchoring at Bristol.

Despite the fact it had been a relatively calm passage, Eleanor was relieved to leave the open sea and enter still waters, where the steep wooded River Avon gorge wound upriver to the town and where exceptionally high tides allowed shipping to anchor safely and securely. She had hardly eaten whilst on board, the motion of the ship leaving her nauseous and dizzy, her first steps onto land seeming heavy and awkward after the heaving deck. But now, the Southern air felt warm and gentle, the soft breeze no longer feeling as if it would scour her skin and with the horizon thankfully fixed in one place Eleanor eyes could re-focus. She had never seen so many ships gathered in one place, anchored hull to hull in a forest of masts and so much activity and noise. Here commodities like cloth, timber, iron, wool, tin and fish arrived from all over England to be shipped out to Ireland, France, Spain and Portugal, in return for wine, spices and oils. The clamour of the thronged streets was a new and somewhat terrifying sensation for Eleanor, who stood amazed at the sight of the old bridge over the river, precariously topped by four and five storey houses, packed together like books on a shelf. 'They look as though they are about to topple into the river!' she exclaimed to her husband as they embarked on the quayside.

After a welcome night at an Inn beside the harbour, where the food tasted more appetising than usual now they were on solid ground, Hugh and Eleanor's party set off Westwards. Following the Somerset coastline, riding hired mounts, they stopped each night at Axebridge and Bridgwater, then at last into Devonshire and Coldridge manor where they were to meet with Sir Thomas. Eleanor enjoyed the changing scenery, though the byways were busier than in the North and she felt a noticeable oppressiveness in the air that evidenced how far South they had come. The narrow roads meandered interminably through lush and wooded countryside, villages hiding homely and protected amongst hillocks and moors and in the distance the sea shining and serene, as if it were made of silver, edged by sands of gold.

It took them three days before they arrived at their destination, saddle-sore and dust blown, the cool of the old manor a refreshing relief. Passing through Wembworthy they had called briefly on Sir John Speke to ask him for directions to Coldridge. Thomas's letter had told them Speke could be trusted. He was related by marriage to Sir James Tyrell, Steward of the Duchy of Cornwall, Richard III's faithful and trusted knight, who in 1483 had sheltered the sons of Edward IV in his safe house at Gipping Hall in Suffolk.

At Coldridge manor, deep in the Devonshire hinterland, Hugh's knock was answered by a housekeeper who ushered them into a small parlour. Hugh told the woman he had an appointment with the estate's Parker John Evans and after a few minutes a servant boy appeared and was instructed to show them the way to the park keeper's cottage. Arriving at the modest building, they were admitted into a compact living room by a young page, who proceeded to stoke the fire and then left to fetch refreshment.

'The parker will be back shortly' he told them. However, within minutes another visitor appeared at the door, grinning excitedly, having ridden over from Culmstock where he had been residing since his flight from Stoke.

'Hugh!' Thomas exclaimed delighted to see his cousin, as they embraced.

'Thank God you're alive, Thomas!'

'Aye, it was a close-run thing, though poor John perished in the bloodbath.'

'Aye, we heard. I'm sorry'. Hugh commiserated, as the two men stood back and studied each other, Hugh clapping Thomas on the back enthusiastically and Thomas acknowledging Eleanor with a nod of recognition. Sir Thomas Broughton had noticeably aged, from when Eleanor had last seen him at Masham with Lord Lovell, a greying beard disguising his jawline, not unlike his cousin's. She could see he had lost weight but at least he was alive and relatively unscathed, having been amongst the very few who had escaped capture after Stoke.

'You look well Hugh, though perhaps suffering from a few too many indulgences!' Thomas quipped, patting Hugh's stomach playfully. Hugh smiled and retaliated with an equally personal rejoinder.

'And you look as if you could do with a good meal Thomas!', he grinned, before turning to introduce Eleanor. 'My wife Eleanor, I believe you have met?'. Eleanor shook Thomas's hand and smiled.

'I am delighted to see you again, Sir Thomas'.

'You're punching above your weight there Hugh! I'm surprised she accepted an old curmudgeon like you!' Thomas winked at Eleanor.

'There were plenty of young soldiers eyeing up Lady Lovell's maid at Masham!', Hugh pursed his lips, suppressing a pang of jealousy, at the thought of his wife being an object of desire to men no doubt more virile than he and slightly annoyed at his cousin for pointing it out. 'Welcome to the Broughton family my dear', Thomas continued grinning, kissing Eleanor's hand, before sitting himself down and gesturing to the page to bring ale.

The conversation switched to the battle at Stoke, the eventual rout and how the boy John had been taken in place of Edward and denounced by Tudor as an imposter named Lambert Simnel. Thomas explained to Eleanor with some amusement, that the name might refer to John being an illegitimate son of King Edward IV's mistress Jane Shore, whose maiden name was Lambert and Simnel being an Easter cake, might allude to the fact the rebellion emerged at Easter. After expressing some mirth at the ridiculous name, Thomas went on to describe how he and Lord Lovell had managed to escape capture. At the mention of Francis, Eleanor, suddenly unguarded, sat forward anxious for news.

'Is he alive then Sir Thomas?' she interjected eagerly - *if Lovell lived, she would have to get word to Anne.* Thomas sighed deeply, regarding Eleanor solemnly.

'I rather fear not, my dear. Pray do not get your hopes up, he was sorely injured and I can't see him surviving for long after I left him'. He went on to describe his flight with Francis, their time at Abingdon Abbey and how the Viscount had insisted on returning to Minster Lovell against all advice.

'He insisted I leave him there and carry out a task he had entrusted to me, which is why I am here. I have heard nothing from him since and I can only assume he is dead, of which I am almost certain, given the grievous state I left him in. He could hardly stand, poor man. I take it Lady Lovell had no further news?' he enquired of Eleanor.

'Nay sir, nothing at all but what you tell me is more than we knew and will be some closure for Lady Lovell. She will know now not to hold out further hope.'

'I'm sorry my dear.' Just as he spoke, the door opened and a young man came in, stamping the dust off his boots and throwing his hat onto a chest, as a long-eared spaniel ran over to the guests wagging its tail enthusiastically. Thomas stood up, as did Hugh and Eleanor, assuming from Thomas's reaction, the newcomer had some rank. However, this man was modestly dressed in forester's garb and wore no jewellery or fine adornments on his plain woollen clothes.

'May I introduce our Parker, John Evans', Thomas announced. Hugh shook the man's hand slightly awkwardly, thrown by the deference his cousin appeared to show this park keeper but Eleanor stood stock still, suddenly struck dumb. As the tall young man turned towards her, she felt herself wanting to bend her knee and utter the words 'Your Grace', for the face that stared back at her appeared to be the spitting image of Edward IV, those same sapphire blue eyes, those flowing golden locks, that classic physiognomy! Instead, she stood open mouthed in surprise, the memory of the day the handsome monarch had stood before her at Middleham Castle all those years ago, flashing before her.

'Eleanor!', Hugh nudged his wife's side, forcing Eleanor out of her reverie. She remembered her manners, regained her composure and held out her hand. 'Pleased to meet you sir'.

'Welcome to Coldridge Manor' the young man replied politely, his voice soft and well spoken, not the heavy local tongue expected of a Devon forester. Undeniably a man of breeding, Eleanor couldn't help but wonder what he was doing down here in rural Devonshire managing a deer park. He looked as if he would have been more at home at Court, or back in the Great Hall at Middleham. All she could see in her mind's eye was Edward IV sitting in front of her, scanning her up and down with that same winning smile, that classic Plantagenet bearing. Despite this man's attire, however, there was something about him that also reminded her of Richard, just as Edward had done, all those years ago. No-one could deny the House of York was a handsome gene pool and that same family likeness now appeared strangely present in this man. A fleeting thought flashed up in Eleanor's mind that perhaps this was another Royal bastard, conceived away from the marriage bed by one of those sons of that charismatic house. He certainly must be very close in age to Edward IV's eldest son, who had been spirited away to safety along with his brother after Richard's coronation. *It could almost be him!* Eleanor shuddered, quickly dismissing the embryo of an idea intruding into her thoughts.

After exchanging pleasantries, Hugh excused himself and beckoned to Eleanor to go with him. Forcing herself to look away from the young man's compelling likeness, she obediently followed her husband to the accommodation provided for herself and Hugh in the manor house, where they would spend the night before leaving with Sir Thomas in the morning.

As she lay in bed that night, however, she kept seeing that face, hearing again the incongruous name that somehow didn't fit. *John Evans?* Repeating it to herself, over and over as her husband snored, Eleanor sat up on her elbows with a start. *Evans? E.V. Edward V! Surely not!? Evans was a Welsh family name. Hadn't Edward V been brought up in Wales at Ludlow, as the Prince of Wales?* She stared into the darkness as outside her window an owl hooted resoundingly across the park. Eleanor wondered if Thomas Broughton knew the young man's real identity for she was sure John Evans was a pseudonym but she felt it imprudent to ask him until she had gained his confidence and they could speak privately. It did seem more than co-incidence however, that the youth was here in this remote Devon manor, the very same which was owned by Thomas Grey, half-brother of Edward V and where Robert Markenfield had been sent in '84 on an important mission for the late king. *Could this be where the young Prince had been living all along? Wasn't Gleaston Castle in Furness, also owned by Thomas Grey, where Edward V sheltered before Stoke? Nay, Eleanor, be realistic! You're allowing your imagination free rein*, she argued with herself, though the more she thought about it the more conceivable the possibility became.

Sinking down beneath the covers, Eleanor smiled to herself at her wild fantasies. Whoever this young man was, it was not her place to question it and even if she had somehow stumbled upon a secret, it would never leave her lips. She was good at keeping secrets, especially now, when innocent lives were forfeit for the most spurious of reasons and Tudor's spies were everywhere. *Tudor! Ugh!* She mouthed a sneer of distaste. *How dare he call himself king of England! A man of such doubtful lineage who with the help of self-seeking traitors had wiped out the last of the Plantagenet line and forced England to bow to a man of such insignificance; a man whose paranoia pushed him to eliminate every possible threat to his precarious crown.*

Chapter Sixteen

After a day's rest, Eleanor and her husband set off for Bristol once more but this time accompanied by Sir Thomas, dressed as one of the accompanying men at arms. If anyone asked, he was to be known simply as Tom Parker, a Northern soldier of no particular note, certainly no knight of the realm with a price on his head. The night before they had dined with John Evans but the conversation had been general, though the young man was evidently well educated and informed, his impeccable manners at odds with his profession. Hugh had questioned him about his background but the answers given were vague and after several jugs of ale Hugh, somewhat annoyed by the young man's reticence, turned his attention to his cousin. However, Eleanor couldn't get the enigmatic parker out of her thoughts and she longed to know if her suspicions were correct.

The return ride to Bristol was tedious but uneventful and they were soon boarding ship once more at Bristol docks, the merchantman fully loaded with cloth and wine bound for Ireland. Sir Thomas and Eleanor spent the voyage mostly confined to their beds, both being unseasoned sailors but Hugh sat up with the captain and first mate drinking the contents of a crate of Portuguese wine, before collapsing in a stupor beside Eleanor as the dawn came up over the horizon. She was almost surprised he hadn't managed to cast himself overboard as more than once he had lurched across the forecastle to relieve himself at the prow. She felt bad for imagining such an incident. She didn't wish Hugh harm, her life was comfortable and she could want for nothing as his wife but part of her yearned for love and tenderness and maybe just a little excitement, not just the jealousy of possession Hugh afforded her. Looking across at her replete husband, uttering a silent plea for forgiveness, she scolded herself for her improper thoughts. *You have made your bed Eleanor!*

She rose and went up on deck, attempting to control the nausea that refused to subside. Sir Thomas came to join her and they gazed out across the water, where to the East the dark outline of the Welsh mountains faded into the mist and to the West a thin shadow of land marked the distant coast of Ireland. Ahead of them lay the silhouette of the Isle of Man, like a giant's stepping-stone cast midway into the Irish Sea. Eleanor had heard the legend of the battle of the giants; one from Ireland and one from Scotland, who it was told, tore up columns of basalt to make a causeway between their lands, evidence that could still be seen in extraordinary hexagonal rock formations marching into the surf. Sir Thomas had seen them on his voyage from Ireland with Lord Lovell, his description to Eleanor sounding almost beyond belief that such structures could exist in the real world and not just in folklore.

Eleanor determined to ask the personable knight about the young parker at Coldridge but first she wanted to hear more about the battle of Stoke and what had happened to the much-lauded German mercenaries and their commander. She kept her enquiries general, hoping Thomas would not of course imagine she had someone specific in mind. The weary chevalier described the initial charge and the confidence his men had displayed engaging with Oxford's troops. The fighting had been fierce, as brutal as any he had experienced, with the Germans mowing down dozens of men with their two-handed swords but gradually the Irish, despite their courage, fell in great numbers. Only lightly clad, the kerns were no match for Tudor's longbowmen and cavalry and seeing their comrades cut down, panic set in and they fled. The Germans fought on but were outnumbered by fresh forces, eventually conceding the fight, once their commander Schwartz was slain, Lord Lincoln fatally injured and Lovell assumed dead.

Eleanor could see Thomas struggled with his emotions as he told Eleanor of his brother and she ventured to put her arm around this courageous knight into whose family she had lately married. She decided not to pursue the matter further for now. He put his hand on hers and smiled gently at her. 'I fear Hugh falls short of deserving you, my dear. I hope you are not unhappy.'

'Nay sir, thank you, sir, I am grateful to my husband and lead a comfortable life. I have no cause for complaint'. Thomas held her gaze with a tender stare and she looked away uncomfortable, as though he could read her innermost feelings. He clearly knew his cousin as well as she did.

'That's not what I asked Eleanor'. He observed her for a moment in silence, then dropped his voice to a whisper. 'I know my cousin my dear. Do not be afraid to ask for help if you need it'. He squeezed her hand supportively and she felt her cheeks colouring at his inference. She decided this was her chance to broach the subject of the young man at Coldridge, by way of diversion.

'Sir Thomas may I ask you something?'

'Of course, my dear'.

'The young parker at Coldridge, John Evans, is he related to the late king? Edward, I mean?' Hugh stiffened and frowned, his voice suddenly suspicious and guarded.

'Why do you ask?'

'I met King Edward at Middleham and the likeness is uncanny, they could be....'

Eleanor stopped abruptly, as Thomas held his finger to her lips and gripped her arm firmly. 'Do *not* share that thought with anyone Eleanor, I *mean* it, anyone at all! Not even Hugh, do you understand?' he admonished somewhat forcibly.

'Aye sir, of course' Eleanor replied, her eyes watering with the abruptness of Thomas's response. 'Forgive me sir, …I..didn't mean to…' Thomas's voice softened and he let go of her arm. 'I know you are loyal Eleanor, Francis told me so and he told me why. I know about your daughter – now you have seen John. Your assumption as to his real identity is correct. Francis sent me here to ensure his safety and afford him safe passage out of the country but he declined. I have done my best.' He exhaled with a long-drawn-out breath, touching Eleanor's hand gently. 'We must keep each other's secrets, you and I, …to the grave'.

'Aye sir, as God is my witness, I will ne'er speak of it again'. If Eleanor held any doubts in her mind about the origin of that young parker they were now dispelled. She knew she had solved the mystery of the young man's Royal birth. She was a custodian of a secret entrusted to her by one of Richard's most loyal supporters, which meant ultimately by him. Nothing on this earth could induce her to betray that trust.

Arriving back at Millom, Eleanor felt the drop in temperature as they stepped onto the exposed Cumbrian shore but the cooler air was welcome, fresh and restorative, consistent with the ice cold water running off the fells, pure and clean. The quietude of the North country came as a relief, such a comforting contrast to the busy thoroughfares of the South, the clamour of Bristol docks and the cloying heat of dust filled roads. Up here in the wide open spaces, she felt she could breathe again.

Eleanor's life continued in much the same vein as the year turned. She performed her duties for the Huddlestons with diligence and her obligations to her husband with the deference expected of her. Though, as his wife, she was now his equal, years of subservience had ingrained in her a respect for age and position, a hard tendency to abandon. She had learned to cope with Hugh's moods and demands, distancing herself whenever necessary to avoid his ill-humour. As a diversion, she visited Sir Thomas often at Witherslack and he became like a father figure to her, giving advice and sharing memories. She found she could talk to him candidly without fear of reproach and he would answer her truthfully. The loyalty of local folk ensured that the knight was able to live in anonymity amongst his tenants, the authorities never guessing the veteran rebel of Stoke had returned to his home turf.

Although many local people knew Sir Thomas by sight, nobody gave him away. When government agents came enquiring after him, they were told Thomas Broughton had disappeared down South and died of his wounds. Lately, however, one of Henry's men had returned, dissatisfied with the answers he had been given. He brought with him one of Oxford's soldiers, a veteran of Stoke, who claimed he was able to identify Broughton and together they frequented the taverns and hostelries, offering generous rewards and scrutinising every middle-aged man they encountered.

Tom Parker, as he was now known, was drinking in an ale house at Cartmel one evening, when the two agents walked in. Immediately recognising Oxford's insignia on the younger man's clothing, Thomas, instantly alert, attempted to hastily finish his drink but he had been spotted and Oxford's man was now watching him intently, as he got up and walked to the door. The older agent was enquiring from the other clientele the identity of the man who a moment ago had been drinking, to be told he was simply a local farmer but the younger man followed Thomas outside.

'Well if it isn't Sir Thomas Broughton!' he sneered triumphantly, drawing his sword. 'You're under arrest!'.

'I don't know what you're talking about, my name is Parker', Thomas replied, hoping his bluff would be enough to dissuade the soldier, while casting around for some assistance but the street was empty. The man held his arm locked behind him and Thomas could feel he was strong, as the soldier called out to his companion but with no response the tavern door remained firmly shut. The younger man was becoming agitated as he pinned Thomas against the wall, the point of his weapon jabbing the fugitive knight's side. Thomas was debating whether he could take on this soldier alone, but with his dagger just out of reach from his free arm and his other immobilised, he was at a distinct disadvantage.

Hearing the tavern door open a moment later, he fully expected the king's agent to complete his arrest but instead, a group of local men charged out and set upon the soldier. Thomas, now freed from the man's grip, ran for his horse tethered nearby, jumped into the saddle and galloped away without looking back. *That was too close for comfort* he decided. He must be more careful in future. He hadn't recognised the soldier but the man clearly knew him, so he must have been with Lincoln's men at Stoke and presumably been offered pardon in exchange for loyalty to Tudor.

Meanwhile, the locals with whom Thomas had been drinking, disarmed the soldier, gagged him and tied his hands, dragging him away down an alley, where they held a knife at his throat should he attempt to alert his companion. The agent, who had until now been prevented from leaving by the crowd inside the tavern, ran out to find the street empty and no sight nor sound of his colleague. Cursing, he went back inside and addressed the drinkers angrily.

'If any of you are found aiding and abetting a traitor, you will pay with your livelihoods and most probably your life', he threatened, only to be met by jeers of derision.

'There be nay traitors here, we be all honest folk', a man with a broad Cumbrian accent piped up, 'you'd best be lookin' in your own back yard if its traitors ye be seekin'. Amidst guffaws and gleeful applause, the agent stalked off angrily in search of his comrade who had since disappeared.

A couple of days later a troop of the king's militia raided every dwelling in the vicinity without success. The Augustinian Priory at Cartmel, founded in 1189 by Sir William Marshall was searched in case the fugitive had found sanctuary within its hallowed walls but Sir Thomas was nowhere to be found and neither was the soldier. Fortunately for Thomas, the agent hadn't actually heard his man at arms identify the knight by name and after a fruitless search the scout gave up, though he remained baffled at the disappearance of the young man, who had presumably set off in pursuit of a likely outlaw and had become lost. Enquiries offered little information, except that a soldier had last been seen making his way across the sands of Morecambe Bay at low tide and a week later a sallet was found washed up on shore at Arnside. It was assumed that the man had drowned, caught out by the incoming tide and treacherous quick sands of the bay. Local honour was such that nobody was tempted to betray one of their own, let alone accuse anyone of the murder of one of the king's men.

Upon calling at Millom Castle, Hugh grudgingly received the king's delegate, assuring the man there were no traitors at large in the area and pledging co-operation, though he could barely disguise the hint of insincerity in his voice, which was picked up by the agent. 'Harbouring traitors and conspirators is a serious offence, punishable by death' he reminded Hugh, narrowing his eyes and regarding the Marshall with obvious suspicion. Hugh answered with a stony stare as he showed the man out, making little attempt to hide his dislike.

'Cleave to the crown!' the agent cautioned, as he spurred his horse in action and rode off, though suspecting these duplicitous Northerners would do no such thing.

Cleave to Tudor's crown indeed! Not while I still have breath in my body! Hugh muttered at the oft quoted phrase, spitting in contempt as he watched the agent ride away. Like many he knew that more worthy claimants waited in the wings should Tudor fail. There had already been two pretenders for his crown and the de la Poles were still biding their time, the spark of hope hitherto smouldering in many a Yorkist heart.

Eleanor made the occasional trip over to Wensleydale to visit her son and grandchildren. William had grown into a healthy teenager and keen huntsman, so very like his father Eleanor smiled fondly. Her heart had skipped a beat when she saw him, for in a fleeting moment she imagined he was Will, her words of greeting sticking in her throat as a sudden wave of emotion overcame her. *Dear, sweet, gentle Will,* who so loved the landscapes of Yorkshire and the creatures who depended upon it. A man who had been snatched from her too soon by the very nature he cared for but who now lived on in his son, eagerly training a young peregrine to come to his call and take his bait, just as his father had done.

At the farrier's dwelling in Wensley, the Dinsdale's now had two boys; their firstborn Richard, being quickly followed by Robert. Eleanor delighted in her grandchildren and her daughter's happiness, which was plain to see. Bess's slim figure had filled out with childbearing into womanly curves but Eleanor could still see in her eyes, the reflection of the nobleman who had given her life, smiling back at her.

Whilst in Wensleydale, Eleanor made an impromptu visit to Ravensworth, accompanied by her brother James. She felt obliged to tell Anne Lovell what Sir Thomas had told her and that it was unlikely Francis had survived his injuries. Somewhat shocked at Anne's pallid complexion and frail appearance, made even more pronounced by the drab religious garb she wore, Eleanor persuaded the Viscountess to walk in the grounds to get some air and bring colour to her cheeks. Besides, Eleanor judged, it would be better to be out of earshot from anyone in the castle who might overhear their conversation. Leaving her brother to refresh himself in the kitchen, the two women strolled in the parkland. Eleanor related everything Thomas had told her and how it would be unwise for Anne to hold out further hope for her husband. Anne was cheered however, that Francis had expressed a wish for pen and paper with the intention of writing to her.

'I knew he would try to get in touch', she beamed at Eleanor but then realising no such letter had ever been received, lapsed into melancholy once more. She was however, pleased to hear Sir Thomas was alive and returned home, her solemn vow never to reveal that information, understood. Eleanor left feeling she had given Anne some solace but saddened at the shadow of the young woman the Viscountess had become, one who had once been so full of hope. She could not help but recall Anne's cousins, the delicate and sickly Neville sisters who had both died young and she hoped Anne would not follow them before her time.

Chapter Seventeen

𝕴n the Spring of 1491. A young boy had landed in Cork from Portugal and was entertained by the Earls of Desmond and Kildare, as a Yorkist prince, returned to claim his birthright. Acknowledged as none other than Richard Duke of York, the youngest son of Edward IV, who had disappeared with his brother in 1483, the lad would find himself celebrated by many heads of state including king James IV of Scotland, Charles VIII of France, Margaret, Duchess of Burgundy and Maximillian the Holy Roman Emperor, as a true son of Edward IV and the heir to the English throne. Richard had been living incognito in Tournai since 1483, awaiting his coming of age, having then moved to Portugal under the care of Sir Edward Brampton and his wife, from where he had first sailed to Ireland.

Upon hearing news from Ireland of a second pretender, Henry Tudor sent for his mother Lady Margaret Beaufort to come to court and keep an eye on his wife, who may have been tempted to assist the young man claiming to be her younger brother. Faced with another figurehead for rebellion, Henry imparted his fears to his mother, who was at the same time keeping a close watch on the dowager queen Elizabeth Woodville, confined in reduced circumstances at Bermondsey Abbey.

Margaret was a frequent visitor to Elizabeth, whom she saw as a threat to her son's rule, the Yorkist ex-queen having been suspected of being in correspondence with her sister-in-law Margaret of Burgundy. If anyone could identify the new pretender as her son Richard, it was Elizabeth. Richard of York had several identifying marks including a defect in his left eye, facts which could easily be confirmed by his mother. Margaret regularly took gifts of wine for Elizabeth, who soon became ill and conveniently for Henry, died in June '92 at only fifty-five years of age, though despite this sudden occurrence nothing untoward was suspected. However, many harboured private doubts about the involvement of the king's scheming mother, who had succeeded against all odds in propelling her son towards the highest station in the land and would stop at nothing to keep him there.

To Henry's chagrin, the next news from France confirmed that young Richard of York was being feted as King of England by Charles VIII, in a surprise reversal of allegiance, the French king having since regretted backing Tudor's invasion of England in 1485. The nervous king Henry's answer to the French was to send a force to Calais in the autumn of 1492 and from thence to besiege Boulogne. After several weeks Charles agreed to make peace with Henry, pay him a pension and as part of the treaty of Etaples, to cease supporting the pretender – this seeming a small price to pay, in order to nullify the threat of invasion. Instead of handing over the Prince to Henry however, Charles ensured Richard's safe passage out of France. Tudor now began his campaign of misinformation, referring to Richard as Perkin Warbeck, after the family who had sheltered him and presenting the youth as another imposter. The young man had been brought up in Flanders by the Warbeques and Henry did his utmost to discredit the teenager and reveal him as a fraud.

After being expelled from France, Richard was taken in by his aunt Margaret of Burgundy, who recognised her nephew's obvious kinship and striking similarity to her brother Edward IV. Meanwhile, to make his point that this young man should not be recognised as the Duke of York, Henry bestowed that title on his three year old second son, who bore his name.

In 1494 the king had summoned the Earls of Kildare and Desmond to Greenwich, where he entertained them in an effort to ensure their loyalty, his gesture serving as a reminder to them of the perils of supporting another pretender. While Perkin Warbeck was being hailed in Europe, Henry brought the young man Lambert Simnel to the dining table to serve the Irish Lords, as a pointed reminder of what had happened to their supposed 'king'. To his chagrin and vexation, however, the lords failed to recognise the youth as the boy they had crowned in Ireland in 1487 leaving Henry discomfited. It was left to a servant to point out Lambert's identity to the guests, the king remaining convinced he had the genuine pretender in his custody, along with the real Earl of Warwick.

With news of the return of Richard of York, poised to claim back his throne, James IV of Scotland was only too pleased to unsettle the usurping English king and offer his support to the pretender. Encouraged by this, many Yorkists flocked to aid young Richard and even Sir William Stanley who had betrayed Richard III at Bosworth, now backed the new claimant, swearing to stand by him if he invaded, a volte-face which was to cost Stanley his life, his execution taking place in February 1495. *What a tragedy*, Eleanor reflected bitterly, *that Sir William was not of this mind ten years ago at Bosworth, when his support might have saved king Richard! How sad that a man's life should hang on the fickle whims of another, for with the Stanley's support Richard would surely have been victorious and history would be set on a different path.*

Despite Henry's best efforts, favoured as the heir to the English throne by European nobility and now equipped by Emperor Maximilian, Richard of York sailed for England with a small fleet but was repulsed at Deal and again in Ireland where the citizens had been harshly punished for supporting the Lambert Simnel rebellion. Eventually landing on the West coast of Scotland, Richard was welcomed by James IV at Stirling in November 1495. James immediately took to the handsome, well educated, genteel young man, who was of a similar age as himself and whose Plantagenet looks, perfect English and knowledge of his father's Court, confirmed to all he was who he claimed to be. Even Sir Robert Clifford, who had been sent by Henry Tudor to spy on the young pretender, could not deny his credibility.

Early in 1496 having attracted the attention of both men and women at the Scottish Court, Richard married Lady Catherine Gordon, a cousin of the Scottish king and daughter of the Earl of Huntley. Catherine, a much-acclaimed beauty, now honoured as Duchess of York, and the 'White Rose of Scotland', was equally enamoured of the young Prince, the couple's devotion being plain for all to see.

By September, two vessels arrived in Scotland from Burgundy transporting a force of German, French and Flemish mercenaries, bolstering King James's army and before long they were advancing across the border in the name of King Richard IV come to claim his inheritance. Assuming English locals South of the border would flock to support their rightful king, the army were surprised at the negative response. Unfortunately, they were met with resistance from Englishmen holed up in pele towers well used to dealing with border raids, to whom this appeared no different to any other incursion in the face of zealous Scotsmen, who when confronted with opposition, soon resorted to their usual practice of burning, looting and killing indiscriminately.

Richard riding out with the advance cavalry, aghast at witnessing the savagery displayed by the Scots in killing his countrymen, recoiled in horror. Far from being a soldier like his father and uncles before him, the young Duke of York's refined and amicable persona, preferred the trappings and good manners of courtly life; his slight, boyish physique, evidence of not having been brought up to fight. Having never experienced bloody warfare at close hand, this peaceable Prince was left appalled and dismayed, turning his back in distress, declaring he would rather renounce his crown than gain it at the expense of such misery. With no assistance forthcoming from the people of Northumberland and with Ralph Neville's well equipped English army fast approaching from Newcastle, the chastened Scottish king was left with no choice but to retreat, his dwindling resources having been spent.

Meanwhile in Cornwall, a protest had begun over a punitive tax imposed by the English king to pay for the Scottish wars, a cause this independent state adjudged nothing to do with them. Not only this but Henry had stopped the Cornish tin-making industry and suspended local privileges, in an effort to centralise it. Rebelling against this injustice, by June 1497, a force of 15,000 protestors had advanced from the West Country to Blackheath, led by Lord Audley but the rebels were quickly defeated by the Royal army and their leader beheaded.

Richard by now had outstayed his welcome in Scotland. The king, mindful of his own meagre resources and the threat of Henry's well-equipped English army poised to oppose him, agreed with the young pretender, that he should leave. By August '97, after thanking James for his hospitality, Richard set sail with his wife and companions for Ireland, on a ship ironically named *Cuckoo*, the name generating some mirth amongst Richard's enemies supporting Henry Tudor, who regarded the pretender as an imposter. After an abortive siege of Waterford castle, Richard found himself abandoned by the Irish lords, who already having paid a heavy price for their support of Lambert

Simnel, were loath to repeat such a risky venture. Encouraged by the recent uprising, he made instead for Cornwall, landing on 7th September, leaving his wife in the safety of St. Michael's Mount. Joined by many thousands of disgruntled Cornishmen, the Duke of York proceeded to Bodmin, where he again proclaimed himself King Richard IV and was received as such.

Chapter Eighteen

Before setting out towards Exeter, young York, now calling himself Richard IV, had received an invitation from Robert Markenfield to make a detour to the deer park at Coldridge. Markenfield was acquainted with Sir John Speke of Wembworthy, who lived nearby and had supported the recently defeated Cornish rebellion and might be called upon for aid. Now with another force approaching from Bodmin Moor, where the rebels had hailed Richard of York as king, Robert decided his Parker John Evans should meet this intrepid young man to warn him of the dangers. Not only that, Robert suspected the close blood affinity between these young men and he wanted to test his theory.

'There's someone you should meet, your Grace', he informed Richard in his missive delivered to the commander of the 8,000 strong army of Cornishmen camped at Okehampton. Knowing the Markenfields as loyal Yorkists, Richard accepted the invitation and with a small party of riders made his way to Coldridge Manor, set in its extensive deer park in the valley of the River Taw, its' previous owner Sir Henry Bodrugan having recently disappeared.

Upon welcoming Richard, Robert Markenfield was immediately struck by the young man's family resemblance to the house of York. Whilst refreshing his guest with food and drink, he studied him carefully. There was little doubt in Robert's mind, this man was a Plantagenet from his looks, bearing and manner of speaking but all the proof he needed lay with the man he had sheltered since the battle of Stoke. Leaving Richard's escort in the manor kitchen's, Robert escorted his visitor to the huntsman's cottage in the grounds of the manor, where they knocked and entered a small room, in which a welcoming fire blazed and a young man sat at a desk writing. He was dressed in plain forester's clothing, his blonde hair, the same shade as Richard's falling to his shoulders, his slim frame, that of a man in his late twenties.

'Sire, this is my Parker, John Evans', Robert announced to Richard, as the man turned to face him. Richard stared nonplussed, his mouth dropped open and he felt a lump rise in his throat, he knew that face, the same hooded blue eyes, the same scar on his jaw, where the surgeon had treated a painful infection, their father's unmistakeable genes reflected in those classic features.

'Greetings, little brother! Not so little now I see!' Edward stood up and held out his hand as Richard stepped forward into his brother's heartfelt embrace.

'Ned!' he gasped, standing back to look at his long-lost sibling. 'What are you doing here in this remote place? Why are you dressed like that?' he frowned perplexed, casting his eye over the huntsman's simple attire.

'It's a long story Dickon but I go by the name of John Evans now. This is my home. Pray sit down, we have much to discuss Dickon. It's good to see you brother!'

Robert excused himself and left the brothers to talk. He felt satisfied his hunch had been correct and though happy to bring the siblings together, he was acutely aware of terrible consequences for them all, should this subterfuge come to light.

'I heard you had been taken at Stoke and put to work in Tudor's kitchens!', Richard queried, attempting to make sense of his brother's situation.

'Nay, that was John, - 'Lambert', as the king called him. He was our natural half-brother, Dickon, born to one of father's many mistresses!' he grinned rolling his eyes. 'We used him as a decoy, enabling me to get away unobserved with Bodrugan. Sir Henry brought me back here. I've been here ever since'.

Edward seated himself and reached for a flagon of mead, pouring a measure into two leather tankards, offering one to his brother. The last time the Princes had seen each other was at Gipping Hall in Suffolk in late 1483, where at 9 and 12 years of age, they had been sheltered by Sir James Tyrell before preparing to go their separate ways after their Uncle Richard's coronation. Now they were men, no longer unsure of themselves or reliant on others to guide them. Minors no more, they knew their own mind and could decide their own fate, both having been hailed England's rightful king, albeit ten years apart.

Richard studied his brother thoughtfully as Edward described his return to Ireland, his coronation, landing at Furness and sojourn at Gleaston, before his escape with Sir Henry after word came the battle was lost. Richard in turn expounded on his time in Scotland and Ireland and his ambitious plans to overthrow Henry Tudor. His little brother's obvious enthusiasm for such a perilous endeavour, perturbed Edward, who took a deep breath, regarding his sibling with serious scrutiny.

'Why are you persisting with this Dickon? Can't you see its hopeless?' he sighed resting his elbow on the arm of the chair and his fingers against his temple. 'Our parents have gone. There's not enough Yorkist support left to fight another battle with the king. Tudor has the luck of the devil! Damn him! Our sister is queen, so our father's blood will live on in her children…. Let that be enough Dickon.' Edward ran his hand through his hair wearily.

'But Ned...' Richard was about to respond but Edward interjected.

'I've had my fill of fighting. Its done! Cousin John gave his life for me, as did so many loyal Yorkists. Lord Lovell is gone, Christ knows where, though I suspect he's dead too. It seems the Irish have given up on us both. The rest have pledged to Tudor. It's been too long Dickon. I've had enough.'

'But Ned, I have eight thousand men now!' Richard replied in exasperation, dismayed at his brother's demurral and resignation to the life of a commoner. 'The Cornishmen are with me and more will come when they hear of our success! Once we have Exeter it will encourage others to join us! Aunt Margaret is backing us, as is Maximillian.'

'The Cornish rebellion has already been thwarted once Dickon!' Edward reminded his brother.

'For God's sake, Ned! *You* are the rightful king!' Richard insisted. 'You know Uncle Richard considered re-instating your legitimacy when you came of age! Don't you remember? He spoke to us about it. Seize your birthright brother! I will stand aside for you!'.

'Nay, Dickon. I no longer desire it. It's been ten years! I am content to live out my life here in anonymity. I have a good life here as Parker. No-one knows my true identity except a very few and they won't betray me... I wish you well brother and I am proud of you but leave me out of it!' Edward appeared resolute. Richard stood up in frustration, steadying himself with two hands resting against the fireplace, finding it hard to contain his exasperation.

'Christ Ned! What has happened to you? You could be king of England, yet here you are in some remote corner of Devonshire, dressed in park keeper's clothes, being addressed as John instead of your Grace!' Richard hated to see his brother attired so plainly, in denial of his patrimony, when he himself was risking all for their cause. He almost felt ashamed of Edward's obduracy. *Surely the House of York deserved better?* He tried another tack, appealing to Edward's conscience. 'Don't you feel you owe it to father?'

'Do *not* lay *that* at my door Dickon!' Edward reprimanded, suddenly irritated at the censure, especially coming from his younger brother. 'You forget, I hardly knew father. I grew up at Ludlow in Uncle Anthony's care. You know something Dickon...', he leaned towards his brother, lowering his voice, 'Uncle Anthony told me a secret about father that proves Uncle George was right all along!'

'What?!' Richard frowned nonplussed, recalling the time of Uncle George's execution, the whispers and the unsettling gloom that had descended upon the household, the raised voices and Uncle Richard's angry departure, so bewildering to a four-year-old.

'What are you talking about?'

'Apparently our grandfather Richard of York's mistress was our father's mother, not Duchess Cecily. That's why he was so much older than his siblings.'

'So father *was* illegitimate after all?!'

'Aye, and Edmund too but grandmother Cecily adopted them and brought them up as her own'.

'Pfft! ... that's a lot to take in Ned.' Richard exhaled slowly, his mind racing. 'I'm not sure I can believe it!'. He would need time to process such a revelation.

'Well Uncle Anthony said he thought I should know and I had no reason to doubt him. Why would he lie? *He* was more of a father to me than the king... I loved him.' Edward eyes misted over and he looked away before forcing himself to re-focus on his brother. 'T'was different for you Dickon, you lived with our parents'.

'Aye. Father was always kind to me and I *did* love him but I used to worry about mother. Richard gazed into the fire. 'I often saw that Shaw woman in father's chamber; sometimes Lord Hastings was there too. It disgusted me. I used to wonder why mama put up with it. You know, I saw her slap father once! He slapped her back, threw her down on the bed and ripped her dress apart. I ran off terrified but the next day they appeared as if nothing had happened.'

'Huh' Edward scoffed, 'she was queen. That was enough for her. She knew as long as she tolerated father's whoring she could get whatever she wanted!'

'Uncle Richard hated it. He was rarely down at court. I only saw him once. He was always so serious and disapproving. Father told him at dinner to take the poker out of his arse and relax a little! '

'Ha! Did he now?', Edward guffawed grinning. 'Uncle Richard never could take a jest'.

'Nay, he wasn't amused' Richard agreed, 'though everyone else was! Even so, our sisters liked him, especially Bess, she was *always* giving him the eye... though I doubt he noticed'.

'Ha!,' Edward chuckled, heaving a fatalistic sigh. 'Now they're all dead and Bess is Tudor's queen! Thank God they didn't know it then! Father would be turning in his grave!'.

'That's *exactly* why I've come back Ned! I feel I owe it to him to try!' Richard retorted irritably. 'I remember when father died, you were as upset as I was but you *couldn't wait* to be king!'

'Aye, of course! I was angry at Richard for taking over and arresting our maternal uncles but I understand now, he had no choice. It was father's dying wish his one remaining brother assumed control as Protector, though I wish he had taken less heed of that traitor Buckingham! Uncle Anthony might still be alive and Lord Hastings too, if it weren't for that duplicitous toad whispering in Richard's ear!' he sighed, his brother nodding in agreement. 'However, I was too young to rule and mother's family should not have tried to ignore father's wishes and side line Richard, they had no right…. I see that now'.

'But, you and I have that right *now* Ned and I'm going to claim it, with or without you!'

'The moment has gone Dickon. I'm not who I once was and I have no desire to go back there. Too many men have died in my name already. I'm glad you still have ambition though Richard. You are more like father in that respect, though I can see you are no soldier – too pretty by far!' he quipped smirking. Richard rolled his eyes and broke into a sheepish grin.

'So I have been told! Aye. I admit, I am no use on a battlefield. I abhor violence, it sickens me, however, I am *not* a coward' He shuddered, closing his eyes as an image of the slaughter he had witnessed on the Scottish border, came to mind. 'I may not have been trained to fight as you were but I have strong men who will do battle for me, as they would for *you* Ned!'

'I've been down that path and it's a dead end, *my* dead end, which I would face from Tudor, should I be located here!' Edward reiterated. 'I fear for you Dickon but I see your mind is made up. We have that in common at least! I pray you have success Dickon, if that is what you wish.' He raised his tankard in tribute. 'I would be happy to serve you as Richard the fourth!', he added with sincerity, drinking his fill, before regarding his brother fondly… 'your Grace!' he saluted chuckling, amused at the irony.

'Huh, Thank you Ned.' Richard smiled, staring ruminatively into the glowing embers, knowing he was beaten by his brother's obstinacy. Edward, feeling sorry to have disappointed his brother, thought to lighten the mood with a change of focus.

'I hear you married a Scottish noblewoman. I trust you are happy together?'. Richard looked up, his face brightening as he pictured his pretty wife.

'You should see Catherine, Ned, she's a real beauty! Men swoon at her feet! When I first saw her, I thought she was an angel from heaven!'

'I'm glad to hear it Dickon. I hope she loves you.' Edward beamed, charmed by his young sibling's passion.

'She does Ned, very much and *I* love *her*. We are as close as any couple could be. I would die for her!' Edward raised his eyebrows.

'I trust it won't come to that Dickon'.

'Me too!' The brothers laughed together and before long said their farewells, each aware of the precarious foundation of their existence but immensely proud of their Plantagenet pedigree; one content to vanish into a life of humble anonymity, one still fuelled by his unalienable right to his Royal inheritance. They embraced and Richard left with his guards, leaving Coldridge deer park to its keeper. '*God speed little brother*', Edward's parting words still resounding in his ears, as he rode away down the narrow Devon lanes, the burden of his undertaking weighing heavily, feeling more alone than ever.

He found himself thinking about his father and Edward's revelation. It struck him that Uncle Richard must have realised that George's claim was just and the impact that must have had on his decision to assume the throne would have been significant. *Of course! He was avenging George, whilst restoring the rightful line of succession!* The semblance of a smile playing on Richard's lips, almost at once twisted into a sneer, as his present reality hit home. *Now a usurper with no such right wears the crown of England, while my brother plays at managing a deer park!*

'I'll show you Edward, if it's the last thing I do!' he muttered stubbornly under his breath. *John Evans' indeed, I wonder who thought that one up?* he pondered, visions of the shock on his father's face, had he been alive to see it, causing him some diversion as he urged his steed forward in the dwindling twilight of a newly risen harvest moon.

Chapter Nineteen

By the Spring of '97, returning from one of her frequent trips to Yorkshire, always with some reluctance, Eleanor found her husband had taken to his bed with chest pains. Despite her administrations and those of local doctors, Hugh died shortly afterwards, drink, rich food and a gradual increase in weight exacerbating an underlying heart condition. Eleanor nursed him as best she could, until one morning she woke to find him cold and unresponsive on the floor. He had got up to relieve himself at the garderobe but had collapsed before returning to bed. Resigning herself to widowhood again, though not without some relief, she set about settling his affairs. Hugh had bequeathed most of his property to his children but to Eleanor's surprise she had been left a small worker's cottage, an allowance and some of his personal effects and silverware. She felt some regret that she hadn't been able to love him as she should but she knew she had given him the companionship he craved and a certain pridefulness in his attractive wife. He had never been unfaithful to her for which she was grateful and she was pleased to have brought some happiness into his final years.

Feeling she had fulfilled her duty by the Broughtons and having no wish to stay on this remote Cumbrian peninsular, Eleanor sold Hugh's cottage, packed up her belongings and wrote to her brothers asking if she may return to Manor farm. She wanted to be near her grandchildren and meet the new addition to Bess's family - a daughter, who had been named Margaret, after her paternal grandmother but who was affectionately known as Meggie.

Visiting Sir Thomas to tell him of her plans to leave, Eleanor remembered she hadn't yet asked him about the German captain and what may have befallen him at Stoke. Now she was single again. she had found herself thinking about the charismatic captain more often. Sitting outside on a bench behind Tom Parker's modest cottage, basking in the summer sunshine, she chatted amiably to the outlaw knight, who offered his condolences to Hugh's pretty widow. Steering the conversation back to the battle of Stoke, after a general enquiry as to the fate of the mercenaries and their commander, Eleanor ventured to ask about Stefan, though she doubted Thomas would remember him.

'Sir Thomas, did you by any chance meet a German captain by the name of Stefan? I don't know his family name but he had distinctive scar across his forehead and cheek'. Eleanor drew her finger across her temple by way of illustration. She held her breath, fearing the worst but nevertheless praying for good news.

'Aye, I recall the man you mean, captain Bauer. A handsome man, very polite, spoke good English.' Thomas confirmed. Eleanor's heart leapt. *Captain Bauer!* He suddenly felt more real, now she knew his name.

'Was he....?' she hardly dared say the word.

'Killed? Nay, not in this battle anyway. He was with the Germans being rounded up and relieved of their weapons when I last saw him. I was too busy making for the river to see what happened after that, though we heard afterwards they were sent home without pay, poor devils!'

'Thank God!' Eleanor breathed closing her eyes, as relief flooded through her. Thomas regarded her quizzically.

'Nay, I mean thank God he survived!' Eleanor laughed and Thomas grinned raising his eyebrows.

'Aha! So you were quite taken with the handsome captain then my dear?' Thomas winked suggestively. Eleanor blushed; fearful he could read her mind.

'Nay, sir, well …aye, a little. We spent some time…erm.. conversing, at Masham and …I liked him'.

'Hmm, conversing is one word for it I suppose!' Thomas smirked and winked again and they both chuckled, 'Its alright my dear, your secret's safe with me!' Thomas grinned patting her knee, knowing only too well what soldiers were like and Eleanor sensing there was little point in denying the patently obvious.

A couple of months later James arrived with two men at arms to escort his sister back to Wensleydale. After saying her goodbyes to the Huddleston's and collecting Pearl from the stables, she bid a fond farewell to Edith, who was sorry to see her mistress leave. Eleanor offered to take her maid with her to Yorkshire but the girl preferred to stay amongst family within the familiar surroundings of home, something Eleanor understood only too well. Instead, leaving Edith a parting gift of pretty hair pins, a comb of carved ivory and some ribbons in a variety of colours, Eleanor set off for Yorkshire with a renewed sense of optimism. Fate had thrown her one more lifeline of happiness and she was going to take it.

Eleanor was coming home, this time not as maidservant in service to landed gentry but back to her birthplace, as a woman of independent means, a mother and grandmother, able to watch her offspring live out their lives in the places she loved. Not only that but now she knew Stefan had survived the slaughter at Stoke, it gave her enough comfort to think that he might still be living in Burgundy and would perhaps remember her fondly. With a sense of closure, she resigned herself to the fact she would never see him again, consigning all thoughts of men to those cherished memories of youth she now deemed behind her.

Chapter Twenty

After having taken part in James IV's brief and unsuccessful campaign over the border, a weary German captain gazed out from the battlements of Edinburgh Castle, his pocket heavy with coin, having been paid for his services to the Scottish king. The crusade into England in the autumn of '96, had been disastrous and instead of the young Prince Richard of York reclaiming his throne in triumph, the youth had retreated in dismay, leaving the Scottish soldiers reduced to their usual indiscriminate killing and pillaging, this appearing no different to any other border raid. Now the pretender had left for Ireland, Margaret of York's Burgundian mercenaries were preparing to return home, another offensive against the English king having ended in failure, though at least this time payment would be forthcoming.

Gazing across to the Pentland hills South of the city, from the battlements of Edinburgh castle, watching the sun sink in the West, Stefan reflected on his life and future. He sympathised with the youthful Scottish king, who had attempted to support the Yorkist Prince but lack of resources, coupled with Richard's reluctance to shed blood for his cause, had embarrassed James and forced him to withdraw. Stefan liked king James, who although much younger than himself, was a patron of the arts and keen on law, literature and science. He had conversed with the forward-thinking monarch, when dining with him, along with his commander Roderick De La Lane and had learned of a new Education Act passed by the Scottish parliament, which made compulsory the schooling of landowner's children in Latin, arts and law. This would ensure that all persons in authority had the necessary education to back up their positions, garner respect and rule the populace wisely.

Although he also felt some sympathy for Richard, Stefan could see this peace-loving young man with his angelic looks and gentle nature was no match for battle hardened troops and determined noblemen, who's support in England for a second presumed Yorkist Prince seemed sadly lacking. Most were too afraid of reprisals from Henry Tudor to risk all in favouring another pretender after the Lambert Simnel failure, despite any loyalty they might feel to the Yorkist cause. Henry's determination to unmask and brand Richard of York an imposter, had had its desired effect.

Now at the end of another campaign, Stefan found himself at a crossroads in his life. The colours of autumn, warm and rich, would soon transform this verdurous landscape, echoing the hues in that lock of hair he had carried with him, since that early summer morn in distant Yorkshire. With a smile of satisfaction, Stefan felt in his pocket, his memento of that unforgettable night at Masham still lay within its pouch, the silken strand's lustre now dulled, its binding ribbon faded and frayed. Somewhere over those hills about eight day's ride, lived the owner of that keepsake, a local beauty, who's fair complexion and cascades of luxuriant auburn tresses had once stopped him in his tracks.

Though Eleanor had appeared to give herself to him in a selfless gesture of solace for a man who may shortly lose his life in battle, Stefan was sure she had found him as desirable as he did her and it pleased him. Miraculously he had survived the bloodshed at Stoke, the violence as brutal as any he could remember, the Irish pitifully ill equipped and exposed in inadequate clothing but plucky and determined, until it became a rout, the kerns falling like scythed wheat before a sickle. Schwartz had gone down bravely, taking out dozens of soldiers before being overwhelmed by force of numbers, whereupon with their commanders all dead, the landsknechts laid down their arms and surrendered. Ever since, Stefan had put his continued good fortune down to that trophy in his pocket, long having vowed to himself to return to England and make its owner his wife.

Immediately, the soldier was filled with a new resolve. Now middle aged, with his best years behind him, Stefan felt he had tempted fate long enough. Most professional soldiers had a life expectancy of months, if not weeks. He had been living by the grace of God for some time now. There was no point in risking all for a few more pockets of silver, when he already had enough for a comfortable life, save for the woman who had occupied his thoughts for nine long years. The time had come. He was not getting any younger. He was back in Britain, he had means, unfettered by allegiance to any one master, he could do as he pleased, choose to fight on or choose to make a new life for himself. The last few years had been turbulent and unsettling; he had fought in Brittany against the French in various campaigns and afterwards for Burgundy in their invasion of Italy. In short periods of inaction, awaiting his next assignment, he had had several amorous encounters with willing females but none of his libidinous conquests so far eclipsed the beauty of his English rose.

His mind was now made up. The retirement he had once envisaged in his home country, seemed less appealing now he had a fresh focus within the pastoral realms of England. Smiling at the new prospect opening up before him and pressing the lock of hair to his lips, he hurried down to his quarters to prepare for a journey tomorrow. He would speak to commander De La Lane tonight and in the morning collect his belongings, before encouraging his sturdy Iberian war stallion to put as many miles as possible between this great Scottish capital and the gentle vales of Yorkshire to the South.

As dawn broke, after bidding farewell to his comrades, Stefan stowed his clothes, armour, several swords and a crossbow into the panniers slung across the Galloway pony, he had hurriedly purchased. Then mounting his faithful black steed Galahad and with the pack pony on a leading rein, set off towards the borderlands. It was a Sunday morning and as the church bells of Edinburgh rang out summoning the faithful, he left the city and his military life behind. His company would even now be boarding ship bound for home, looking forward to an indulgence of wine, women and raucous song before the next assignment loomed but to his surprise, he felt no remorse or nostalgia; instead, he felt liberated, ready for a new adventure and with any luck a new love.

Keeping to the Great North Road his route followed the coastline of Eastern Scotland, over the border to Berwick and on to Newcastle, after which it lay further inland towards Durham and Darlington, where Stefan knew he could veer West to Wensleydale on roads he had travelled before. Dressed in his landsknecht wams and hosen, the striped, slashed unform and helmet marked him out as a formidable opponent, skilled in all forms of offence and defence. He estimated any would-be opportunist attacker would think twice about confronting him, given the reputation for grim violence that the European mercenaries had earned.

All at once the thought struck him, he had no idea where Eleanor lived. England being such a small kingdom, he had assumed she would be easy to find but now he had to admit he was unsure where to look. He knew she had been in service with Lady Lovell and he realised he would have to make further enquiries when he reached Yorkshire. Nothing had been heard of Viscount Lovell since the battle of Stoke but with local nobility well known. he felt confident somebody would be able to direct him.

Another thought nagged at him as he rode. *Suppose Eleanor had re-married?* After all, it had been many years since their night of passion, and with no word of him, she would have presumed him dead, his name not being listed as missing after the battle. *Would she even remember him and would she even want him after all this time?* A woman as fair as she would in all probability have been claimed by a suitor before now and would surely have long since sought a partner to share her life. She would be older too, perhaps the passions of youth will have subsided with the approach of middle age?

Doubts began to plague Stefan, he felt deflated and ashamed of himself that he should be so presumptuous as to think Eleanor would still be available, let alone still want him. Showing his years, his hair now streaked with grey at the temples, his body not as toned as it was, though constant wielding of heavy weaponry ensured he was still muscular and strong where it counted. He had suffered an ugly wound where an arrow had pierced his thigh but with quick extraction and the administrations of an expert Italian surgeon, it had healed well enough.

Should I turn back? He argued with himself. *Nein, that solves nothing. I will go on with my quest and should it prove fruitless, I will think again, after all, I am a free man, bound to no-one - I can do as I please!* He felt cheered at his reasoning and grinned to himself at the thought of Eleanor appreciating the fact his manhood still functioned as it should and he could still show her how much he desired her. Filled with the warm glow of lustful anticipation, he relaxed and began to admire the pretty countryside he rode through, more arable than the dense forests of his homeland.

He passed through villages and skirted farmland where peasants toiled, stopping briefly to stare at the colourfully dressed stranger. The last wheat and barley harvests were done, the fields were under the plough and turnip crops were being planted, while children foraged in the birch woods gathering sticks for the fire or were put to work in the orchards picking ripe fruit. Stefan would stop regularly to rest the horses, partake of a drink and chew on some dried meat and on one occasion was offered some fruit by a group of curious children, who had stood to gawp in curiosity at this odd-looking traveller.

'Are you a soldier mister?' a scruffy looking pre-pubescent lad enquired boldly, his intonation displaying the distinct North-eastern twang of the region, a group of girls giggling timidly behind his back.

'Ja! I am.' to which further mirth ensued at his unfamiliar accent.

'Where are you going?'

'I'm going to York shy'are' he tried to pronounce the county name like a local but it sounded awkward and from the stifled titters, clearly the children thought it amusing.

'You've got a way to go then mister'.

'Would you like an apple?' a young girl stepped forward holding out a ripe red fruit.

'Danke, fräulein' Stefan took the apple and rummaged in his purse for a small coin which he flicked towards the group. As they scrambled for the coin squealing with delight, a peasant woman in her mid-thirties approached, eyeing him suspiciously. She was dressed in a plain woollen kirtle laced tightly over her bosom; her hair hidden under a threadbare linen bonnet from which untidy strands had escaped. It's auburn hues, similar to Eleanor's, appeared dull and unwashed and her face and hands bore the signs of hard labour, though her cheeks were flushed with the rosy bloom of country life.

'What is your business here sir?' she enquired haughtily but at the same time somewhat taken by this handsome stranger.

'I'm just passing through madam. Good day to you'. The woman ushered the children away, casting a fleeting glance behind her. Stefan smirked, taking in her well-rounded figure as she smiled back coquettishly. He lay back on the grassy bank, closing his eyes against the sun, munching his juicy apple, images of pretty russet haired women playing on his mind.

He awoke with a start, as an owl screeched in the tree canopy above him. A cold wind moaned in his ear, the peasants were gone and dark clouds obscured the sun. He hurriedly re-mounted, trotting along the track cutting a straight path through extensive woodland on either side, his senses suddenly alert. It would be getting dark and sooner here under the tree canopy than on the open road. He must find somewhere for the night. There was no choice for now but to follow the rutted highway but a lone traveller was always a target for vagabonds and thieves, especially so in woods where trees and undergrowth provided perfect ambush territory. No sooner than he had deduced the danger, he started, for suddenly, as if on cue, a woman ran out in front of his horse, causing the beast to rear up, unsettling the packhorse beside it. Easing the skittish animals to a stop, Stefan saw it was the peasant woman he had encountered earlier. Her hair hung loose about her shoulders and her bodice hung open where the laces had been undone. 'Help me sir!' she cried breathless as Stefan dismounted.

'Are you hurt fräulein?' he enquired with concern but just as he moved towards her, a trio of well-built young men emerged from the undergrowth, knives and sickles at the ready. Stefan cursed himself for his foolishness. *Dummkopf!* The oldest trick in the book and he had fallen for it! The woman had clearly marked him out as a target for robbery, surmising he would have a good deal of coinage stashed about him for his travels and she had brought reinforcements to relieve him of it. He shot her a glance of loathing and turned to face his attackers, one of whom was about to cut the reins of the packhorse. Unfortunately for them, these simple peasants had never encountered a time-served mercenary before and in a flash of hardened steel all three, lay prostrate on the ground, blood pouring from a variety of wounds, their own workaday weapons lying impotent at their feet, having had no chance to draw blood.

The woman screamed and stood aghast, her hand over her mouth, shaking involuntarily at the unexpected show of violence. In her simple ignorance she assumed her victim would simply yield when outnumbered by younger men and this would be an easy snatch. Angrily thrusting his bloodied sword into the earth, Stefan leapt at her, grabbing her arms, and pushing her to the ground, kneeling over her, trembling with rage, mostly at himself for being so gullible. With the soldier's dagger blade pressing against her throat, threatening to break the skin, the woman fully expected to be at the very least violated, or killed, or both. She had seen what this man could do and it terrified her. 'Mercy!...' she breathed panic stricken, as Stefan's eyes bored into her with loathing. He held her arms down with his knees, the dagger in his right hand still held against her flesh, while with his left he felt for a silver coin in his pocket. She clearly thought he was about to unloose his hose but instead he sneered contemptuously.

'Is this what you want? *Hundin!*' he scowled through gritted teeth, jamming a silver coin into her cleavage. 'Fear not fräulein, you won't be getting anything else from me, no matter how much you beg! *Hure!*'. He released her roughly before leaping back into the saddle, both animals needing little encouragement to put distance between him and his would-be muggers. As he relaxed into his ride, he chuckled to himself. *That's one fräulein who won't be so quick to repeat her little pantomime!* He felt a pang of conscience for her three companions, though they would most likely live to tell the tale. He knew only too well the hardships these peasants faced to maintain their simple lives and he blamed himself for his imprudence. *I will be more mindful next time*, he vowed.

Chapter Twenty One

Upon leaving Coldridge, encouraged by Edward's good wishes and filled with renewed resolve to earn his brother's pride, Richard of York led his forces in an attempt at besieging Exeter. However, despite his steadfast commitment and purpose his offensive failed, ending in a humiliating retreat to Taunton, where faced with the Royal army's superior numbers, Richard had no choice but to seek sanctuary at Beaulieu. His inexperience as a commander and his subsequent flight during the night left his demoralised company leaderless and surrounded, having no option but to flee or surrender. It seemed the lessons of Stoke, the Scottish campaign and recent Cornish uprising had been well learned. It was time to admit defeat.

Given promise that his life would be spared, and that of his wife, who had by this time been betrayed and captured, Richard gave himself up. He was brought to London in November, to be paraded through the streets, pilloried and mocked as an imposter. Lady Catherine, meanwhile, upon being brought to Henry who, immediately captivated and astounded by the noblewoman's beauty, had her placed her under the queen's care. In a further blow for the couple, Henry had engineered a peace with James IV, leaving Richard and Catherine without the Scottish king's support and now at Tudor's mercy.

Dismayed, Richard accepted his brother had been right. Their cause was indeed hopeless. His grand plan to claim his birthright lay in tatters, all his efforts in vain, his supporters melting away in the face of overwhelming opposition. The house of York lay vanquished, their great dynasty consigned to the annals of history. He thought about his brother's words and wondered how many more secrets his family had hidden from him. Both his mother and grandmother were now dead, so he couldn't ask *them* if Edward spoke the truth, though it hardly mattered now. God had seen to it the house of York was undone. As the last of his line, he had done his best but it was not enough. He could ask no more of loyal men who had risked all in his name. Too many were already dead, it was time to stop. All he could do now was to trust in the king's clemency. Sadly for him, no such dispensation was forthcoming.

Richard maintained his Royal provenance throughout whilst he was kept at Sheen Palace, until in need of an excuse to punish the young man he called Perkin Warbeck, the scheming English king allowed his prisoner to escape. Upon recapture at Sheen Priory three days later, where the fugitive had claimed sanctuary, Henry brought him to Westminster to be put in the stocks and ridiculed before sending 'Perkin' to a windowless cell in the Tower, to be starved, tortured on the rack and beaten. Despite a promise to the Prior to treat his captive well, the injuries Richard sustained especially to his face, were an attempt by Tudor to make any identification impossible.

Broken in body and spirit, his wretched prisoner signed a confession stating he was simply an imposter, the son of a boatman from Tournai who had been used to impersonate Richard Duke of York and therefore no threat to Henry. This confession, Henry was only too pleased to publish, having been in mortal terror that the young man who had imperilled his sovereignty, would dethrone him and reveal his own spurious claim as untenable. Should either one of Edward IV's sons have been found to have survived, it would undo all Henry's carefully promoted propaganda that Richard III was a murdering tyrant who had killed his nephews - the lie upon which Tudor's invasion had been supported and endorsed. Doubts had already begun to set in amongst the nobility, many now bemoaning their backing of this unworthy usurper whom they had raised to majesty but at whose hand they could now be impoverished.

Henry's queen was never permitted to see the man who claimed to be her brother, for if she had, it may have been the unwelcome proof Henry dreaded. Lady Catherine who was seen as an innocent bystander in Perkin's deception, remained at Court, though prevented from ever returning to Scotland, saved perhaps, by her beauty and shared maternal grandmother with Henry.

With Richard of York in Tudor's hands and Yorkist hopes dashed once again, the nobility of England had no choice but to settle down to Lancastrian rule. With two failed claimants, another bid for the throne seemed unlikely. Henry VII already had two male heirs and it became apparent with every passing year the Tudor dynasty would endure. As time marched on, the impetus for change was lost and acceptance of the status quo for many now proved the easier option.

Faced with the need to eliminate all possible claimants to the throne of England, a condition of his agreement with Spain, Henry condemned 'Perkin' as a traitor and following another specious escape plot, linked with the other young man in the Tower, assumed to be the Earl of Warwick, both men were executed in November 1499. That sorry youth, having spent much of his young life in captivity and without an education, was hardly a threat but the king couldn't take the chance of Warwick becoming a figurehead for yet another uprising, once Perkin had been disposed of. The supposed escape plot by the two prisoners being Henry's justification for their execution, which might otherwise be construed as murder.

Henry's heartless actions had now cleared the way for his son

Arthur to marry Catherine of Aragon, no other claimants poised to contend the crown, a prerequisite of the betrothal agreement. Nevertheless, many believed the death of the last surviving Plantagenets, to have brought a curse down on the Tudor king for the calculated and unnecessary slaughter of innocents, a belief borne out years later by the eventual failure of the Tudor succession.

Chapter Twenty Two

Around the time Richard of York was landing in Cornwall, Stefan Bauer was making his way South through Newcastle, Durham, Darlington and thence to Richmond. From enquires made along the way, he was eventually directed to Ravensworth Castle where he was told he would find Lady Lovell and hopefully, Eleanor.

Arriving at the seat of the Fitzhughs as light was fading, the mercenary dismounted and enquired at the gate after the Viscountess. He was ushered into the parlour and stood waiting while a page went to convey his message. The castle felt cold and gloomy and Stefan shivered, his stomach in knots, wondering if Eleanor was somewhere within these walls and if she was, would she even want to see him? After waiting what seemed like an eternity, a petite, pale faced lady with an elfin face, dressed in the plain grey gown and russet headdress of a vowess, entered the room and stood before him, as the page announced 'Lady Lovell, sir'.

'May I help you sir?' Anne enquired, surveying the visitor's unusual clothes and recognising the unmistakeable garb of a landsknecht mercenary, noting his facial scar, as Stefan bowed and held out his hand. 'Captain Stefan Bauer, I am pleased to meet you, Lady Lovell. I served your husband at the battle of Stoke my lady. My sincere condolences for your loss.'

'Have you come to tell me news of him?' Anne asked, instantly alert, observing him wide-eyed, her heart racing at the mention of her husband and clutching the crucifix at her waist for reassurance. *Had Francis been confirmed dead? Is that what this man had come to tell her?*

'Nay my lady, forgive me, I come on another matter'. Anne's face fell and she sat down disappointed.

'Pray be seated sir'. Stefan sat down opposite her, while she indicated to the page to bring refreshment for her visitor. Now recalling seeing this man speaking to her husband at Masham, Anne was pleased to see he had survived, though the memories he stirred were painful and she had to stop herself from wishing it was Francis and not this stranger seated before her today.

'Did you see my husband after the battle? she ventured, hoping Sir Thomas Broughton had overstated Francis's injuries to Eleanor.

'Nay madam, I lost sight of him after our initial charge'. Anne nodded pressing her lips together stoically before remembering to enquire his purpose.

'What brings you here captain Bauer?' she heaved a fatalistic sigh, for clearly there was no further news to be had about her husband.

'I have come to enquire after your maid servant Eleanoore, my lady. Is she still with you?' Anne looked up surprised, a quizzical frown creasing her brow. *Why would this German soldier be seeking Eleanor?*

'Eleanor is no longer with me sir. She returned to serve the Metcalfe's at Nappa Hall before she re-married and she now resides with her husband at Millom.' she told her guest. 'He's Marshall for the Huddleston's.' she added, endeavouring to be of help. Stefan swallowed, he felt like he had been thumped in the chest. *Eleanor had re-married!* His worst fears had been realised. *She was another man's wife!* Anne could see the news had shaken the soldier. He appeared deflated and she could sense he wrestled with his emotions. He stood up.

'Forgive me, my lady, I am sorry to have troubled you.' But Anne was curious and not ready to let him leave. She stood up as the page brought a flagon of ale and a tankard, which she filled and handed to Stefan.

'Here, pray refresh yourself before you go Captain Bauer.'

'Thank you my lady'. Stefan took the tumbler and Anne noticed his hand shook. She placed her hand gently on his arm.

Did you meet Eleanor at Masham, before the battle at Stoke?' she enquired, thinking back to that last night she had shared with Francis and how Eleanor had seemed strangely elated the following morning.

'Aye, madam. We enjoyed an evening together and I have thought of her many times in the intervening years. I was hoping to…' he stopped, unable to say more, the disappointment hitting home as the words caught in his throat. Anne smiled to herself. *I knew it!* She could quite see how Eleanor would have fallen for this handsome soldier and she decided there was no harm in affording him some solace.

'Her daughter married the farrier in Wensley. If you call on them they may have news of Eleanor', Anne offered commiseratively, feeling sympathy for this man who was clearly disheartened, having come searching for Eleanor in the hope of resuming their relationship. 'It's been ten years sir. A lot can happen in ten years.' she added, attempting to defend Eleanor's actions in re-marrying.

'Aye madam. I am aware of it and I expected as much. Thank you for your assistance my lady'. He drank his fill, put the tumbler down and held out his hand in farewell. 'I shall not trouble you further Viscountess'.

'If Eleanor should return, do you have a message for her?' Anne asked as she took his hand, knowing Eleanor would enquire likewise if she heard this man had come looking for her. Besides, Eleanor had come to tell her about Francis and now she could return the favour.

'Tell her,.. 'he hesitated, 'Tell her, I still have it! She will know to what I refer'. He smiled and Anne raised her eyebrows and chuckled.

'With pleasure sir'. She watched him at the casement, wondering what it was he still had, *some keepsake of Eleanor's no doubt*, as the page showed him out and he mounted his horse. He looked back, saw her at the window and doffed his cap respectfully before trotting away into the twilight. She waved pensively, a tear tracking down her cheek, as a pang of jealousy caught her unawares. She had tried to cast all thoughts of Francis away but this man had brought them to the fore once more, the sudden rush of envy taking her by surprise. *Dear Lord, if this man lived, why not Francis?* Not only did Eleanor have another husband but now a suitor as well! *Oh, Francis what befell you? Why did you not come back to me? Why does the good Lord not favour ME?* she besought her maker in a fit of self-pity, before running to her prie-dieu and sinking to her knees in contrition for her covetousness.

After a restless and somewhat depressing night at a local hostelry in the town, Stefan made his way over to Wensleydale. His quest was over, he would have to decide what to do next with his life but first he would call on the farrier Lady Lovell had mentioned, before leaving Yorkshire. He wanted word to reach Eleanor that he had come looking for her and had not forgotten her and besides, there was always the slim chance she might wish to see him again despite having re-married. Perhaps if he saw her one more time, he reasoned, he would rid himself of his obsession and he could move on?

The road soon became familiar. Stefan delighted in seeing Wensleydale again. His army's long march through the vale had stayed with him and he found it unchanged, though it had been summer then and now it was high autumn, the colours as he had envisaged, reflecting that lock, of auburn hair still tucked into his doublet, resting against his heart. Perhaps he could find another English rose to share his life within this tranquil dale, for he had already decided to stay and make this place his home. There would be plenty of work for a trained military veteran amongst retainers of the local nobility. He could learn to be content here.

As he neared Wensley, he could see the turrets of Middleham Castle on its hill across the valley, the red dragon of Wales still flying aloft, the sight of which had caused no little disgruntlement amongst the Yorkshiremen marching with him on their way to oppose the Tudor king. He gazed over to the familiar slopes of Penhill and Westwards, beyond Bolton Castle, towards the head of the dale, where somewhere behind those distant Cumbrian hills the woman who had fuelled his fantasies now shared another's bed. As he rode on, he struggled to dismiss that image so annoyingly repeating in his mind's eye.

Passing Wensley church, he soon located the farrier's dwelling and forge close by, where he dismounted and led his horses to the water trough by the side of the road. Galahad was in need of new shoes anyway and if the young man he could see working at the anvil was Eleanor's son-in-law, what better person to employ as messenger? Robert looked up as the stranger approached. The last time he had seen one of these colourfully dressed men at arms was all those years ago at the battle of Stoke and he was curious to converse with the man. 'Good day to you sir, may I be of assistance?' he enquired of Stefan, putting down his hammer.

'Thank you, my horse needs shod'. As Stefan came into focus, both men momentarily stared at each other, before simultaneously breaking into a grin of recognition.

'Lord Scrope's farrier is it not?' Stefan held out his hand in greeting.

'Aye, sir, Robert Dinsdale. And you sir, were commander Schwartz's captain were you not? I remember you! I'm glad to see you survived *that* blood bath!'

'Me too!' Stefan smiled embracing the younger man warmly. 'Stefan

Bauer. Aye, Robert, of course! I saw you had been taken by the Earl of Oxford! Good to see you back here!' The two men sat down and shared their memories of that fateful day and the loyal friends they had lost. They were both aware however, the tide had turned and it was better to accept Tudor rule was here to stay. Robert being young enough to adapt, build his business and raise a family and Stefan having no particular loyalty to whoever sat on the throne of England, so long as he was able to make a living.

As they chatted, two small boys rushed out of the cottage followed by a young woman who could only be their mother, resting a babe in arms on her hip. Stefan stopped talking, momentarily dumfounded. The woman resembled a younger version of Eleanor, her hair lighter but with the same honeyed hues, yet something about her seemed strangely out of place amidst this scene of rural industry and domestic chaos. Stefan sensed this woman's origin was beyond than that of a simple peasant woman, she had a certain bearing and grace, a hint of an aura more noble, her grey/blue eyes soft and distant, her strong chin redolent of the handsome Plantagenet dynasty who had ruled England for over 300 years. He stared transfixed, a fact not unnoticed by Robert, who was struck by a sudden covetousness for his pretty wife.

'My wife Elizabeth' the farrier introduced Bess proudly, as she nodded in greeting. Stefan could hardly speak, all he could see was Eleanor, for this was undoubtedly her daughter.

'Captain Stefan Bauer, madam, I am pleased to meet you', he managed, swallowing the lump in his throat, as Bess smiled back with Eleanor's smile.

'So, Stefan,' Robert interjected, somewhat irritated at the captain's engrossment with his wife. 'What brings you back here?' Stefan forced his eyes away from Elizabeth and the likeness to her mother that had caught him unprepared.

'I was employed by the Scottish king to be part of his invasion force in support of Prince Richard of York. However, the campaign was a failure and my services are no longer needed' he replied somewhat absently, still mesmerised by the young mother.

'Aye, we heard about that. But what I meant was, why are you back here in Wensleydale, when you could have returned home to Burgundy?'.

Stefan realised he would have to explain his mission but to do that fully, would compromise Eleanor's reputation - he would need to be tactful. Addressing Bess directly, he chose his words with care. He did not want her thinking badly of her mother.

'I met your mother Elizabeth, when we camped at Masham, before the battle of Stoke. We spent some hours conversing and she told me of her life here. I determined to return to this peaceful place should I survive. I was hoping to …renew our acquaintance but I fear I have left it too long'.

'Ten years is certainly a long time' Robert commented wryly, raising his eyebrows.

'Aye and I hear she has re-married and moved away. I hope she is well'. Bess and Robert exchanged glances, which were not lost on Stefan, who looked up quizzically, holding his breath. *Was it bad news?*

'She is well', Bess confirmed, seeing the soldier exhale in relief…'but she is no longer wed, she is widowed .. again'.

'And she has returned. She lives nearby.' Robert added, noting a look of astonishment and elation light up the soldier's face, the man appearing nonplussed. The couple could see from his sharp intake of breath, the news meant more to Stefan than his casual enquiry indicated and evidently Eleanor had meant more to this man than he was admitting to.

'Excuse me… a minute', Stefan rasped, his voice suddenly hoarse, his hand covering his mouth to stop his lip from trembling. He strode back to his horses, steadying himself against Galahad's flank, his heart thumping so loudly in his chest he imagined the whole of Wensley could hear it. He felt as if it were about to burst, he was shaking and needed to steady his nerves. He closed his eyes. *Eleanor is widowed! She is free! She is nearby!* It was though he had suddenly been raised up from the depths of despair to the dizzy heights of euphoria. He took deep gulps of air to calm his heartbeat before facing the couple once more but he couldn't stop himself from grinning at the prospect of finding Eleanor, *not only single but living here in this very valley!*

'Where might I find your mother, Elizabeth? I would very much like to call upon her, if you think she would see me?', he asked upon returning, deliberately steadying his words so as to appear outwardly calm, when inside he was in turmoil.

Of course, she would be delighted, I am sure. She is at Manor farm about two miles away.' Bess grinned, aware from his face the news was welcome. *Two miles away!* Stefan could hardly believe his luck.

'Leave the horses with me to be shod, Stefan, you may come back for them later', Robert offered, noting Stefan's eagerness to depart.

'Danke …thank you, thank you!' was all the soldier could manage as he collected his saddlebag while Robert proceeded to point out the way to the farm. Thanking the couple once more, Stefan strode off eagerly, leaving the diverted pair chuckling to themselves.

'Well, if that's not love I don't know what is!' Bess remarked. 'Mother will be so surprised. I must admit I did wonder if she had met someone that day at Masham. She seemed different when she came back… and he *is* very handsome!'

'He must be nearing fifty!' Robert observed somewhat testily at his wife's

appraisal of a man he considered too old to be of interest to women.
'Oh, you men and your ego! Why do you all assume you have to be young to be attractive?' Bess laughed. 'Besides, mother is in her mid-forties now. He is perfect for her!'

Chapter Twenty Three

It had been many years since Eleanor had awoken with that indisputable feeling that her life was about to change. This fine autumn morning though, she felt it again. *Was it just because she was back at Manor Farm? No, it was something else.* It was not as if there was any hope of a Yorkist restoration now, with Richard of York imprisoned in the Tower and his support melted away - no this was different, Eleanor was sure, this time fortune's destiny pertained only to her.

She rose and dressed, greeted her brothers and sisters-in-law at breakfast as usual but her stomach churned with an unexpected nervousness, which she could not fathom and her food lay untouched. Sipping a little milk to settle her stomach, she set about organising her day. She didn't need to milk cows, churn butter or harvest vegetables, they had boys and girls for that but years of service was a hard habit to break and to admit to the truth, she enjoyed having something constructive to do. She began peeling some apples for a fruit pie, as the sun streamed in through the split stable door, separating the kitchen from the yard. The top section had been left open, inviting the last of the season's lambency to warm the flagstone floor.

She wasn't thinking about anything in particular, as the apple skins curled from her knife and dropped onto the table, when there came a knock on the door frame. Assuming it to be a peddler come to sell some wares and sighing phlegmatically to herself, she cast her eyes around for cook to attend to him but there was no-one about. After casually rinsing her hands in a bowl of water and wiping them dry on her apron, she stood up and went to the open door, the sudden movement causing her to feel lightheaded. The autumn sun suspended low in the sky, shone so brightly into the shadowed kitchen, it dazzled her. Eleanor raised her hand to shade her eyes and peered into the light. The man was silhouetted against the glare, the beams radiating around him she thought, like heaven around an angel.

'What are you selling sir?' Eleanor narrowed her eyes in an attempt to focus as the man moved to one side and leant against the door frame, arms folded, a beaming smile lighting up his face.

'My heart, Eleanoore, if you will have it', he said quietly. Eleanor gasped. She felt as if her heart had stopped. She knew that voice, the way he spoke her name, that German accent was unmistakeable, she knew that handsome face, those piercing blue eyes. *It can't be! Can it? After all this time?*

'Stefan?' she whispered incredulously, hardly daring to hope. Eleanor's head spun, she suddenly felt faint, while in the glaring light she saw him wink at her and then everything went white as she lost consciousness. In a second, he had caught her in his arms as her knees gave way and she fell into his embrace. Stefan gazed down at his lovely English rose, every bit as beautiful as he had remembered, as her cap slid to the floor spilling cascades of rich auburn hair over his arms and he smiled. He kissed her parted lips gently, laying her on the settle, watching her until she opened her eyes and saw that the phantom she had imagined was real and his lips were moving.

'I've come back for you, mein liebling', he declared tenderly, as Eleanor beamed a smile so wide and welcoming it took his breath away.

The End

Author's Conclusion

I wrote this sequel to *Maid of Middleham*, as any defence of Richard III inevitably involves the fate of the Princes in the Tower. That clichéd mystery, so beloved and treasured by Tudor historians in their vilification of Richard as Shakespeare's murdering tyrant, which despite enduring for over 500 years, still remains unproven today. In writing *Cleave to the Crown*, as a continuation of Eleanor's story, I hope to plant in reader's minds the very plausible possibility and in my opinion, the most probable, that the sons of Edward IV survived beyond 1483.

Readers of *Maid of Middleham* will know I have previously set out my reasons for Richard's innocence of the heinous crimes to which he is attributed. I cite his religious piety, family loyalty, love for his people, undoubted courage, military prowess and desire to do the right thing, all for which there is contemporary written evidence. Following his brother Edward's death in 1483, Richard was left with an impossible task, not only to unite a divided nobility but to form a stable Government whilst keeping his brother's children safe, against those wishing to take control and rule illegally whilst the heir was still a minor. Nobody wanted a return to the power struggles that took place during the reign of Henry VI. The illegality of Edward IV's marriage, though seen by some as a convenient excuse, was a fact, which the Queen's family attempted to conceal and which forced Richard to take the action he did when it came to light.

As next in line to the Yorkist throne after Edward's children were found to be illegitimate, Richard took the only possible course of action to save the country from anarchy and chaos, by accepting the throne. As Protector, he had every right to do this, his accession approved by Parliament. Should he refuse, a less eligible candidate would have been offered the crown. In lawfully deposing his brother's children, Richard still needed to keep them safe from harm or kidnap amidst rebellion and treachery, despite in doing so laying himself open to rumour and slander by those seeking to bring him down.

Henry Tudor's invasion was sanctioned in no small part, by malicious talk that Richard had murdered his nephews, declaring him therefore not fit to be king. However, there is not one shred of evidence for this wholly unnecessary crime and indeed Richard's love for his family and deeply held religious beliefs render such an act laughable. Why do so many believe that the disappearance of the two boys from the Tower equals murder? The answer lies in Tudor propaganda and Thomas More's embellished history, based on the word of Richard's mortal enemy, Archbishop Morton. Domiciled in Morton's household, More, who was only 5 years of age when Richard succeeded to the throne, had only the staunch Lancastrian's prelate's word on which to base his chronicle. Coupled with the need to please King Henry VIII, More's history, had to reflect Tudor thinking and ensure Richard III was seen as culpable in the murder of innocents.

In our search for the truth however, besides murder, there are equally strong reasons for the boys' disappearance, which need to be considered - the fact that the princes needed to be kept safe from those who saw fit to unlawfully crown a bastard child, or from those who wanted them dead, in order to accuse Richard of the crime, to usurp his throne and theirs. Interestingly, the fact Thomas More left his work unfinished, in my view, leads me to wonder whether he may have harboured doubts about the veracity of his imaginative work, as a serious historical treatise. Did he acknowledge it as propaganda and have second thoughts about publishing it?

If the princes were dead in 1483, as history would have us suppose, why then did Henry Tudor invest so much time and effort into seeking out the pretenders and exposing them as fraudsters? (Note: The word 'pretender', does not infer the English 'to pretend'. The word is based on the French *pretendre*, meaning 'to claim', therefore for 'pretender', read 'claimant'). Having re-legitimised Elizabeth of York, in order to marry her legally, Henry's actions also legalised her brothers at the same time. Consequently, the Tudor king had the strongest reason of all to make sure they were dead, or he would have lost his tenuous hold on the crown.

Do people not think it strange that during Richard's lifetime, nobody formally accused him of murdering his nephews? Despite Buckingham's failed rebellion and his own personal tragedy, Richard's first parliament was progressive, setting him on course to consolidate his reign. Only after he died on Bosworth field did the Tudors set in motion their campaign of disinformation, to malign their predecessor. They did everything they could to discredit Richard as justification for Tudor's usurpation, an employment of spin so successful it still endures today.

In this novel, I propose my strongly held belief that the young 15-year-old pretender, later known as Lambert Simnel, crowned in Ireland in 1487, was indeed Edward V, the son of Edward IV. I believe there was a clever plot employing an imposter of a similar age and appearance, who could have been an illegitimate son of Edward IV by one of his many mistresses. Rumours that the youth who was crowned may have been the surviving Earl of Warwick confounded the issue, though he was younger than his cousin. The two young men were brought to England with Lord Lovell and Lord Lincoln's army to depose Henry Tudor at the battle of Stoke. Should they be victorious Edward V could claim his birth right, however, should the campaign fail, as it eventually did, the imposter could be allowed to be taken captive, allowing Edward to escape to Devonshire. I suggest this is what happened and Tudor was able to expose the imposter he dubbed Lambert Simnel as a fraud and set him to work in his kitchens. My story proposes that Edward V lived quietly in anonymity, as Parker at Coldridge Manor in Devon, his army never having been able to re-group in the face of the king's superior numbers and fear of reprisals amidst the nobility. I will return to him shortly.

The fate of Francis Lovell remains as mysterious today as it did then. Apart from a possible sighting of him crossing the River Trent, after the battle of Stoke, nothing was seen or heard from the Viscount, despite extensive enquiries. My story therefore includes an anecdote passed down as legend which describes an intriguing discovery made in 1708. Workmen renovating a chimney at Minster Lovell, knocked through into an underground vault, which had lain undiscovered for many years. Inside the vault was the skeleton of a man still seated at a table, but which apparently disintegrated on contact with the fresh air. Upon the table lay paper, book and pens ready for use, indicating he was an educated man and by the quality of his clothing it was assumed this must be Lord Lovell, though we will never know for certain.

As for Perkin Warbeck, my story asserts that this unfortunate youth *was* indeed the real Prince Richard of York, as feted by the king of France, the Holy Roman emperor, James IV of Scotland and Richard's aunt Margaret, Duchess of Burgundy. It is impossible to believe Henry Tudor's ludicrous claims that a young Dutchman brought up in Flanders could swiftly be taught the English language so fluently and without a foreign accent, as to be passed off as a Prince of England. The young man's knowledge of English courtly life amidst the Yorkist family, his mannerisms, his looks, his distinguishing features and his education, all served to substantiate his claim.

In desperation, after Richard's failed invasion of Devonshire and eventual capture, Henry Tudor resorted to ridicule, assault, torture and finally murder, in order to discredit Richard and rid himself of this contender for his throne. To have a young man beaten to an unrecognisable pulp, shows there must have been no doubt in Henry's mind as to the pretender's identity. There are two possibilities here, either it WAS Richard of York, or another youth was substituted in his place and the real Richard sent into anonymity, like his brother. Either way, Henry ensured identification was impossible. Tudor used every possible means to invalidate Richard of York's claim, including forcing him to sign a false confession, a tactic he later used against Sir James Tyrell, who was made to confess to the murder of the Princes in the Tower on Richard III's orders. This so-called evidence would today surely be thrown out of court as obtained under duress.

To me, Henry's actions point to a man terrified of losing his crown, knowing full well he had little entitlement, determined to eliminate every possible drop of Plantagenet blood from the succession. It is my strong belief that the young man, Henry referred to as Perkin Warbeck, was indeed Richard of York. He was sentenced to be executed along with his fellow prisoner in the Tower, assumed to be Edward of Warwick, Richard's cousin. Then came the torture and disfigurement of Richard, designed to disguise his looks. This despicable treatment of two innocent young men, ensured there were no more challengers for the English throne waiting in the wings, a prerequisite which formed part of the agreement for Catherine of Aragon to marry Henry's son Arthur.

My story also proposes that Edward of Warwick was substituted for another child, although there is no historical proof of this. I simply inserted it as a tantalising hypothesis. One narrative of the time relates that George Duke of Clarence sent his son away to Ireland at a young age and instead brought up an imposter at Warwick castle, his intention to return his son to England to claim his birth right, when the boy came of age. We do not know the truth of what happened to George's son, although it is assumed the young man Henry Tudor executed, was Edward of Warwick. It is interesting to note that Richard III passed over Warwick as his heir, in favour of John de la Pole, Earl of Lincoln. Edward was under his father's attainder but Richard could have reversed that, had he wished. Did he perhaps know something about the whereabouts of his brother's son? To me, a contemporary statement that the boy 'could not tell a goose from a capon', suggests the boy in the Tower, whoever he was, had no clue as to what was going on and may have been an imposter.

George Duke of Clarence always maintained he himself was Richard Duke of York's rightful heir, due to his brother Edward IV's illegitimacy and went to his death because of it. I venture to suggest in this novel he was right, though this is pure conjecture. It does seem odd though that Cecily Duchess of York would consider confessing to adultery but this is understandable if we consider it may not have been *her* adultery but the Duke of York's infidelity! Opinion is still varied on this point, though another unexplained action by Edward in 1469 raises concerns. Why did he suddenly banish Cecily from her luxurious castle at Fotheringhay and send her to Berkhamsted, a poor substitute, after she saw off her son George at Sandwich before his marriage to Isobel Neville? Was she in fact condoning rebellion against his brother? This deprivation might make sense if Cecily was indeed Edward's stepmother and not his birth mother. If it should eventually come to light that Edward was in fact illegitimate, not only will it exonerate George but it will simply underline and validate Richard's inalienable right to succeed, as his father's only remaining legitimate son.

To return to Edward V, the recent discovery of a tomb in a remote country church in rural Devonshire, offers tantalising clues as to the possibility of Edward's survival into maturity, under a false identity. St. Matthew's church in Coldridge, only accessible by cart track in the 15th century, was attached to the Manor of Coldridge, just North of Exeter, owned by Thomas Grey, Marquess of Dorset, Edward V's half-brother. Interestingly, Thomas Grey also owned Gleaston Castle in Furness, which could possibly have been used as a safe house by Lovell's rebels before the battle of Stoke. It is clear Henry Tudor also had his suspicions about Dorset's allegiance. In 1484, Elizabeth Woodville, Edward's widowed queen, wrote to her son urging him to return to England and two days after she came out of sanctuary, Robert Markenfield was sent by King Richard to Coldridge on an important mission. Soon afterwards, a John Evans arrived in the village having been granted the title Lord of the Manor and Parker of the deer park. Significantly, no evidence of such a man exists before this.

One hypothesis, as suggested by this novel, is that after the battle of Stoke in 1487, Edward V went to ground, kept safe by the anonymity afforded him as John Evans, Parker of Coldridge deer park. In 1511, Evans built a chantry at St. Matthew's church where a stained-glass window was commissioned depicting Edward V, a crown and other intriguing clues. Firstly, we must ask why in this remote and little-known hamlet of Devonshire, is there a window dedicated to Edward V, when only two other glass portraits of him exist, one in Canterbury cathedral? What makes this remote church significant?

Below the window, John Evan's tomb effigy appears to gaze up at the stained glass, where the image shows a large crown floating above Edward's head, with the Duke of York's emblem of the falcon and fetterlock at its centre. The chantry was built in 1511, and intriguingly, the ermine, worn only by Royalty, is shown dotted with 41 tiny deer in place of the usual markings. Subtracting 41 from 1511 equals 1470, the year of Edward V's birth. A second face is seen in the corner of the window where the man, also wearing ermine, holds a crown. His face and hair suggest a likeness to Edward V and on his chin a scar echoes a similar scar on the tomb effigy.

The tomb itself offers further clues. On the shield, the name John Evans is misspelt as 'Evas'. One interpretation is that EV stands for Edward V and AS refers to the Latin asa, meaning in sanctuary. Below the name, an inverted etching appears to depict the word 'king', indicating that things upside down are to be kept secret. Below that, are nine etched lines, could this be the year of Henry Tudor's death in 1509, when Edward V should have become monarch? There are other clues around the church such as Rose of York motifs on the floor, in itself unusual for a Devon church. Yorkist Sunnes in Splendour adorn the roof trusses and stained glass and odd carvings depict Tudor women with snake like tongues, a device indicating untruths, or sins of the tongue. If one of these heads represents Margaret Beaufort, Henry Tudor's mother, I would not be surprised.

Why all these strange clues should be found in such a remote place, appears to me to tie in with the fact Coldridge was owned by Thomas Grey and with the knowledge that Richard III sent Robert Markenfield to this very place on a secret mission in 1484, I suggest, this cannot be merely co-incidental.

There is yet another fascinating theory about the survival of the Princes in the Tower, based on extraordinary clues to be found in Hans Holbein's painting of Sir Thomas More and his family in 1528. On the far right of the image, a young man stands in a doorway or portal, representing Dr. John Clement, who by close analysis of the many visual devices across the painting, is indicated to be the surviving Richard of York, heir to the Yorkist throne. John Clement married More's adopted daughter Margaret and lived with the family for a time. The words 'Johanes heresius' painted above his head signify *'John the rightful heir'* and the artist has represented him as half his age by various means such as the stopped clock and has incorporated Yorkist symbols such as the sun in splendour. John is wearing a sword and buckler. (*Servants don't wear swords*) The spoke of a wheel is *'rai'* and the rim is *'jante'*, a split-homophone of *'régente'*, and *'le bouclier du régente'* means 'buckler of the king'. There are too many clues to delve into here but interestingly More's fool, the only figure facing outwards, is shown to have an uncanny resemblance to Henry VIII. An examination of Dr. John Clement's life reveals the strong possibility he could have been Richard of York. He is described in the Louvain University register as *'of noble birth'*. If this is the case, then the young man executed by Henry VII was an imposter and the real Richard either escaped or was permitted to go free in exchange for his life, provided he never resurrected his claim. It is not inconceivable that Elizabeth of York pleaded to her husband for her brother's life. Interestingly a John Clement was listed as taking part in a feat of arms, along with other nobles against Henry VIII in 1510, something a commoner would not have been selected to do.

Regarding Edward V, the death in 1528 of Sir Edward Guildford, standard bearer to Henry VIII, appears to be referred to in this painting and a further examination of this man's life also points to the possibility he was the eldest son of Edward IV. His daughter Lady Jane Guildford, Duchess of Northumberland's tomb bears the inscription 'right and noble excellent Princess' which could only mean she was either the daughter of a king, or the wife of a Prince, the former being the only possibility.

Did Edward V eventually leave Coldridge, for the sake of either safety or deception? Was he taken in by Sir Richard Guildford and hailed as his son Sir Edward Guildford? After Edward's death, his grandchildren the Dudleys, considered themselves heirs to the throne, with Guildford Dudley (Lady Jane Guildford's son) married to Lady Jane Grey, the nine days queen. Guildford's brother Robert Dudley, Earl of Leicester subsequently courted Elizabeth I.

It is said therefore, Sir Thomas More was commissioned to write his *History of Richard III* as a smoke screen to detract from the continued existence of the Princes, thereby halting further search. This imaginative work had the added advantage of discrediting the last Yorkist king, at the same time as hailing the Tudors as the saviours of England. Further endorsed and validated by Shakespeare's imagination, More's account has since found its way into history books as fact, despite none of its pronouncements ever having been proved or corroborated.

To me, this concluding period of the Wars of the Roses, is the most fascinating in our history, with claim and counter claim, rumour and deception, treachery and secrets, truth, lies, loyalty and betrayal. Much written evidence has been deliberately destroyed and we are left with puzzling clues and anomalies, with which to fill in the blanks. With hindsight, Richard III may not have always made the wisest decisions but in the tumultuous times he lived, when faced with plot and counter plot, rumour and insinuation, treachery and perfidy, he did what he believed was best to stabilise a divided nobility. He lived through some of the most violent times in British history and having lost all the people he loved, at just 32 years of age stood alone against an invader, dying with the utmost courage and valour. The fact he has been vilified ever since, without any effort by traditional historians to refute the calumnies, is beyond tragic.

As a committed Ricardian, I am passionate about seeking the truth about Richard III and the disappearance of the Princes in the Tower. I applaud Philippa Langley in her tireless search for evidence with the *Missing Princes Project.* I fervently hope she can eventually prove what many of us suspect, that Richard III was entirely innocent of the crimes attributed to him by the Tudors. I believe he has suffered the worst miscarriage of justice in British history, aided by the dramatic fantasies of Shakespeare's imagination and those historians who persist in maligning a courageous, undoubtedly loyal and God-fearing young statesman.

Bridget M. Beauchamp

STOP PRESS: Just as this book was about to go to print, Philippa Langley has published her research into the missing Princes and has found irrefutable evidence that both Edward V and Richard of York survived Richard III's reign. Edward V was crowned in Ireland and so called 'Perkin Warbeck' was indeed Richard of York, who returned to claim the throne of England.

Author's note: Cleave to the Crown is a work of fiction. There is no evidence to suggest there was ever a woman of Eleanor's description, or that she had a child by Richard Duke of Gloucester, or met with Francis Lovell and other noblemen. However, the historical figures woven into this story were real people and the historical events described here are based on fact, along with some of my own suppositions and opinions.

Recommended reading:

The Survival of the Princes in the Tower *by Matthew Lewis – History Press*
Richard of England *by D.M. Kleyn – Kensal Press*
The Lost Prince *by David Baldwin – Sutton publishing*
The Last White Rose *by Desmond Seward – Constable*
The Secrets of the House of York *by Marylynn Salmon – Liberty Corner Press*

THE RICHARD III SOCIETY

Readers interested in joining the **Richard III Society,** whose aim is to promote research into the life and times of Richard III, secure a reassessment and raise awareness, may do so through their website online at **www.richardiii.net** The annual membership fee includes the Society's annual publication *The Ricardian Journal* and a quarterly *Ricardian Bulletin* magazine, packed with informative articles, photographs, letters, book reviews, details of forthcoming events and merchandise for sale. There are numerous affiliated local Richard III Society Groups and Branches around the UK and internationally, where members can meet regularly for talks, discussions, visits to places of interest and social occasions.

MAID OF MIDDLEHAM
By
Bridget M. Beauchamp, Arcanum Press 2022

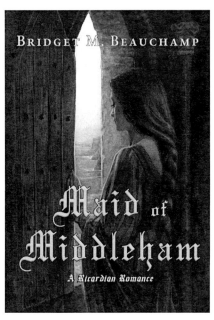

ISBN: 978-1-3999-41 40-2

The author intended her first Ricardian novel MAID OF MIDDLEHAM to be read before CLEAVE TO THE CROWN. Maid of Middleham begins Eleanor's story, when she first meets Richard Duke of Gloucester as a teenager, at Middleham Castle in 1468. Eleanor falls in love, bears Richard a child, weds another man when Richard departs, is twice widowed and eventually re-unites with Richard for the last time before the battle of Bosworth in 1485. The plot follows Eleanor's life in parallel with Richard's, as he marries Anne Neville, becomes king and eventually falls in battle - a story of love, loss, desire, duty and death, played out in the tranquil surroundings of Wensleydale.

Edward V stained glass,
Coldridge Church 1511

Stained glass image,
man with crown 1511

John Evans tomb effigy at
Coldridge Church (C16th)

'Perkin Warbeck'
(aka Richard of York) (C16th)

Edward IV (C16th copy)

The Thomas More family portrait by Hans Holbein 1528,
from Nostell Priory

All truth passes through three stages.
First, it is ridiculed.
Second, it is violently opposed.
Third, it is accepted as being self-evident.

Arthur Schopenhauer 1788-1860